IRONHEART

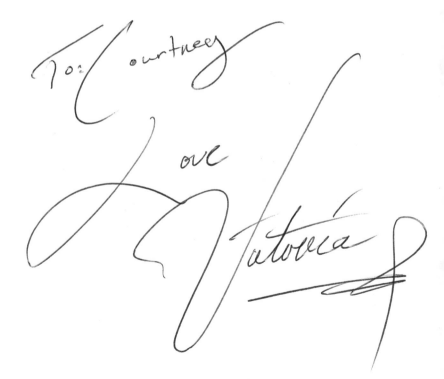

To: Courtney

Love

Vatoria

IRONHEART

By Victoria Kasten

Original cover art by James Krom
Natural Images

Photography by Scott Briggs

IronHeart
Copyright © 2007
Victoria Kasten
All Rights Reserved

First Printing • 750 copies • Nov 2007

Library of Congress Control Number: 2007908043

ISBN: 978-0-9788850-4-5

Published By: Victoria Kasten

www.epicscrolls.com

Printed in the USA by
Morris Publishing
3212 East Highway 30
Kearney, NE 68847
1-800-650-7888

Dedicated with love to my best friend
Sara Enderle

Call me, and I will run to be at your side
Command it, and I will build you a castle among the stars
Love me, and I will be yours forever
Be faithful unto me, and I will die for you
I will remain loyal to you throughout the ages
My heart ever seeks you, my love

- Utomian Song -

1

The sun edged over the Oppolo Mountains, and its golden rays beamed down over the sleeping city of Ichoda. Lifting his dew covered snout the big watch bison bellowed from his place on the Eastern Hill. The sound echoed through the valley, arousing the citizens of Ichoda from their stalls and sleeping mats.

The palace became lively with the hurrying about of the servants. Windows of houses and barns were opened to let in the cool morning air.

Jiro the falcon, who was the town crier, flew through the streets screeching, "The watch bison has proclaimed the sunrise. Everyone awake! Today is the day of the Great Tournament!"

Those words seemed to have a magical effect on the still weary citizens. Animals and humans alike seemed to come alive with those words. Instantly, the streets were filled with excited chatter.

Ichoda was the capitol city of a land called Leyowan. It was a beautiful country, lush and green with all kinds of vegetation. Ichoda was the centerpoint of the beautiful world that animals and humans alike called their home.

In Leyowan, a human could be expected to live 150-200 years. The animals could be expected to live that same amount or even longer.

Surrounded by other countries, Leyowan was the most sought after by the other nations, especially the Western Lands of Morbia. A dark, foreboding place, Morbia was ruled by an evil bear, Orluc, who commanded hordes of jackals, hyenas, foxes, wolves, and birds of prey.

Many times, the Morbians had attempted to force their way into the land of Leyowan and build their own cities. However, they had always been easy to drive away.

The Great Tournament was an annual event hosted by the Royal Family of Leyowan. The Tournament was a mock battling grounds in which young military hopefuls could prove their worth. The challenge was open to all species and races. The winner of each duel was accepted into the Ichodian Army.

This year would be no different, the people hoped. They loved the Tournament, and waited patiently for it all year. The participants especially were impatient for it to begin.

As the herds of animals and groups of people began to mill around the large arena used for the Tournament, a loud trumpet blared from the palace. The palace balcony which overlooked the arena was suddenly occupied by the King, Queen and Princess of Leyowan.

King Jarlir bowed to his applauding subjects. He helped Queen Elaria, who was expecting a child soon, sit down on her throne. Princess Kikpona waved and smiled to the people and animals below.

The Royal Family was human, but they ruled fairly over man and beast alike. The Queen's soon to be born child was

2

hoped to be a boy, so that Leyowan would have a king to replace Jarlir when he died.

Princess Kikpona was a very bright, happy girl. She was sixteen and loved her country with a passion.

King Jarlir's gaze swept over the participants lined up against the fence of the arena.

"Honored guests, we welcome you to the 113th Great Tournament! My family has held this event for over forty years.

Revered participants, we honor you with our respect for your courage. This event is not meant for the faint-hearted. We wish you good fortune. Let the Tournament begin!"

The applause was deafening. Hooved animals pounded their feet against the cobblestone that surrounded the arena. Humans whistled and clapped.

Princess Kikpona whispered something to her father and slipped out of the balcony quietly. Queen Elaria watched her leave worriedly.

The first contestants were two half-grown bull calves. They shook their short horns at each other threateningly. They pawed the ground and bellowed. Suddenly, the smaller of the two charged. He knocked the older calf over in a single neat sweep of his horns.

Bellowing, he held the bigger calf down with his front feet. A trumpet blared, and the young calf reared up in a victorious gesture. His eyes were bright with excitement. The crowd thundered their approval at such a swift victory.

The calf stood before the balcony, waiting to receive his acceptance from the King.

Jarlir smiled at him and stood. "What is your name, young victor?" he asked. The calf raised his head.

"I am Atoru. My father was the great Captain of One Hundred, Toru the Black Bull," he said proudly.

Jarlir smiled broadly. "Well, Atoru son of Toru the Black Bull, you are welcomed with honor and respect into the army of Ichoda. In honor of your father's sacrifice of life in the battle of Espoda, I replace him with you, as Captain of One Hundred."

The calf's eyes shone with gratitude. "I will serve you proudly, my King," he said. The crowd roared again. The calf exited the arena, and stopped when a human in full armor blocked him.

"Welcome to the army, Atoru. I do hope you can keep a secret," said a familiar voice. Atoru gasped. It was Princess Kikpona! The princess and Atoru had been best friends since birth. The two of them had grown up romping around in the meadows of Ichoda together, dreaming up wild adventures.

"My Princess! You are competing?" he asked in total confusion. The Princess had never attempted anything like this.

She smiled. "I want to prove to my father that I am worthy to be his Army General, and be leader of the whole army. If I accomplish this, you will be my Second Commander."

Atoru's eyes widened. Second Commander was the second highest leadership in the entire army. He bowed respectfully and intoned the battle blessing of Leyowan.

"I wish you strength and a clear mind, my Princess."

Kikpona sighed. "Atoru, you are as dear to me as any brother could be. Do not speak to me as though you do not know me."

Atoru shook his head. "Forgive me, Princess Kikpona. But I am bound by law to be respectful of you. The punishment for disrespect is ten lashes with the whip. I really do not wish to carry welts through life as a symbol of dishonor. Your father may be kind to those that keep the law, but he is very hard on those who disobey it."

Kikpona laid a hand on the white star that decorated the black calf's forehead. She smiled at him.

"My father is very lenient with me. I have the power to pass judgment also, you know. I will never let him harm you."

Atoru smiled. "Aye Princess, it is so. But if you do not hurry, you will miss your pairing. And look whom it is you are competing against! You will surely be tested in strength and thought," he said.

Kikpona looked to the other side of the arena, and saw a tall boy being suited up in armor. The boy was none other than Erondir, the blacksmith's son. Erondir was big, very boastful, and the city's most dreaded bully. He could wield a sword faster and harder than anyone.

Kikpona gulped. She had not expected such deadly competition. But she raised her chin in defiance. It would just prove her worth all the more when she defeated him. She gripped her iron spear tightly. Atoru looked worriedly at her.

"Be careful, Princess," he warned quietly. She nodded in determination. Her knuckles turned white from the ferocity with which she gripped her weapon.

The arena gatekeeper turned to her. "Enter, participant," he said. Kikpona was surprised not to hear him refer to her as Princess. Then she remembered the protective helm that covered her face. The golden eagle wings that formed the crest on her breastplate glowed from the sun's warm rays.

She strode hesitantly onto the arena sand. Erondir approached her, a wicked smile on his face. They met in the center of the arena. They bowed in a sign of respect to each other, and then to the king and queen. Kikpona felt strange bowing to her father, who did not even know whom it was that dared to challenge the strong son of the blacksmith.

With the formalities now finished, they circled, Erondir flipping his sword around in his hand. Kikpona saw how confidently he handled the blade. She felt insecure for a moment.

She looked down at her spear. The long smooth shaft of the weapon sat comfortably in her hand, ready for battle as soon as she was. The sharpened spearhead glinted in the sunlight.

Kikpona suddenly felt strong and brave. She advanced towards Erondir, and twirled her weapon. He raised his sword and she blocked it with the spearhead. They strained for a moment, each trying to throw the other off balance. Erondir whispered in her ear.

"I will break you into so many pieces the crowd will have to sift sand to find them."

Kikpona felt her temper rise at his assessment of her ability. "Do not so lightly challenge me, Erondir son of Eledor."

Erondir laughed jeeringly, and let go of her spear. She stumbled backwards, and barely regained her footing. She felt fury rising at his mocking laughter. She rushed towards him, spinning around in circles and flipping her spear.

Kikpona whipped her spear in a circle and made a stab for Erondir's breastplate. He blocked it easily with his sword and brought his weapon up sharply. Kikpona dodged just in time to miss the blade, which would have severed her left arm.

Her opponent laughed again and raised the sword above his head, bringing it down on the spear shaft. Kikpona quickly retaliated by flipping the handle end of her slim weapon up to knock Erondir in the face. He stepped back with a grunt of pain.

Kikpona waited until he was back in his stance before going into a half crouch with her spear. Her ice blue eyes watched Erondir carefully through the slits of her helm. The boy flipped his blade around in his hand and made a sideswipe

7

for her neck. Kikpona leaned backwards as the sword sliced through the air barely an inch from her throat.

Without giving him time to prepare for another attack, Kikpona lunged upwards and jabbed Erondir in the abdomen with the blunt end of her spear shaft, and then brought it down on his shoulder, sending him down to his knees.

Disbelief filled Erondir's eyes as he felt the cold iron spearhead against his throat. Grudgingly, he dropped his sword in submission. The crowd thundered.

Kikpona heard Atoru bellowing louder than all the rest of the onlookers. She smiled at her friend, and stepped forward to receive her praise from her father. The King stood, and she saw his smile at her.

"What is your name, victor, that we may praise you properly? Do remove your helm, so that we may look upon one who is so skilled with a weapon."

Kikpona hesitated. She bowed her head, and slowly removed her helm. Her mahogany red hair flowed down to her hips, and radiated light from the sun's rays. Her blue eyes slowly rose to meet her father's.

"Father, it is I."

The quiet sentence placed a spell-like hush over the crowd. Disbelief was evident in the faces of all the spectators. But Kikpona's greatest surprise was the look on her father's face. Instead of pride, there was disappointment.

"Kikpona, you have disgraced yourself. You are a princess, not a warrior. You have no place in the army, but should be here in the palace beside your mother."

8

Kikpona's anger rose. Her cheeks flushed with a red tinge that did not fully express her rage.

"You know I was chosen, Father. The Ancients chose me as your successor. Yet you still hope that the son you've always hoped for will come and replace you as King. You deny my rightful place as the heir to your throne."

King Jarlir stared at his daughter. He knew what she said was true. But such a disrespectful outburst was punishable.

He bowed his head. Though she was his daughter, he knew what he must do. He raised his right hand, and began to speak.

"Kikpona, you have disobeyed the laws of respect to your King. I must fulfill my duty to see such disobedience dealt with."

Kikpona's disbelief was profound. She didn't believe the words she was hearing. The crowd stared in equal surprise at their King. Though the law must be upheld, many could not believe the harshness of the King's voice.

Jarlir finished the sentence in a quiet voice. "Disrespect from a royal is much more serious than a commoner. Banishment from Ichoda and ten lashes with the whip."

Two guards came forward to take Kikpona. Her armor was removed and left in a pile on the ground, leaving her dressed only in a shirt and breeches and looking like a perfect commoner. Her blue eyes stayed locked to her father's brown ones. The betrayal and anger in her eyes was too much for the king. He had to look away.

The guards led her out of the arena. They pushed her through the crowd of sympathetic eyes. She heard her father accepting Erondir into the army. Shock settled in, and Kikpona felt drained and weary. She followed the guards meekly, all the defiance gone from her spirit.

Atoru followed them. He stopped the guards, and said, "I will accompany the princess to the dungeons. She will need a guard," he finished, his eyes downcast.

The guards shrugged in acceptance, allowing Atoru to join them, and then continued towards the dungeon gates. The dungeon had been delved into the side of the mountain, and went down deep into the earth, into darkness. Kikpona looked at the gates, rising up over the path, their iron hinges capped with spikes.

The gates opened to admit the small group. Kikpona's guards handed her over to a mute jailor, who gripped her arm tightly. He led her down the stone steps and through many winding narrow hallways, until they came to a door at the end of a hallway. Through the door was a cell.

Kikpona was pushed inside, and the door closed with a crack behind her. Kikpona did not attempt to rise. She lay on the cold stone, her fists clenched. Tears squeezed through her tightly closed eyelids and slipped down her cheeks.

Atoru stood behind her, silent. He had the freedom to leave if he wished. But he eased himself down with a grunt, and laid on the floor behind Kikpona. He said nothing, because he knew that the Princess was embarrassed for him to see her cry.

The tears gave way to sobs, and Kikpona knew grief that she had never known before. She couldn't believe her father would do such a thing to his own daughter. And her mother was pregnant. Kikpona just knew it was a boy... a Prince for her father to love and set on the throne of Leyowan.

.~.~.~.~.~.~.

Night fell. Kikpona knew that the Tournament was over by now. New soldiers had been added to the army, and the crowd's hunger for excitement would be sated for a time. But did they disagree with her father? Kikpona wondered how many of them were on her side.

Many of the people loved her. The Princess was not someone who stayed in the palace. She had always mingled with her people and tried to become one of them. But how many of them knew of the prophecy? The people may have disagreed with the king, but would they fight for her.

Kikpona lie there, listening to the sound of Atoru's grunting snores.

.~.~.~.~.~.~.

An hour later, the cell door creaked open, waking Kikpona with a start. She bolted to her feet, and looked towards the door. She saw two masked men standing there, waiting to take her. She closed her eyes.

Kikpona felt hands grip her arms and begin pulling her out of the cell. She walked along the hallway in silence.

Reaching another iron door, the two men pulled it open. Inside was the torture chamber. Kikpona shuddered at all the weapons and instruments laying on tables and hanging from the ceiling and walls. She turned to see Atoru standing behind her.

"If my strength will aid you, it is yours for the taking," he said. The encouraging look in his eyes made Kikpona's heart falter. She knew what waited.

Atoru turned and stood outside the door. As it closed, Kikpona got one more glance of his sympathetic eyes. Then she was forced towards a pair of chains at the back of the room. Her wrists were encased in the shackles, and the chains were raised. Her hands were pulled up, and her eyes were covered with a blindfold.

She heard the first crack of the whip, and felt a searing pain shoot through her back. She gritted her teeth, determined not to show her pain.

Outside the door, Atoru listened to the crack and snap of the whip. He flinched every time he heard it.

He marveled at the Princess's silence. Suddenly, a wild fury filled him at the injustice of it all. How could King Jarlir treat the Chosen One this way?

He stomped his foot angrily, and his nostrils flared. He pawed at the stone floor. But he knew that to attempt to rescue the Princess would mean certain death for him. And Kikpona needed him alive and well.

12

Suddenly he heard the Princess cry out. His heart felt heavy at the sound. He wanted to stop his ears to her cries. But he couldn't.

He paced up and down the hallway. He passed cell door after cell door. Suddenly he heard a whisper come from one of the doors.

"Guard?"

Atoru stopped, and went back to the door that the voice had come from. He listened, and heard heavy breathing on the other side. Atoru replied hesitantly.

"I am Atoru, bodyguard of the Princess Kikpona," he said.

The voice spoke again. "Princess Kikpona is here? Why?"

Atoru quickly replied, "She angered her father by entering the Tournament, and he had her sent her for punishment!"

The voice was silent for a moment. The heavy breathing quieted.

"How dare he. She is the Chosen One. Yet he still denies her of her throne. Is there no one to fight for her?"

Atoru shrugged. "I do not know. I am with her to whatever end, but I do not know if there are others that share my loyalty."

The voice spoke. "I do. The Princess Kikpona holds my loyalty to death itself. She fought for me when her father sent me here."

Atoru gasped. "Quetoro?" he asked.

A sigh sounded from the cell. "I am the same. It has been many years since my name has been spoken by any."

Atoru couldn't believe this. Quetoro was a red stallion, a Hupeg Horse, a mighty warhorse first bred by the Ancients for battle. These horses were much stronger and faster than the normal equine breeds.

Quetoro had been the Army General of Ichoda's army, but had been accused of attempting to poison the King. Because of this, he had been sentenced to a lifetime of solitude in the Dungeon.

The voice once again came from the other side of the door. "Atoru, there is a desk outside my cell door and to the left. On it will be a ring of keys. The warden has been absent for some time now. It is his midday mealtime. Bring them here and unlock the door."

Atoru looked hurriedly for the desk and found the desired keys. He grabbed the ring in his teeth and looked at the objects it held. He found one he thought would work, and picked it up with his mouth. Inserting it into the keyhole in the door of Quetoro's cell, he turned it slowly. The key grated in the lock and the door swung open. Atoru gasped at the sight of the stallion.

The horse was thin, his ribs showed, and his mane and tail were matted and ragged. Long scars covered his body, and bruises and fresh cuts were visible. But the wild fire in his eyes had not dimmed throughout the years of seclusion.

"Great One," Atoru bowed in respect. The horse raised his head proudly, and nodded in approval.

14

"Thank you, Atoru. Where is Princess Kikpona?" he asked. Another whip crack sounded from the chamber. Atoru flinched.

Quetoro's eyes darkened and narrowed. He strode out of his cell stiffly, and marched up to the chamber door.

"Atoru, we must rescue her. We cannot let her fall prey to the fancy of those evil villains. They will kill her."

The black calf gasped. "We can't leave her there, then. We must save her. I will not live with myself if she dies."

Quetoro didn't wait to hear more. He lunged at the chamber door, striking it with his hooves. The old wooden door was weak, and it splintered under the power of the stallion's anger. The horse stepped back as Atoru advanced on the door for a second attack.

The door fell in as Atoru's strike landed upon it. The whipping men inside shouted in surprise as the red stallion and black calf bolted through the doorway and headed for them. Quetoro looked at them angrily, his nostrils flaring. He spoke to them in a low ominous voice.

"Step away from the Princess and you will not be harmed."

The guards looked at the intruders and moved away from the Princess, but grabbed two swords from the wall and advanced on the horse and the calf.

Atoru slammed his short horns into the stomach of the first man. As the human doubled over in pain, Atoru lifted him off his feet, and threw him into the wall.

Quetoro reared up in front of the second man, who fell instantly as the sharp hooves hit their mark. The two animals both looked around for the Princess. They saw her then, still chained in the dark corner, blood pouring down the back of her shirt. Atoru felt nauseous at the smell.

Quetoro slammed his hooves against the chains, breaking them in two. Kikpona fell to the floor with a thud as she was released. Atoru rushed to her side.

"Princess?" he pleaded softly. "Stay with us. You are the Chosen One. Your people need you."

A soft moan escaped her lips. Atoru threw his head up in delight. Quetoro's old face creased into a smile.

"She is alive. Come, we must get her to safety," the stallion said to Atoru, who was still amazed that she was alive.

Atoru managed to get his horns under the Princess' limp form, and lifted her up onto Quetoro's broad back. Quetoro shifted his charge slightly with his nose, so that she was sitting on his back and leaning forward onto his neck. Atoru looked slightly doubtful about the arrangement.

"Do not worry, Atoru. She will be safe and sound. My gait is smooth and will not move her."

Atoru was still not fully convinced, but the two animals started off with their precious burden.

They journeyed back up the stairway to the gates. Atoru pushed one of the heavy portals open. The creak was loud, and Quetoro exited the dungeon very quickly, disappearing into the trees on the left side.

16

Atoru waited to see if any sleeping villagers would rise to see what the noise was. Hearing and seeing no one, Atoru slipped out after Quetoro. He left the dungeon gate open, to avoid making more noise.

As they entered the forest next to the gates, Quetoro led the way into the thick brush, away from Ichoda.

2

They traveled for many hours, until the first few rays of light began shining through the trees. Kikpona made no sound, and Atoru was beginning to worry about her.

Quetoro stopped. He huffed, his nostrils flaring. They had been trotting the whole way, and both animals were exhausted. Quetoro motioned for Atoru to help him with Kikpona.

Atoru caught her on his horns as she slid off of the red stallion's back and gently laid Kikpona against a tree. Her red hair flowed in a scarlet river down over her shoulders. Atoru turned her over slowly so she was lying on her stomach.

Quetoro came over with a mouthful of chewed leaves. Atoru looked questioningly at the older animal. Quetoro patiently explained.

"These leaves contain a healing poultice when crushed, and will soothe burns and wounds, as well as help the scabs form. They will ease the pain for a while so she can rest easily."

Quetoro nudged the back of Kikpona's shirt up. Atoru caught his breath quickly. Red welts covered the Princess's white skin, and caked blood covered her.

Quetoro smoothed the crushed leaves over the welts, pulled Kikpona's shirt gently over her wounds, and stepped back.

"Leave her be now. She needs to rest if she is to recover fully."

The two animals bedded down nearby, and soon all three friends were sound asleep.

.~.~.~.~.~.~.

Kikpona opened one eye. Her vision blurred for a moment, and then she opened the other eye. She looked around at the lush jungle forest, and frowned in surprise. Where was she? She rolled over, and gasped. She suddenly became aware of a surging pain in her back. Even that small movement brought discomfort. It all came flooding back to her memory. The Tournament, her duel, her father's sentence, the dungeon…the beating.

Kikpona frowned again. The beating was the last thing she remembered. How had she gotten here?

Then she saw a familiar face sleeping nearby. The newly risen sun shone through the branches of the trees and created a sort of halo around the young black calf's white horns.

"Atoru," she whispered. Her voice sounded like a frog's croak. Atoru grunted in response.

"Just a moment more, Dam," he mumbled groggily. Kikpona bit back a giggle. The cows, horses and other animals of that type referred to their mother as Dam, and their father as Sire.

"Atoru," she said again, this time louder. The black calf's eyes opened, and he saw her looking at him. He frowned in confusion for a moment, and then his whole face lit up happily.

"Princess! You're awake!" he said, his lips lifting slightly in a smile. Kikpona nodded slowly. She tried to sit up, and grimaced.

"Do not strain yourself too quickly, Princess. You don't want to ruin what Quetoro has done," he warned his face full of concern.

Kikpona stared at him. "Quetoro?" she asked in surprise. She remembered how angry she'd been at her father for believing the false accusations against the big red stallion. Quetoro had been accused of attempting to poison Jarlir. Kikpona had fought against the judgment, but to no avail.

Atoru nodded. "The very same. I found him in the dungeon while you were in the chamber. I found a key and let him out, and we both broke the door down on the chamber and rescued you. We killed the men who were beating you. No one saw us... I don't think. They...they were going to kill you," Atoru said, his eyes misting.

Kikpona smiled at him. He walked over and lay down beside her. She reached over and rubbed his white star.

"You're the best friend anyone could ever have, Atoru."

The calf looked away, pleased yet embarrassed. He grunted in reply. A loud cracking of brush was heard suddenly, and a red stallion broke through the jungle growth.

"Well, Princess, it seems as though you've decided to stay with us," Quetoro said, a pleased look on his face.

The old red horse bent his neck around to embrace her lovingly. Before his imprisonment, Quetoro had been Kikpona's tutor and one of her closest friends.

He had also been the High General of the Ichodian Army, the most revered position in the country after the Royal Family.

Quetoro finally nudged her in the stomach gently. "There now, don't strain yourself too much. You'll undo all the healing, and then where will we be?"

Kikpona rubbed the tears from her eyes and leaned back against the tree.

"Oh, Quetoro, it is beyond my wildest hopes that I have been united with you again. How I have missed you," she said. Quetoro nodded his head, his red mane falling over his eyes.

"And fine friends you have made since our parting," he said, motioning towards Atoru, who had watched the entire proceedings.

The black calf ducked his head in embarrassment. Kikpona smiled at him.

"Aye, Atoru is my best friend. His loyalty means more to me than all the kingdoms in the world."

.~.~.~.~.~.~.~.

Meanwhile, back in Ichoda, Erondir raced up the palace entry steps. He pounded on the heavy wooden doors with a clenched fist.

A serving girl opened the door. "Yes, sir?" she inquired with a curious look on her face.

Erondir quickly spoke his message. "I must see the King. It is most urgent!"

The serving girl's eyes widened and she motioned him in. She led him down the marble hallway to a large door and knocked politely.

"Come in," the King's voice came from within. The girl opened the door and stepped inside.

"The young master Erondir is here to see you, my lord. He says it is most urgent."

The King frowned. "Bid him enter."

Erondir entered the room, and bowed respectfully. King Jarlir motioned the servant girl out. When she left, he looked expectantly at the strong lad in front of him.

"Speak your message, Erondir."

The tall young man obeyed quickly. "Early this morning we found the dungeon gates open. The steward said that he found the torture chamber door broken in, and the two whipping men were dead. Also, Princess Kikpona's cell was empty."

King Jarlir buried his face in his hands. "So the lioness breaks free from her chains. I had hoped that she would

23

remain there until such a time when I could establish my son as King. Then she would be less of a threat to his deity. But now…"

Erondir continued, "My lord, there is more. The Captain of One Hundred, Atoru, was also found missing today. He was one of the Princess's closer friends, and it is suspected that he may have aided her escape. And the worst of all, the High General that you imprisoned, Quetoro, has escaped from the dungeon. They were traced as far as the jungle."

King Jarlir's head came up at mention of his ex-general. His eyes were wide with surprise and dread.

"Quetoro? He is still alive? And now he has been freed. There is a threat that I had hoped to destroy for all time. Are you certain that he is the one who escaped?"

Erondir nodded. Jarlir sighed heavily. He tapped his fingers against the table beside him.

"Well, there is only one course of action. Send three of our Jungle Raiders into the forest, and find them. Kill Quetoro, if you can, but bring back Atoru and Kikpona alive. And keep this concealed."

Erondir bowed and left the room. King Jarlir's knuckles turned white as he clenched his fists. Another soft knock sounded at the door. The king looked up to see Elaria quietly enter.

"What is wrong, my lord?" she asked him quietly. Her dark eyes were emotionless as she gazed at him.

"Elaria, my love, please do not stress yourself. But it would seem…" Jarlir hesitated. How could he tell her that Kikpona had disappeared? She would insist that he find her immediately.

"Our dear daughter has taken her own life. I didn't know until just now. There was nothing I could do."

The Queen's eyes widened as her face became a mask of horror. Her fists doubled and she ran from the room. She kept running until she had reached the door to the palace courtyard.

Elaria went down on her knees in the midst of the rose gardens and beat her fists on the dirt. Tears ran down her cheeks, and her eyes were filled with a helpless grief.

"No! My daughter, my child! Dead?" she whispered, her voice breaking. Her hands found their way to her pregnant belly. She looked down, silently aching for the unborn child who now would never know his sister. Emitting a strangled cry, she gave way to sobs of despair.

.~.~.~.~.~.~.~.

Kikpona laughed at Atoru. The black calf was trying to dislodge a large branch from his horns. He had gone into the jungle to look for food, and had run into a tangled mass of vines and branches on his way back. The green vines clung to his face and horns.

The black calf shook his head and dragged his horns against trees, trying to dislodge the debris.

Finally, Kikpona motioned him over. He stopped beside her, and extended his nose. She reached up and pulled the vines from his face.

"Many thanks, Kikpona," the calf said. Upon her request, he had quit calling her Princess now that they were beyond the fear of being punished.

Kikpona shrugged. "If you had hands, it would be much easier," she said teasingly to the calf. Atoru snorted.

"But if I had hands, then I would look rather like a fool now wouldn't I?" he said with a grin.

Kikpona laughed again. The sound of galloping hooves broke into their reverie of laughter. Quetoro charged through the undergrowth and slid to a stop, his sides heaving. Kikpona held onto Atoru's left horn and pulled herself up stiffly.

"What is wrong, Quetoro?" she asked worriedly. The red stallion took several deep breaths, and then spoke.

"Your father has sent Jungle Raiders in after us. Their orders are to take you and Atoru alive back to Ichoda."

Kikpona frowned. "They do not know you escaped, then?" she asked. Quetoro got a dark look in his eyes.

"They were also ordered to kill me," he said. He snorted and stomped his hoof in anger. Kikpona gasped.

"But my father, he wouldn't!" she said desperately, trying to believe her own words. Quetoro shook his head.

"Yes, Kikpona, he would, but none of that matters now. We must leave here at once, or they will find us very soon."

Kikpona frowned. "But where can we go? We have no allies within hundreds of miles of here! We would have to go all the way to another country to find safety."

Quetoro shook his head again. "There is a place here in Leyowan that would offer us protection. It is a forbidden place, and only animals and people in greatest need may use its safety. A place ruled by a great elephant tribe, one that Jarlir has not dared to attempt to find."

"Where is this place?" Atoru wanted to know. Quetoro motioned eastward.

"It is east, about three day's journey. I do not think the Princess could make it that far."

Kikpona put her hands on her hips stubbornly. "Do not underestimate my strength, old friend. I am sturdy enough to make it, if I ride on your back some of the way."

"Well, we can't stand here talking about it," Atoru said. "We should start off right away, or else we'll be overtaken."

Quetoro agreed, and with Atoru's help, Kikpona managed to climb aboard the red stallion.

"It is a great honor to sit astride such a fine mount," she told Quetoro. The stallion blew through his nose in pleasure.

"Many thanks, Princess. You have a kind tongue and a gentle heart," he said. Kikpona smiled in gratitude for his praise.

"All thanks to you for that. You were a good teacher," she replied. Quetoro didn't answer, because they heard the sounds of the Jungle Raiders bounding through the trees some ways off.

27

Atoru led the way at a strong canter through the jungle eastward, heading away from Ichoda.

Kikpona found Quetoro's gait to be very smooth and easy to ride. She held on to a fistful of his red mane, and clung to his sides with her legs. But even that small effort made her blink back tears of pain. Her back was still very sore. Quetoro kept glancing worriedly at her over his shoulder.

They kept up the canter, until Quetoro stopped suddenly. He raised his nose to the air, and smelled the wind. He snorted.

"We are being tracked," he said. Kikpona felt a terror rise in her. If only she had a spear...

Jungle Raiders were black panthers, equipped with sharp spiked armor. They were some of the most elite and deadly warriors in all of Leyowan. The King only sent them after the worst sort of criminals and traitors. Kikpona felt tears sting her eyes.

She thought about her mother, expecting her second child any day. If it was a son, her parents would have all they had ever hoped for. Anger coursed through her like a wildfire. She swung her leg over Quetoro's back and leaped to the ground, ignoring the renewed throbbing of her back.

She grabbed a strong branch from the ground, and stood waiting, her blue eyes snapping like sparks.

"Let them come, and I will show them the wrath of the Chosen One!" she said hotly. Quetoro and Atoru stopped and pivoted to run back to her, their faces lined with total astonishment.

28

"Princess! What are you doing? We must flee from this place!" said Atoru in a wild panic. Kikpona shook her head vigorously.

"We cannot outrun those servants of darkness. We must stand and fight or else perish. Quetoro cannot outrun them with me upon his back," she said. Atoru stared at her.

"But I...my horns are not even full length yet. I am still a calf," he said. The fright in his eyes was evident. Kikpona placed a hand on his star.

"If my strength will aid you, it is yours for the taking," she said, echoing his very words from the torture chamber doorway. Atoru's head came up, his eyes plainly stating his disgust with himself.

"I would take nothing from you, Princess. It is my own lack of courage that fails my strength."

And with that, the three fugitives stood in a line, ready for battle. The steady soft footfalls of the panthers were audible as they advanced towards their quarry.

Suddenly, the black raiders appeared, their eyes glittering under their spiked helms, and their claws exposed. Their fangs were bared as they growled fiercely. The largest of the three stepped forward.

"King Jarlir has sent us to fulfill his orders. We seek the Princess Kikpona, the Captain of One Hundred, Atoru, and the traitor Quetoro."

Princess Kikpona raised her chin. "I am the Princess. You may tell my father that I will never submit to his betrayal of the prophecy. As far as I am concerned, he forfeited all rights to me when he sent me to the dungeon, disregarding what my fate might be."

The panthers growled at that, anger evident in their glittering eyes. The largest spoke again.

"In that case, we are ordered to kill you all," he said. He bared his fangs and leaped for Quetoro's throat.

The red stallion reared and slammed his hooves into the armored attacker. The panther fell to the ground, moaning.

The other two assassins attacked Atoru and Kikpona. Whirling, Kikpona brought her branch down on the panther's head. He yelped and fell back before leaping for her again. Kikpona brandished her makeshift weapon and slammed it down on the panther's back. He fell to the ground, dead.

Quetoro's panther was proving difficult. The big stallion danced about, evading the outstretched claws. The attacker lunged for the horse's legs, and found himself borne up into the air by the sharpened horns of the black calf. Atoru slung his head to the side, throwing the panther up and over the cliff's edge.

The last assassin took advantage of Atoru's momentary distraction by swiping his bared claws across the calf's side, creating gaping wounds. Atoru huffed painfully and barely kept his footing. Quetoro's hooves came into play and he knocked the panther aside. The dark killer knew that with his two companions lying dead, he stood little chance against the determined defenders. He turned and raced back toward Ichoda as fast as his legs would take him, disappearing into the thick brush.

30

Atoru shuddered. "I can't believe I just survived my first battle," he said shakily. Kikpona laughed.

"What? Atoru, son of the great Toru the Black Bull himself, is afraid? I have never heard such a strange thing," she said teasingly.

Atoru humphed at her. "Excuse me, but you…didn't…I…" the calf couldn't come up with a good enough answer.

Kikpona glanced at Quetoro. The red stallion was looking away towards their path of travel. He had a faraway look in his eyes.

"Quetoro?" she said quietly, hoping to catch his attention. But the red stallion's eyes were captivated by a memory. His nostrils quivered slightly. Kikpona reached over and put a hand on his glossy neck. He jerked, and looked at her.

"Oh. I am sorry, my dear. I simply remember another battle that took place a long time ago. It was the day when my Sire was killed by Morbians. I will never forget the sight as long as I live."

Kikpona looked up at him sadly. "I'm sorry, Quetoro. You've never told me of your father, but judging from you, I can tell that he was a brave and noble horse," she said, trying to provide a little comfort.

Quetoro shook his head, irritated with himself.

"We will not talk more of it now. Let us be going. Soon your father will send more raiders, and we cannot fight a group larger than this one."

The other two agreed, and with Kikpona settled comfortably on Quetoro's broad back, they set off eastward once again.

.~.~.~.~.~.~.

The Black Panther raced into the palace, brushing past the serving girl who had opened the door.

"Where is the King?" he asked her gruffly. Frightened at the dark raider's presence, she pointed towards the study. The panther bounded towards the door and pounded his front paw against it.

"Enter, enter," came the admittance from within. The Raider slipped through the door, and stopped in front of King Jarlir.

"My lord, Kikpona and Atoru the Captain of One Hundred have escaped with Quetoro the Betrayer. They killed my two companions, and only I have returned," he finished with a growl.

King Jarlir banged his fist down on the table. His fury was evident in the scowl on his face and the hard set of his eyes.

"Why does my daughter keep evading my reach? Just when I think she is trapped, she manages to slip through my fingers. My son will never be safe until she is locked away somewhere. Send messengers to all my cities and outposts. Alert the guards there and tell them that I will give 3,000 gold pieces to whoever brings her to me alive."

The panther bowed and left to carry out the order. A serving girl quickly entered the room after him.

"My lord! Come quickly! The Queen is giving birth!" she said breathlessly. King Jarlir quickly rose and hurried down the hallway after her.

3

The three travelers pushed wearily on through the jungle. The midday sun was not quite so hot because of the shade of the trees, but all three were weary and thirsty. Suddenly, a long, faint trumpet blare sounded. Then another, and then another.

Kikpona looked back towards Ichoda. "Quickly, go to the cliff's edge, Quetoro! We can still see Ichoda from here!"

Quetoro turned course and went to the side. He stopped at the cliff's edge, and Kikpona looked out towards Ichoda. She saw the city afar off. She saw the palace rising up against the cliff face. More trumpets sounded.

Kikpona did not have to ask her companions what to make of the strange actions of the Ichoda citizens. She knew.

"My brother has arrived," she said quietly. Quetoro nodded. Atoru snorted in disgust.

"The Imposter has arrived, you mean."

Kikpona shook her head. "He cannot control his heritage, Atoru. He will be raised and told that he is the rightful King. And they will never tell him that he has a sister."

Atoru looked up at his Princess. A tear meandered down her cheek, and her eyes watched Ichoda with an evident longing.

Quetoro and Atoru said nothing. The Princess's grief was something neither of them had any words of comfort for. They knew that at this time it was best to be silent.

"Princess, we should be going," Quetoro said softly. Kikpona sighed, wiped her eyes, and nodded.

"Yes, Quetoro. We can leave now. I just wanted to know."

.~.~.~.~.~.~.~.

That night, the three companions bedded down in a secluded patch of short, leafy trees. Atoru nudged some of the brush and bushes around and stomped on them to flatten them. Quetoro and Kikpona watched in amusement as the black calf walked around and around in circles to make his bed just right.

"You missed a spot," said Kikpona teasingly. Atoru huffed and glared at her. Quetoro shook his head from where he had laid down in a small nest of huge leaves.

Kikpona scooted over towards the black calf. She lay back against Atoru's warm belly.

"You make a good pillow, Atoru," she said, her eyes sparkling in merriment. Atoru blew through his nose, which was his way of chuckling.

"And pray tell, Princess, what it is that has put you in such a fine mood this evening?"

Kikpona's smile disappeared. "I have a choice between crying and laughing. And I do not wish to be undesirable company, so I have chosen the later."

Quetoro sighed. "Ahhh, Princess. It is unfortunate that one so young must be burdened with problems of the adult nature. I'm afraid that all the tutelage I could provide would not have prepared you for this. I am truly sorry."

Kikpona shook her head. "I am enjoying myself, actually. I mean being here with you and Atoru. The two of you are all the company I could ever wish for. And I've always wanted to live out in the wild like this. It's not so bad."

Quetoro smiled. "It is admirable that you are able to see the good through all the evil. Perhaps you have learned something after all."

Kikpona laughed. "Yes, *hhateh*, I had a good teacher," she said. Hhateh was the word for "master" in the Ancient tongue. All the young nobles and royals of Leyowan were required to learn some of the language, if not all of it.

And for Kikpona, learning the language was like playing a game. She loved all the old words and symbols. She had learned to write and speak the entire language by age nine.

Atoru huffed again, and his eyes drooped slightly. His tail whisked a fly away, and he stretched out his neck on the ground.

"I am going to sleep now. This day has been very tiring," he said quietly. Soon, his snores filled Kikpona's ears. But

37

tonight they were a safe, welcome sound. She closed her eyes, and fell asleep.

.~.~.~.~.~.~.

King Jarlir sat at his study table, his head in his hands. The flickering candle beside him was burning the inch or so of wax left in the holder.

A quiet knock sounded at the door, and a heavily robed Queen Elaria entered the room. She sat down opposite her husband, and placed a hand on his arm.

"Jarlir, look at me," she commanded softly. The King lifted up his head and gazed into her dark eyes. She sighed, and looked at him carefully.

"You told me that you had her sent to the dungeon and whipped as a traitor. And now, she is dead. Why did you do it?"

Jarlir looked at his concerned wife. Her pale cheeks told him how tired and weak she was. The spirited glint that had always sparkled in her eyes was absent. He did not even have to ask of whom she spoke.

"Dear one, Kikpona was never a very mentally strong child. She was always so defiant and would become angry if we did not give her what she wanted. I don't know what she was thinking. Perhaps she didn't want to live in the shadow of her brother," he finished.

Queen Elaria's narrowed eyes sent a cold chill through Jarlir. Her shock at his uncaring words was so evident that King Jarlir barely held an innocent look on his face.

"Why did you send your own daughter to that horrid place?" the Queen asked. King Jarlir looked down, and took her trembling hand in his bigger one.

"I only wished to keep her quiet for a while. My love, if the people had started thinking about what she had said, Jathren, who is our own son, our flesh and blood, would have been denied the lordship of Leyowan. And I wasn't about to see that happen."

Queen Elaria's cheeks were wet with tears. She shook her head, and closed her eyes tightly in distress. She couldn't believe what she was hearing. Did her husband care so little for Kikpona?

King Jarlir drew a deep breath. "And also, my love, remember that Kikpona is the daughter of a dead imposter. A tribute to the foolish fantasies that you call romance. She was not even of royal blood... as you are not."

Elaria scowled at him, her beautiful face contorting into an angry frown. She jerked her hand away from him.

"How could you talk that way!" she said. "She is as much of royal blood as you are! She is the daughter of a man whose family ruled this country long before your great-grandfather was even born! Kikpona may not have been your daughter, but she is mine! And I never told her she was not yours. She treated you as though you were the very rising sun! Do you care so little that you despise her even now? She is dead!"

King Jarlir sighed again, but a fire began to light in his eyes. "Perhaps, but I would rather have the path to the throne clear for Jathren than be afraid of her threatening his life. She felt very strongly about the old prophecy, and would have stopped at nothing to take Leyowan as her own. I was not about to see my country in the hands of a common girl!"

Elaria stood up, her eyes flashing. "How *dare* you! If you remember correctly, husband, I was once just such a girl. Your father married me to you because of my beauty, and because my father was his closest friend, even though he was a mere tent maker! And as for Cyus, he was the only man who ever loved me for something other than my beauty!"

King Jarlir vainly attempted to soothe his wife's anger. He looked up at her pleadingly.

"Elaria, love, please consider! I never wanted any wife besides you. I love you, and always will. Kikpona is better to us dead than living. Do you want your son to be killed by her because of a prophecy that means nothing?"

Elaria stared at him. "True prophecies mean everything, Jarlir! Is your heart turned to stone? Do you care nothing that your daughter is dead? She was my daughter, and you make it sound as though she was worthless! If it wasn't for our son, I would leave you here in this castle all by yourself!"

With that, she marched out the door and slammed it shut behind her. Jarlir slumped in his chair. He had really made a mess of things.

But he knew that if he had told her the truth, she would've insisted that he bring Kikpona back. And he wasn't willing to do that. The princess's determination to be Queen scared him. Jathren was the rightful King, and no commoner was going to tell his father otherwise.

.~.~.~.~.~.~.

"Kikpona! Wake up, Princess!"

Atoru's voice broke into Kikpona's sleep. She opened her eyes and quickly sat up.

"Atoru, what is it?" she asked. He looked excited.

"The tribe is here! We are barely three miles from the haven. Quetoro has gone ahead to speak to them, and I am to bring you to them!"

Kikpona's interest was piqued. She stood up, and rubbed gently on her back. She followed Atoru into the thick trees, and began to hear drumbeats, and chanting.

They entered a little clearing, and Kikpona saw a herd of elephants standing in a semi-circle, all stomping up and down, creating a drumbeat sound against the hard packed earth. All of them were far more majestic than anything Kikpona had ever seen or imagined before in her life. Their tusks were adorned with two bronze bands that encircled the ivory. Red and black paint decorated their faces, ears, trunks and legs.

When they saw the red-haired girl standing before them, they all inclined their great heads toward her in respect. Kikpona smiled and curtsied back in acknowledgement, but inside she felt as though her stomach was turning flips. All these magnificent creatures, who could kill her with a single thrust of their tusks, were paying homage to *her*.

Suddenly, a couple of them blew a trumpet-like blast through their long trunks, and the group separated in the middle to create a path for an elephant that was at least a foot or two taller than the others. Red and gold paint created mystical patterns over his face and trunk, and his huge tusks were encircled by bands of gold and silver. Four brass rings hung from his left ear, and two from his right. His eyes were old and wise, and he looked at Kikpona with a welcoming smile.

"Welcome, Chosen of the Ancients. We are loyal to you, for we believe that the Ancients are wisest of all the living or dead, and their wish is our command. I am Pernog, the leader of this elephant tribe. All who are beneath me now are beneath you. Do with us as you wish."

Kikpona felt tears prick the back of her eyes. Such great beasts, submitting to her without question... She bowed in respect to Pernog.

"Many thanks, your loyalty is accepted with gratitude and respect, Magnificent One," she said to the old animal. Pernog's eyes lit up in surprise at the unexpected and very grand title that Kikpona had addressed him with, and he nodded his head in appreciation. Quetoro appeared behind Pernog.

"Come, Kikpona. We will take you to your new home," he said. The Princess smiled and stepped toward him.

42

Quetoro led Kikpona back behind the circle of elephants and into the trees. The tribe followed them a short ways behind, their heavy feet pounding the earth, the sound warming Kikpona's heart.

The lush jungle was so beautiful. The three miles of walking went by quickly for Kikpona, because everywhere she looked, there was something to see. Flowers in every shape and color bloomed on the ground and on the vines that grew up into the treetops.

Monkeys chattered at them from the branches of the tall forest monarchs, which rose up like dark brown pillars into the clear blue of the sky. Huge leafy bushes leaned out over the dirt path, brushing Kikpona's cheek as she passed by them.

But the greatest surprise of all was yet to come. Quetoro led her through a thick overgrowth of bushes and out into a clearing. The clearing was the size of the city of Ichoda, and everywhere there were large elephant dwellings, accompanied by hundreds of smaller huts. There were many different species of animals that were milling around the clearing. And Kikpona was also surprised to see several humans.

The large Selmar Mountains loomed high above them in the distance, veiled by hazy clouds. Suddenly, a vision passed before Kikpona's eyes, of a great walled city, flanked by watchtowers, grand turrets and spectacular main gates...

She shook her head as the vision cleared and Pernog's voice broke through her daydream. The large old elephant was speaking to the inhabitants of the haven, who had gathered around to hear him.

"My friends, our prayers have finally been answered. We will end the days of the tyrant Jarlir and bring a new ruler to the throne of Leyowan. I give you our future Queen, the Princess Kikpona of Ichoda!"

Cheering broke out, and Kikpona felt her heart leap. These were her subjects, and this was the beginning of a new time…her time. This was where she would build her own city.

The very next morning, Kikpona was awoken by Quetoro, who motioned for her to follow him.

They moved out of the village and then around the side of a gigantic rock. Quetoro looked back at his charge, and then disappeared into a slit in the stone. Kikpona followed, slipping through the narrow doorway to what appeared to be a cavern.

There was a short hallway that delved deep into the rocky outcrop. Kikpona felt a strange tingle start its way up her spine. There was something very mysterious about this place, yet it also held an aura of age and history.

When she came out of the hallway and stepped into a huge room in the cave, she caught her breath. All around her was the glitter of gold.

Gold coins littered the floor, creating an almost supernatural light all around the room. Treasure was stacked up against all four walls almost to the ceiling, from all different countries and origins. There were pure golden bowls, silver necklets, golden baubles of all types and sizes. Heavy oaken chests sat open, displaying a dazzling array of jewels; sapphires, rubies, emeralds, and diamonds.

The young princess looked at Quetoro. "How can my father not know of this treasure? Surely he would have taken it to Ichoda had he ever found it."

Quetoro nodded. "He knows nothing of its existence. The Ancients were very clear that it belonged only to the Chosen One, and that only that ruler could use it for the good of Leyowan. The elephant tribe has kept it a secret for that very reason."

Kikpona moved slowly around the room, her fingertips brushing the priceless treasures. She knelt down in front of a golden statue of a stallion, standing proud and alert. The horse's sides were inscribed with runes proclaiming the loyalty and spirit of the species.

The Princess' eyes were wide as she took in everything. Quetoro stepped toward her and spoke softly.

"There is enough here to buy an entire country," he said meaningfully. Kikpona looked at him with a determined glint in her eyes.

"Or build one."

Her words brought a surprised look to the red stallion's eyes. But then admiration and approval replaced the former expression. Kikpona smiled, and turned to the center of the room, and amazement overcame her.

There, in the center of the room, was a statue of a kneeling Ancient, withered and old, yet his stone face looked wise and noble. His robes were plain, common and tattered. But in his stone hands sat a golden crown, more beautiful than anything Kikpona had ever seen. The gold circlet was twisted around a silver band, with red and black gemstones set in between the two metals.

It was the most glorious piece of treasure that Kikpona could have ever imagined. She gasped as a sun ray beamed down through the skylight to illuminate the crown. She realized that the statue had been placed perfectly so that the morning sun would strike it.

"This is worth more than all the lands of Leyowan!" the Princess exclaimed. Her hand ventured nearer, and she extended a hand toward the precious piece.

Quetoro instantly was at her side, his muzzle restraining her hand. "Be careful, Kikpona. We know what the Ancients prophesied. But this crown can only be worn by the Chosen One, and we must make sure that is you before you dare try to wear this crown. The Ancients made mention of a curse to anyone who wore this and was not the rightful ruler."

Kikpona's eyes were fixed upon the beautiful crown. Her mind was held by it as if a spell had been cast on her.

"What sort of curse?" she murmured. Quetoro watched her worriedly. He stepped between her and the crown.

"Kikpona, do not dare to touch it. It is only yours if the Ancient's prophecy says so."

Kikpona glared at him. Her eyes flashed in anger. "Ahh, so now you too, are beginning to doubt me. Just like my father. Perhaps you should bring out the whip right now, Quetoro!"

The red stallion stared at her. He looked shocked for a moment, and then disappointment became embedded in his eyes. He shook his red mane, and trotted out of the cave, his hoof beats reverberating throughout the stone walls.

Kikpona could not believe her own words. She had just disrespected the very animal that was the reason she was still alive. She sank down against the cave wall, her own voice echoing in her mind.

"Perhaps you should bring out the whip right now, Quetoro!" The words circled endlessly in her thoughts, and resentment of herself began to form deep down inside her.

She had spoken to him as though he were a worthless pawn that could not think for himself.

Kikpona stood up, and walked outside. As the fresh air hit her face, blowing her red hair back, she sighed. How could she have been so careless? She saw Atoru waiting for her. He looked at her expectantly.

"Why did Quetoro leave like that?" he asked her quietly. Kikpona looked at him. But the concern in his eyes was too much. She had to look away.

"I said something I should never have even thought, and it hurt him. I cannot believe I was so careless," she replied. Atoru nudged her arm sympathetically.

"You do not make your mistakes better by keeping silence," he told her. Kikpona nodded.

"I know. You're right, Atoru, as always. I will go speak to him now. Did you see where he went?"

Atoru nodded, and motioned off towards the woods, over to where the cliff's drop off was. Kikpona smiled nervously at him and hurried off in that direction.

She pushed through the trees, following the hoof prints that were embedded in the soft dirt.

She came to the cliff's edge, and there was Quetoro, looking down over the Magiro Valley.

"Quetoro," she said softly. The red stallion did not answer. His red mane blew back into the wind, and his tail gently lifted in the breeze. Kikpona bit her lip. She didn't rightly know what to say. She knew that no amount of words could ever undo what she'd said.

Kikpona knelt down on the ground, and held out her arms in front of her in the submissive bow she'd seen her father's servants do to her. In doing so, she lowered herself to the obscure position of a slave.

"*Hhateh,*" she said pleadingly, tears running down her face. Quetoro turned and looked at her. His eyes were filled with betrayal and hurt.

"Kikpona, you cannot rule a country without loyal and devoted subjects. If you strike the hearts of your subjects,
48

they will not fight for you. I thought you were old enough to know that. Has everything I have taught you led to this?"

Kikpona's traveled up to look at him. "May I beg for your forgiveness, Quetoro? I have wronged you, and what I said is unforgivable, I know. But please, do not hold it against me forever."

Quetoro's eyes softened. "Even the very wisest of all beings make mistakes. You cannot be perfect. That quality is found only in the Creator. So do not try to be perfect, because you will fail. Rather, accept your mortality and do the best you can."

Kikpona rose to her feet, and faced her mentor. She reached out a hand and touched his nose lovingly.

"Quetoro, without you, I would not be able to face mortality. If you had not taught me, I might be a ruler just like my father, or even worse. It pains me to know that I have some of his lesser qualities running through my blood."

The red stallion looked away. "It is time that you knew the truth, Kikpona."

The Princess frowned. "What truth?" she asked, confused. Quetoro looked at her again. His eyes were steel hard and he looked at her with firm resolve in his eyes. When at last he spoke, his voice bore a hard edge to it.

"King Jarlir, if he may be called a king, is not your father."

Kikpona's eyes widened. Her hand went to her mouth, and she gasped. Her eyes narrowed.

"What do you mean, he is not my father?" she said suspiciously, her eyes watching Quetoro's. She still wasn't sure that she'd heard him right.

"Your mother, the beloved Queen, was the daughter of a tentmaker. She was in love with a man called Cyus, a good, kindhearted young man. The two of them were making plans to be married, but Elaria's father saw that the young King Jarlir's eye had fallen on her," Quetoro began.

"So he forced his daughter to marry Jarlir, who disregarded your mother's love for Cyus, and took her as his wife. They were married when she was only sixteen years old. She was heartbroken, and swore never to enter his bedchamber because of what he had done to her. Cyus ran away, and was not seen for three years."

Kikpona sat down against a tree. Her mind was whirling with the shock of it all. She had never remotely even suspected this. Quetoro paused momentarily, as if remembering the story, and then continued.

"So a few years passed, and when Elaria was nineteen, Cyus came back to Ichoda, and when Elaria learned of it, she began sneaking out of the castle every night. Jarlir knew of this, but said nothing, wishing to let her think she was getting away with these midnight meetings. Well, you can guess what became of that. One day, Elaria found out that she was with child to Cyus. In her fear of being discovered, she acted like she had fallen in love with Jarlir. But the King wasn't fooled. He knew exactly whose child it was. However, Elaria was wise and did not tell Cyus of the child."

50

Kikpona listened. She couldn't believe her mother had been like this once. She seemed so subdued now, submissive to her controlling husband.

Quetoro sighed, and looked over the valley. "When Jarlir told Elaria that he knew everything, she begged him not to kill Cyus. Jarlir agreed on three conditions. One, she would submit to him and act like his wife. Two, the child's true parentage was never to be told to anyone, including the child itself. Three, Cyus would be banished from Leyowan for all time, and Elaria was never to see him again."

Kikpona gasped. "Did she agree?"

Quetoro nodded gravely. "She did, not willing to have Cyus killed. Cyus was banished, and your mother became the true wife of Jarlir. And when the child was born seven months later, her true parentage was hidden from the mind of Leyowan. Cyus disappeared, believing it was his love for Elaria that had forced the King to banish him. Partially that is the truth, but you were the deciding factor. "

Tears ran down Kikpona's cheeks. "I was the child," she said. It was not a question, but a simple accepting statement.

"Jarlir's blood does not run through your veins. It is a far nobler blood than his. For Cyus came from a noble family that had long ago been dethroned by Jarlir's grandfather. Jealousy overcame Jarlir when the Ancient's prophecy pointed to you as the Chosen One. That is why he jumped at the chance to banish you when you spoke disrespectfully to him at the Tournament."

Kikpona clenched her fists as the pieces began fitting together. "And my mother sat there and let him do it. Why did she have a son for him? Why?!" her voice rose until it was a shout. She leaped to her feet and ran off into the jungle trees. She heard Quetoro start to follow her and call her name. But she ignored it and ran.

She ran until she could not run anymore. Then she stopped, breathing hard, and sank down to the ground. She lay in the soft dirt, her fists clenching handfuls of it. Tears rolled down her face.

"Why me?" she asked. The only answer was the soft rustling of the leaves in the trees. Then anger overcame her grief. She looked up at the blue sky, and her eyes narrowed.

"I will build a new city. And I will rule Leyowan."

4

Elaria stood on the roof of the castle looking down over Ichoda. Her black hair blew back in the wind. Her dark eyes were masked in sadness, and tears ran in tiny rivers down her face.

She heard steps coming up the stairwell. She knew who it was without even turning to look. A hand descended on her shoulder, and she flinched away.

"Do not touch me," she said angrily. She moved away from Jarlir. He scowled.

"Stop being so pig-headed, woman! I am regretting taking you for wife. I should never have listened to your father. He gave me a worthless wench as my Queen!" he told her maliciously.

Elaria whirled on him, and her hand rose before he could stop her. She slapped him across the face, hard. He shouted in surprise and anger and put his hand up to cover the already forming bruise.

Elaria's dark eyes sparked. "Do not dare to call me a worthless wench," she said, her voice low. "You banished my love out of Leyowan, killed my daughter, and forced me to give you a son. If anyone should be accusing someone else, it is me. I should have left with Cyus, but I kept my word, which is less than you are capable of!"

Jarlir grabbed her wrist. "You have overstepped your boundaries, Elaria! I have half a mind to send you to the dungeon!"

Elaria struggled as she glared at him. "To kill me as you killed my daughter? Please do, it would be better than life with you!"

Jarlir stepped back as though he had been struck. He stared at Elaria. She moved away, turning her back to him.

"I have never loved you. The only way I could ever bear your touch was to imagine that you were Cyus. You really think I enjoyed being kissed by the very man that banished my love outside the country?" she asked, her voice full of disgust. Jarlir's fury mounted.

"You could be put to death for such treasonous speech, my dear Elaria," he said, all effort to soothe her anger gone from his voice. He shouted down the stairs.

"Guards!"

Two of them came running up the steps. "Yes my lord?" they asked. Jarlir pointed to Elaria.

"Take her to the dungeon and find a nursemaid for her son. He will be taken from her, and she will never lay eyes on him again as long as I draw breath."

Elaria cried out. "Jathren! No, Jarlir you can't!" she said, her eyes wide. Her eyes filled with tears.

"Do not take my son from me also," she said pleadingly. "You have already killed my daughter, and banished my true love. Do not make me give Jathren to you."

54

Jarlir held up a hand to stop the guards. "Then let there be no more of this talk."

Elaria's eyes glinted with a hidden rage so hot and angry that Jarlir stepped back a step. But the look vanished beneath the veil of neutrality that Elaria kept her true self hidden behind.

She turned and left the rooftop, her train sliding down the stairwell behind her.

.~.~.~.~.~.~.

The great elephant chieftain Pernog frowned at Kikpona. "But it is so dangerous!" he argued. She sighed and looked up at him.

"Please, I know that the crown is mine. Let me try it. I would not try it if I thought it would put me at great risk. I know who I am."

The old elephant shook his head vigorously, his big ears flapping against his face.

"No. I will not let you do this. You are too valuable to us right now."

Kikpona tried once more. "But if you think I am truly the Chosen One, then why do you doubt me? I cannot take the crown from its keeper unless I am the Chosen One. Do you not believe that I am the same?"

Pernog lowered his head. His eyes closed. Kikpona could tell he was in deep thought over the matter.

"All right, you may try it. But do not be surprised if the crown rewards you with the curse."

Kikpona stared at him. "What is this curse? Twice now have I heard it mentioned, always in a hushed tone and with hesitation. Why is it so feared? Is it that dreadful?" she asked quietly. Pernog nodded.

"The curse is indeed dreadful. If any but the Chosen One takes the crown for himself, the punishment for such greed is a long slow death that is beyond the worst pain you have ever endured."

Kikpona subconsciously placed a hand protectively over her back. She could still feel the hard scars from the whip.

Pernog sighed again. "Besides, you do not have the one sign that the prophecy clearly states will be upon the Chosen One."

Kikpona frowned. "What might that be?" she asked curiously. Pernog looked at her, his wise eyes fixing on her face.

"The prophecy says: The Chosen One shall bear the mark of malice upon the skin. The Chosen One's flesh shall be scarred with hate and jealousy."

Kikpona suddenly understood. She looked at the elephant with triumph. Her hand lifted the back of her shirt and at the same time she turned around. Pernog gasped.

"My back bears the scars of the malice of my false father, King Jarlir. He had me flogged and sent to the dungeon because he was jealous of me, or rather, where I had come from. I am not his true daughter, but the daughter of Cyus of

56

the family of Rasowe the Mighty Hearted. My blood is nobler than his."

Pernog gently touched the scars with a gentle trunk. "Indeed, this puts my mind at ease. You are the Chosen One, Princess. Forgive my doubts."

Kikpona turned to face him again, and smiled. "There is nothing to forgive. Now that I know the full prophecy, I also am sure that my pain was not for nothing. I am now proved to be the Chosen One. Jarlir fulfilled the prophecy when he thought he was getting rid of me," she said with a laugh. It was a funny thought.

Kikpona walked out of Pernog's wigwam and breathed in a deep breath of fresh air. She walked down to the clearing where all of the dwellings were, and saw Atoru playing with some of the baby elephants. He was chasing them around and then letting them run after him.

Kikpona was suddenly filled with determination. She turned and slipped into behind the rock. She looked back to see if anyone had seen her. When she was satisfied that no one had, she disappeared into the cave.

Entering the treasure chamber, she stepped toward the statue. The crown's gemstones sparkled brilliantly. Kikpona reached out and took the crown from the hands of the Ancient. Raising it, she placed it firmly on her head. It fit her perfectly, nestled comfortably in her scarlet tresses.

Kikpona's eyes were drawn to the hands of the statue. A line was clearly visible now that the crown had been removed. Kikpona removed the square of stone and saw a very old piece of parchment lying within the hollow space. She took it out and read the old script.

Raise your eyes and behold the gifts of the ancients.

The newly crowned queen lifted her eyes and saw a wooden stand directly against the wall in front of her. There were two stands. One held a spear, far more beautiful than any Kikpona had ever handled before. Runes were etched into its handle, and the spearhead glowed. Kikpona removed it and ran her hands lovingly along the smooth iron shaft. She turned to the second stand and saw silken robes and a jeweled belt.

Her worn clothes were discarded and replaced with the beautiful silk. She slowly drew the jeweled belt around her waist and tied the leather cords at the end. As she pulled the velvet cape from its place, another piece of parchment fell from the folds of the fabric. It read:

Look beyond the place from whence came your spear.
Release the fire. Proclaim yourself the Chosen One.

Kikpona's blue eyes searched the gloom beyond the wooden stand. A large, circular protrusion jutted out from the wall, and an iron handle had been welded onto the stone. She reached out and grasped the handle, and twisted it. A great rumbling sound came from beneath her, and the cavern

58

shook violently. Then came a sound that would ring through Kikpona's memory forever.

.~.~.~.~.~.~.

Atoru laughed as one of the baby elephants whacked him on the shoulder with her trunk and then dashed away, calling, "You're it, Atoru!"

Suddenly, there was a loud crack, as if someone had snapped a hundred trees in two. A great "BOOM" sounded from the earth, and smoke billowed up from the rock over the cave. Then, a pillar of fire leaped up into the sky, rising hundreds of feet above the cave from which it came.

Atoru stared. The whole tribe of elephants was suddenly in a wild panic. They ran for shelter, trees, and wigwams, anything they could hide in. The young ones hid between their parents' legs in terror. All of the tribe was horrified at the natural phenomenon that rose into the skies.

Except Pernog. He came over to stand beside Atoru.

"She did it," he said softly. Atoru looked up at him, and then slowly looked back at the cave's entrance.

Jarlir put a forkful of lettuce leaves into his mouth. He chewed thoughtfully, planning his next move on Elaria. What was he to do with her?

A loud thundering blast of noise interrupted his thoughts. He stood quickly, tipping his chair over backwards. He ran to the window, and looked out. To the northwest, he saw a pillar of fire reaching to the heavens.

Then, to his terror, a vision of Kikpona entered his mind. She was wearing a twisted crown, and held an iron spear in her hand. Her eyes spoke to him.

"I will give back to you the pain you forced me to endure. Prepare, Jarlir, for I know your secrets. I know what you have done. Beware of the twisted crown, for your days are numbered."

Jarlir fell back against the wall. His eyes were blinded for a mere second, but his heart was cast into a terror that quickly enveloped his whole body. He sat there, feeling as though the palace walls were closing in around him, choking the life from him.

Then, the vision faded as quickly as it had come, and the fire disappeared into the wild forests of the north. Jarlir gasped for air, and placed a hand over his chest. A servant came running into the dining hall.

"My lord? Are you all right?" the old man asked worriedly. Jarlir stared up at him with panicked eyes.

"She's coming for me!" he whispered. The servant frowned. He reached for the king's arm and helped him stand.

"Come, my lord. You are very weary, and you must get some rest."

After one more suspicious look at the window, Jarlir allowed the servant to help him out of the dining hall.

60

.~.~.~.~.~.~.

Atoru watched the entrance to the cave. There was no sound from within. He began worry. Was the Princess alive? What had happened to her? Had the curse descended upon her because she was not the true Chosen One?

But suddenly, out of the misty entrance, a figure approached. In the figure's hand was a magnificent iron spear. On her head sat the twisted double crown of Leyowan. The terrified elephant tribe had come out of their hiding places to see this wondrous sight.

Kikpona stopped outside the entrance. She was different. Her simple clothes had been exchanged for royal robes of silk and a heavily jeweled belt. Her head shone under the crown. Her hair hung in scarlet rivers down her back, flowing in the breeze. Her eyes were hard as steel, and her face had seemed to grow ten years older in that moment.

Instantly, the entire elephant tribe, along with Pernog, Atoru and Quetoro, bowed to the ground in submission and loyalty to the newly crowned Queen. She looked over them lovingly, and then spoke. Her voice was clear and musical.

"No longer am I Princess Kikpona of Ichoda. I am now Queen Kikpona of Leyowan, your supreme ruler and Lady over all the lands of Leyowan. I ask for your loyalty with love and a promise. I will always reward your service with honor. I will always love you as my own family, and govern you to the best of my ability."

The tribe stood. Quetoro's eyes shone with pride. Atoru looked at his new Queen with a loyalty that was unmatched by any other. And Pernog just smiled knowingly.

A Queen had come to bring Leyowan back to its former glory.

.Ten Years Later.

5

Queen Elaria sat on a stool quietly, watching her ten-year-old son kicking around the leather ball that had been a birthday present from his father. Jarlir had become almost ignorant of Elaria in the past few years, which of course did not bother her in the least. She preferred it that way.

"Jathren! Come here," she called across the lawn. The young boy's face brightened with a charming smile and ran over.

"Yes, Mother?" he asked, giving her a hug. Elaria patted the ground beside her short bench.

"Sit with me a moment, my son."

Jathren obediently sat down cross-legged in the warm grass. He looked up at Queen Elaria expectantly. She smiled down at him.

"Jathren, have you thought about what I said earlier about choosing your animal friend? It is an important decision for you right now."

The boy nodded gravely. "Yes, Mother, I have. But I have so many to choose from, and I like them all very much. I do not know how I shall choose only one."

Elaria laughed. "That is exactly what Kikpona said, so long ago..." suddenly the Queen covered her mouth with her hand, realizing what she had just said. Jathren looked at her worriedly.

"Who is Kikpona, Mother?" he asked curiously. She looked at him, horrified.

"Jathren, you must promise me never to repeat that name, especially to your father, do you understand?" she said.

Jathren frowned. "I promise, but why is it so dreadful?" he wanted to know. Elaria looked out over the castle yard.

"Someday perhaps I shall tell you. But for now, it is best left out of our memories."

Atoru charged. His long horns crashed into the tree, shaking the trunk violently. The tree cracked at its base, and with a loud thud, crashed to the ground. The ring of elephants watching trumpeted their approval.

Atoru turned and bowed slightly as he accepted their accolades. He looked over at the tall woman standing nearby. She smiled at him.

"Well done, Atoru. I do believe you've honored your father's memory. You are a fine warrior."

Atoru bowed respectfully, his eyes shining with pride. "Many thanks, Queen Kikpona. You are most generous."

Kikpona's red hair was piled up on top of her head behind the twisted crown. Two strips hung down to frame her face. Her eyes were still the same hardened steel gray, but now they were wiser and stronger than before.

Quetoro stood at her right side. The old red stallion was now getting slower than he had been in his more youthful years, but a rebellious fire still gleamed in his eyes.

Atoru had changed the most. Instead of his lean, gaunt calf frame, he had now matured into a thick, heavy boned bull. The only thing about him that was the same was his gentle spirit and kind nature.

Behind them, the walls of Kikpona's new city rose high up above the jungle floor. The city was finally done after ten years of hard work to finish it. Throughout those ten years, Kikpona had silently been gathering to her an army of all different species and races, and had established her own city in the jungle. She still lived with the elephant tribe, but more loyal herds and groups were flocking to her new city. She had named it Utomia, the city of promise.

Houses and barns had been raised, and the city was now about half the size of Ichoda. Kikpona was very proud of it, because it symbolized what she had accomplished in the last ten years. Slowly, her army was growing, and soon she would be able to march on Ichoda and take back what had always been hers.

Atoru was her First General, and controlled all of her armies. The only person he answered to was Kikpona herself. Quetoro was her Chief Advisor, and helped her to better rule her people, as well as making battle plans and strategies.

A few Ichodian spies had seen the city, but they had not lived to reach Ichoda again to warn King Jarlir. There were hundreds of Utomian guards that circled far away from the city itself, stopping anyone who wanted to travel in or out of the city.

King Jarlir had become so engrossed with the plans for his son's coronation as King of Leyowan that he had almost forgotten about Kikpona's escape. He had heard so many accounts from people who had said they'd seen her dead, that he nearly disregarded her very existence.

But always there was that terror hovering in the back of his mind. He had never forgotten the vision of her cold blue eyes speaking his death sentence. So far there had been no true battles between the two cities, but of course that was because Ichoda was completely oblivious to the other city's existence.

A cool breeze rustled through the trees. The dark night sky glittered with stars. Kikpona walked silently through the jungle, enjoying a bit of time to herself. She didn't like being surrounded by advisors, subjects and soldiers all the time. She wished that she could just leave for a couple of days and live by herself. She might take Atoru with her, he was good company.

But Kikpona had hardly seen the black bull for four years. He was very busy training the army how to march, think, and fight. He had separated each species into a special unit so they could all work together at the specific skills that they excelled in.

Kikpona missed him. She wanted to go back to the old days, before all of this had happened. Before the Tournament, back to the time when they were very young, and could run where they pleased.

But now she knew that those times were over. She had a responsibility now to Utomia and her subjects. They had given her their loyalty, and she could not abuse it.

The Queen was so engrossed in her thoughts that she was oblivious to what was happening around her. As quick as a flash, a hand slipped around her head and covered her mouth while a dagger was held against her throat with the other.

Kikpona reached down and slipped a knife from her pocket.

"Ahhh... I think not, Princess Kikpona. Why don't you just drop your little knife, nice and slow."

Kikpona stared at the face of the young man that had just come out from behind a tree. She let go of the knife.

"Who are you, and what do you want with me? I have only to scream and seven thousand Utomian warriors will be headed straight for us."

The young man laughed. "Perhaps you are right, Princess. But alas, we are friends, and to harm us would be very poor judgment on your part."

Kikpona scowled. "I would hardly refer to you as friends, seeing as though I'm being held in a death grip with a Sumerilian blade at my throat."

The young man bowed. "As you wish, Royal One. Kero, release her. She is a very good judge of weaponry, it would seem. Besides, it would be a shame to kill one so beautiful, would it not, sister?"

Kikpona was released. The girl that had been holding her captive stepped over to stand beside her brother. She was taller than Kikpona, with dark brown hair and dark eyes that seemed very cold and angry. Her jagged Sumerilian dagger was tightly clutched in her left hand. Two slender sword hilts were visible behind her shoulders.

The young man smiled. "Pardon our rudeness, Princess. My name is Morgo of Halesbra, and I am from South Leyowan. My sister and I come to aid your uprising against King Jarlir."

Kikpona straightened her back and held her chin high. Her eyes met Morgo's without a flinch.

"I am not Princess Kikpona. I am now Queen Kikpona of Leyowan. I am the Chosen One that the Ancients prophesied. I am not conducting an uprising, but a movement to restore my family's name to the throne of this country. I am only taking back what is already mine."

Kero snorted. The girl's expression clearly stated that she thought Kikpona was some fussy and fancy royal whose bark was worse than her bite. Kikpona felt anger rise inside her. Kero met her gaze with a challenging look.

Morgo saw it too and quickly intervened. "Well, Your Majesty, would you allow us to be your humble subjects? We are loyal to you and would like very much to join your army."

Kikpona nodded. "You are very welcome here. If you are not hostile to me, I shall return the same to you. That shouldn't be very difficult to understand," she said looking straight at Kero.

The girl smirked and looked away, but slid her dagger back into its sheath. Morgo smiled at her, and then looked expectantly at Kikpona.

She turned around and led them back towards Utomia. The walk back was silent; none of the three said a word to another.

When they came in sight of Utomia, Kikpona stopped. She looked behind her to see Morgo and Kero staring. The tall stone walls of the city towered above them. Inside, buildings and houses were everywhere. However, all the citizens did their business quietly so as not to attract passerby's.

A large field nearby was being used for training of the army units. At the moment, Atoru was deep in discussion with a group of young steers. At sight of Kikpona and the newcomers, he trotted over. After looking Morgo and Kero over, he turned to Kikpona.

"Kikpona, glad you are back safely. And who, might I be so bold to ask, are your friends here?" he asked expectantly. Kikpona smiled.

"This is Morgo of Halesbra and his sister, Kero. I met them in the woods as I was taking my walk."

Kero laughed. Atoru looked at her. "Something funny, young miss?" he asked quietly. She shook her head, suddenly

71

the look of pure innocence masking her face. Kikpona frowned. She knew that Kero would bear watching. She liked Morgo alright, but his sister...

Kikpona watched as Atoru escorted Morgo and Kero to a guest house beside the palace. Before entering the spacious hut, Morgo turned and grinned at her.

Kikpona inhaled sharply. She didn't know what to make of it. She looked around to see if anyone else was standing nearby. But she saw no one.

Kikpona was flustered. She whirled and walked right into Quetoro.

The red stallion grunted. "You had best watch your path of travel, Your Majesty," he teased her quietly. Kikpona smiled.

"My apologies, Quetoro. My thoughts... are elsewhere, I believe. They are wandering again," she said.

Quetoro shook his head mirthfully, sending his red mane flying. He stepped aside to allow her to pass by him. Kikpona ran into the palace and into her study. Reaching for a book of prophecy, she pulled it from the shelf. Sitting down at her reading table, she opened it.

Flipping through the pages, she searched for what she was looking for. Finally, she found it.

"Ah hah. Here we are," she said to herself. Her finger traced the worn letters as she read.

"*The Queen's right hand will stretch forth to take unto her that which her family has lost, and she will mount the throne of Leyowan and restore peace.*"

72

Kikpona frowned. That was about her, but she thought she remembered something about a dark-haired girl. She looked down the page, and a sentence caught her eye.

"*A woman with dark hair and cold eyes will come into the Queen's trust, and will betray the Queen unto death, unless a friendship is discovered between them...*"

Kikpona gasped. Death? Betrayal? Could this be Kero?

The study door opened with a creak, sending Kikpona flying out of her chair and bracing herself against the wall.

"Kikpona? Forgive my intrusion! Have I startled you?" a familiar voice asked. Atoru's black face peered around the door.

Kikpona breathed a heavy sigh of relief. "Yes, Atoru. You did startle me, but do not worry yourself about it."

Atoru came into the room, his eyes watching her worriedly. She quickly shut the book of prophecies, and put it back up on the shelf with the other books. She sat down in her chair.

"What is it you came to see me about?" she asked in a vain attempt to change the subject. Atoru looked at her knowingly and used his nickname for her.

"Princess, we have never kept secrets from each other. I know that you are hiding something from me, and it is painful for me to see. Have you lost your trust in me, or are you afraid to share your fears?"

Kikpona slumped in her chair. "You know me far too well, Atoru. I have not lost my trust in you. You are my closest friend. I am just afraid to voice my fears, because you may think them…foolish."

Atoru shook his head, a clear signal to her that she was to keep explaining herself.

"I think Kero was also prophesied by the Ancients. It says that a young woman with dark hair and cold eyes will betray the Queen, even unto her death. I am afraid that Kero is that woman, Atoru. I do not wish to be betrayed, especially not to the death."

Atoru frowned. "I understand why you fear her, then."

Kikpona stared at him in surprise. "What? Why do you think I fear her, Atoru? What have I said to make you think that?"

Atoru looked at her. "When you introduced them to me, I saw a look in your eyes that I shall not forget. You do not fear her as a person, but what her person is capable of doing. She is indeed one to watch and observe. I will appoint a spy to follow her wherever she goes, and to tell me all that she does and says."

Kikpona nodded. "Be careful. If she finds out, I may be in greater danger than I am now, as may you."

Atoru bowed. "Don't worry, my Queen. Anyone wishing to cause harm to you will first have to step over my dead body. I am not about to let anyone near you if they are set on harming you."

Kikpona smiled gratefully at him as he left the room. She sighed, and stood up. Crossing the room, she stood in front of the window. She saw Morgo playing with a couple of young boys who were smashing wooden swords together. Morgo was strutting around as though he was a king, and the boys were showing off their "skills". Kikpona laughed lightly.

"Watching my brother, are you?" said a cold, dark voice from behind her. Kikpona whirled, drawing her dagger as she turned. The figure lounging against the doorway laughed lightly.

"Do not fear me, Queen. I am simply a wanderer who is cared about less than a summer's rain."

Kikpona gritted her teeth. "What do you want, Kero? I can tell that you are going to bore me quite quickly with your careless attitude."

Kero straightened. "I have nothing to hide, Kikpona. If you wish to fear me, be my guest. You just disgust me."

Kikpona stared at her. "Disgust you? You speak in riddles, Kero, and it tires my patience. Speak now before I call a guard to escort you from the palace. You should not have entered without permission in the first place. My palace is not your playground."

Kero shrugged carelessly. "I come and go where and when I please, Your Majesty. Do not try my patience," she said with a smug smile. Kikpona slammed her fist down on the table.

"Guard!" she called out the door. A young man in armor came running up to the entrance to the study.

"Yes, Your Majesty?" he asked obediently. Kikpona pointed to Kero, and waved her hands in the air.

"Get her out!" she shouted, her anger boiling over. The guard bowed and gripped Kero's arm. She jerked away, and with one last smug look at the infuriated Queen, she left the room.

Kikpona sank back in her chair. How could she lose her control like that? Kero was very dangerous to her, she now knew. Kero could make her lose concentration and fly into a rage. The prophecy's words echoed in her mind.

"*Even unto death...*"

.~.~.~.~.~.~.

Meanwhile, back in Ichoda, Elaria gently pulled the sheepskin blanket up over her son's sleeping form. She kissed his cheek, and smiled. He was already so much like his sister... strong and determined to prove himself.

A loud footstep sounded just outside the bedchamber's door. Elaria turned to leave, and saw Jarlir standing in her way. He smiled at her. Elaria felt her flesh crawl in disgust.

"He looks like me, don't you think, Elaria?" said the king. His eyes held a distinct look of disgust. She looked up at him.

"No, Jarlir. He looks like his sister."

Jarlir scowled. "Do not mention her in my presence, woman! I do not want to hear another word about her from you ever again, do you understand? I thought I made that clear enough years ago!"

Elaria set her jaw stubbornly. "I will speak of my daughter whenever and to whom I please. You have no hold on me anymore, Jarlir. I disgust myself that I ever let you near me."

The king's anger rose. "Do not push me, Elaria. Very soon I shall decide I do not wish to put up with your impudence any longer, and I will send you away. Then you will be without your son also."

Elaria laughed lightly. "Do not flatter yourself with imaginary power, my lord. You never will send me away, because you know you would lose your son also if you did."

Jarlir frowned. "What do you mean?" he asked. Elaria looked towards the sleeping form on the bed.

"He would hate you forever if you sent me away. You know this, and so you have not taken action on the matter. You would have already banished me if you did not agree."

Jarlir's temper rose quickly, knowing she was right. He shook his head angrily and left the room.

Elaria sighed in relief. For all her confident words, she wasn't at all sure about her or her son's future. She closed her eyes, and the image of a laughing girl with bright sapphire eyes and long red hair entered her mind. Elaria felt tears rolling down her cheeks. Why had Jarlir taken Kikpona from her?

But in the deepest corner of her heart, Elaria knew why. Jarlir hadn't wanted any loyalty towards Kikpona rising up from the Ichodians. She had been a threat to his throne, and he had known it.

But know Jathren was all that was left to keep his sister's memory alive for Elaria. He had the same red hair, the same sparkling eyes, and the same intelligent personality.

Elaria walked out into the hallway of the palace, and crossed the hall to her own chamber. Closing the door behind her, she sank into a chair, and gave way to tears of grief.

.~.~.~.~.~.~.

Unseen to many of the Utomians, a golden eagle quietly soared over the city. His keen eyes picked up all movements, and especially that of a long red haired woman pacing to and fro, listening intently to the voice of a tall red stallion.

The eagle was a spy from Ichoda. He went out every so often to scout the land and bring a report back to King Jarlir.

But this was new to him. He had barely noticed the city, hidden well behind the shadows of the jungle forest. He had only noticed it because he had swooped down low between the trees and seen the huts.

Kesoto the eagle had never seen this city before. And as he stared in amazement at the woman, he suddenly realized that he knew who she was. It was the Princess Kikpona! But hadn't the king proclaimed her dead almost ten years ago?

Kesoto quickly turned and flew back towards Ichoda with all of his speed. But he did not get away unnoticed. Kikpona and Quetoro had been watching him the whole time. Now, the young Queen hurried into the palace, and called for a messenger.

A swift cheetah named Makkiu came running in. "I am at your service, my Queen. Tell me your message."

Kikpona immediately replied. "I have no message. I want you to run as swiftly as you can to Ichoda, and spy on the city. I saw an eagle just leave Utomia, and I am sure it was a spy from Ichoda. I want you to take a mouse with you; one called Papilu, and get him into the palace. He must tell me what the eagle tells Jarlir."

The cheetah bowed respectfully. "Your wish is my command, Queen Kikpona. I shall find Papilu at once."

With that, he left immediately, and after finding Papilu, the two raced off towards Ichoda.

Kikpona paced back and forth in her study, lines of worry beginning to crease her forehead. A knock sounded at the door, and Kikpona turned to see who it was.

Morgo stood in the doorway. "May I enter, my lady?" he asked. Kikpona nodded stiffly. The young man came in, and looked at her worriedly.

"May I ask the occasion for such concerned manners?" he asked. He waited for an answer expectantly. Kikpona sighed.

"Since you've been so helpful with training the army lately, I suppose it would do no harm to tell you. A spy from Ichoda was sighted today, and I sent spies after him myself to see what he will tell King Jarlir. But I am sure that we will no longer have the advantage of surprise."

Morgo closed his eyes. "These are not good tidings, to be sure," he said, and then paused. His eyes opened, and he looked at her.

79

"If you will trust me, my Queen, I would ask you for an occupation in which I could be of service to you. I want to help you."

Kikpona was struck by surprise at his offer. She smiled appreciatively at him. Looking right back into his eyes, she replied, "Yes, you can. Tell Atoru what I have told you, and start arranging the army into herds. Put each kind of animal in its own herd. Pair humans with horses and whatever other animals can and will carry them. Tell the blacksmith to start making weapons. We must prepare for war!"

6

Papilu the mouse jumped off of Makkiu's back at the edge of the jungle surrounding the Ichodian palace. He scurried up to the castle doors and in through a small hole in the side.

Reaching the end of the long palace hallway, he slipped underneath the door to Jarlir's study room. He hid behind a weapon cabinet, and settled in to listen.

The eagle was speaking to his master in quiet tones.

"I have seen the Princess, wearing the Twisted Crown of Kalmenor. She has built a city in the jungle, unseen to us for many years. She is building an army, my lord, one that will crush you if you do not act immediately."

Jarlir sat in his chair, his fingers tapping his chin as he thought. The eagle waited patiently for a reply.

"Send out riders to every province, city and village in Leyowan, and bid the armies there to journey here with all haste. We will give Kikpona a war she will never forget!"

The eagle bowed and flew out the door. Papilu watched for a moment more as an evil smile spread itself over Jarlir's face.

Kikpona sat outside in the field; her skirts billowed out around her. She sighed. If only Jarlir hadn't found out so soon. Granted, she had gotten away with her hidden city for almost ten years, but she only had 7,000 warriors for her army. She was sure that Jarlir would have almost 20,000 soldiers to support his cause.

Kikpona reached up and jerked her hair band loose, letting her red hair spill down around her shoulders. She pulled the Twisted Crown off of her head. To her surprise, it seemed as though a huge weight had been lifted from her shoulders.

But in her heart, she knew why. The responsibility of ruling a city was hard enough, but she had the knowledge that she would soon be Queen over all of Leyowan. The entire country would depend on her.

Kikpona looked at the crown. Its cold beauty was unlike anything else she'd ever seen. The gold and silver intertwined, and the black and red gems sparkling in between.

Suddenly a voice penetrated her thoughts.

"My lady?" shouted the voice. Kikpona didn't look. She didn't want to. She was angry at whoever it was that was intruding upon her time by herself.

"Go away! Your message can wait," she called back. But she soon heard footsteps coming closer. She stood up furiously, and turned to face the messenger.

She found herself face to face with Morgo, who grabbed her arms.

"My lady? Is something wrong?" he asked worriedly. The concern in his eyes softened Kikpona's anger. She fought back sudden tears. Morgo quickly pulled her down to the ground, and she sat in the grass, using all her self control to stay composed.

"My Queen? Please let me help you, you are severely distressed. What is it that torments you so?" he said. Kikpona sniffed.

"I have the doubts and terrors of an entire nation weighing on my shoulders. I haven't seen my mother for ten years, I do not know even if she still lives. My father now knows of my existence here, and he will not hesitate to send an army. He wants to kill me, Morgo. And what is worse, he will pull Utomia to the ground and kill all of my subjects."

Morgo nodded and gently pulled a strand of hair away from her eyes.

"I do not know how you have stood it this long, my lady. But I promise you this; I will do whatever I can to help you with this responsibility. I will always be here for you. You have my unending loyalty."

Kikpona looked up at him, and realization dawned on her. She pushed away from Morgo, and ran towards the palace. She heard Morgo calling after her, but she stopped her ears to his voice and kept running.

She didn't stop until she'd reached the palace, sprinted down the hallway and into her bedchamber. She slipped the lock over the door handle, and sank down against the wall. Blinking back tears of confusion, she slammed her fist down on the wood floor.

"Why now? Why him?" she asked. The only answer was profound silence.

.~.~.~.~.~.~.

Kikpona opened her eyes slightly. Looking around her, she realized she had fallen asleep on the floor of her bedchamber. She slowly rose to her feet, and stretched her arms out. She felt stiff and sore all over. Crossing the room, she looked out the window.

The quiet hustle and bustle of the city had begun. The streets were lined with shoppers, sellers, and soldiers. Kikpona saw Atoru looking right at her. She looked away quickly. No doubt Morgo would've told him about yesterday. Kikpona felt like screaming in frustration.

Atoru came over and tapped on the window with his horn. Kikpona sighed, and opened it.

"Yes, Atoru?" she said. The black bull looked at her stoically. Shaking his head, he replied, "What is wrong, Kikpona? Why have you been so aloof lately? It worries me."

Kikpona shrugged. "I guess all of this stress is getting to me. But do not worry, Atoru. I will be fine…"

The bull looked at her. Kikpona could tell he wasn't convinced. He finally sighed.

"We have been friends for almost thirteen years. Do you not trust me after all this time? Have I not proved my loyalty?"

Kikpona frowned. "Atoru, I do trust you and you have proven your loyalty one hundred times over. I just have some problems that I need to sort out."

Atoru sighed, but didn't push the matter farther. Kikpona decided to change the subject.

"Have the two spies come back yet?" she asked. Atoru shook his head.

"They've been gone two days already, and still have not returned. However, I wouldn't worry. Papilu is wise, and so is the cheetah Makkiu. They will return safely, I am sure of it."

Kikpona nodded. "I hope you are right. I really do not want to lose any of my subjects, especially two that are so skilled. But you are right, Atoru. I shall not worry any more about it."

Suddenly, as if on cue, a shout came from the city gate.

"Makkiu and Papilu have returned!" called the watchman. Kikpona smiled at Atoru.

"Ahhh. Wise as ever, Atoru the Black Bull," she said. Atoru smirked and bowed. Kikpona shut the window and hurried outside the palace to where Makkiu and Papilu were waiting to be heard. She quickly placed her Twisted Crown on her head, and stood before them.

Makkiu spoke first. "My lady, we have seen much and heard much. Your father is indeed in the mind of war. Your mother, the Queen Elaria of Raubea, is soon to be banished to the Dungeon. Your father tired of her many years ago."

Kikpona motioned for him to continue. Papilu stepped in and bowed before speaking.

"My lady, he has sent out riders to all the provinces demanding men and beasts to come to his aid. Very soon his army will be numbered at 15,000 strong. He means to destroy Utomia, and bring you back to Ichoda in shame."

Kikpona laughed lightly. The crowd that had gathered now stared at her in surprise. Why was their Queen laughing at such a terrible tiding?

But Kikpona soon told them. Her eyes sparkled in merriment.

"Back to Ichoda in shame? My father wants nothing but to act like a small child who has been caught stealing, trying to place the blame on another child's head."

The crowd snickered at the humorous explanation. Papilu spoke again.

"What are we to do, my Queen?"

The eyes of all the people and animals were on Kikpona. They waited impatiently for her to decree her judgment on the matter.

The Queen lifted her eyes to the sky. "We will answer his call to war! We will drive him from our city, and send him and his armies crawling to the borders of Leyowan. Who will fight for me?" she shouted.

The roar of the crowd was deafening.

.~.~.~.~.~.~.

Kikpona sat in her bedchamber later that evening, feeling pleased with the response she had received from her subjects. She stood, her plain white nightdress trailing off the bed behind her.

She put her hand on the window sill. Thoughts of war ran through her head, and then a sudden image of Morgo's face. She shook her head.

"Happy, your Majesty?" said a wry voice from the door. Kikpona knew who it was.

"Did I bid you enter into my private quarters, Kero? I do not remember doing anything of that nature."

Kero shrugged. "I do not recall anything of that nature either, my Queen."

Kikpona turned, and saw a dagger in Kero's hand. She stared at the other girl in shock.

"So, this then, has been your plan from the day I met you in the forest. You came to assassinate me. You were the one in the prophecy."

Kero smiled. "Nay, Princess. I was not sent to kill you. I came of my own free will. For I am the Chosen One. You are simply an imposter."

Kikpona smiled. "I think you are confused, Kero, as to which one of us is the imposter, and which is the true Chosen One. I bear the mark spoken of in the prophecy, the mark of jealousy and hate."

Kikpona turned and dropped the back of her gown slightly; exposing the still hard scars she bore from her beating in the Dungeon. She was satisfied to hear Kero's sharp intake of breath.

She lifted up her gown again, and tied the back string tightly. She faced Kero once again.

"So now, you can see that I am the Chosen One," she said with a smile. But Kero's gaze met hers. Kero's hands were raised to her cheeks, and the long wings of hair that always covered the sides of her face were pushed aside. Kikpona gasped.

There, lacing across each of Kero's cheeks, were long scars, blood red in color but long sealed.

"I too, bear the mark of hate. Not from your father, perhaps. Nay, mine came from a much longer past. For years, my family has opposed that of a noble that lived close to us. He took our lands and our crops every year by force, and gave us nothing, leaving us to starve or beg. Finally, my father had no choice but to sell Morgo and me to a slave dealer from another country. The dealer then sold us to the very noble that had ruined my father.

Sir Fagellon was his name. He was very cruel to us, and beat Morgo and I if we did something wrong. My father found out, and came to rescue us with a sword in his hand. Sir Fagellon killed my father, and when I tried to save him, he gave me these as a warning. These scars are made from a Juilorian blade, the weapons of devilry. The blades that leave blood red scars."

Kero's eyes were filled with tears. "I watched him kill my father, Kikpona. That is one sight a daughter should never have to see."

Kikpona crossed the room and circled her arms around Kero. To her surprise, Kero did not jerk away. Kikpona hugged her tightly.

"I'm so sorry, Kero. I never knew. I suspected you had a painful past, but nothing so extreme."

Kero sniffed. "I'm sorry I've been so angry lately. I just thought that somehow being the Chosen One would bring my father back."

Kikpona smiled. "Wait here, I want to show you something."

She left Kero and crossed to her wardrobe. Opening the door, she reached in and brought out a long object wrapped heavily in blankets. She went back to Kero and extended the bundle.

"Open this. It is an old friend, one that I received on the day of my coronation. It was a gift from the Ancients."

Kero unwrapped the blankets, letting them fall to the floor. Her eyes widened as she pulled out the iron spear.

"The Spear of Light," Kikpona said lovingly as Kero traced the runes carved on the shaft with a gentle forefinger.

"I had one before it, but it was much more crudely made... although, I did manage to win my pairing at the Great Tournament. That was the day my father had me banished," Kikpona said with a laugh.

"Strange, since I only told him that I was the Chosen One. Apparently he had a problem with the truth."

Both women chuckled. Kero looked up, and suddenly she knelt down on the floor, face to the ground, and spoke quietly to Kikpona.

"I am your loyal servant, my Queen. I was wrong to disapprove of you. Do with me as you please."

Kikpona reached down and lifted up the other woman. She looked into Kero's eyes, and saw only love and loyalty in them.

"Kero, I am about to give you an honor that you will never have even hoped for. I am going to give you a new name. From now on you will be known as Vanddai the Strong, because of your determination."

Kero blinked in surprise. "But, my Lady! You can only give names to warriors that have proven themselves in battle!"

Kikpona smiled again. "But you have, Vanddai! You have won the battle between good and evil, in your own heart."

Kero, now Vanddai, bowed low to the woman standing before her.

"You are truly a wise ruler, Kikpona. I am honored simply to be your lowly subject."

Kikpona put a hand on Vanddai's shoulder. "Now go, and tell your brother that I wish to see him… in private."

Vanddai's smug grin spread across her face. "I will tell him. Should I tell him anything else?" she said. Kikpona glared half heartedly at her.

"No, just tell him to come in."

Vanddai left the room snickering softly. Kikpona rolled her eyes. She sat down on the edge of her bed. What was she going to say to Morgo?

Suddenly, Kikpona heard a noise begin outside. It was the frantic shouting of watchmen and the bugling of the alarm trumpets!

In that instant, Vanddai shot through the door again.

"What on earth is going on out there?" Kikpona asked, her voice edged with confusion. Vanddai's eyes were wide.

"Get your spear, my Queen! Jarlir has sent a battalion to attack us!" she said, and ran outside. Kikpona stared after her for a moment, and then grabbed her spear from the side of the bed.

Running outside after Vanddai, she took in the scene with a gasp. Outside the city walls, Jarlir's beasts were everywhere, ripping apart huts, killing, and burning. Her army was bravely attempting to stop them, but their courage was failing.

Jarlir's battalion of armored wild boars was making quick work of Kikpona's army. The boars were crazed and in their battle rage.

Kikpona gripped her spear as a huge male boar came racing for her. She twirled her spear above her head and brought the shaft down on the beast's face. He roared and fell forward.

Kikpona slammed the spearhead down and the boar breathed his last. She raised her weapon in triumph and shouted.

"Soldiers of Utomia, rally to me and we will show these traitors the meaning of death!"

Immediately animals and humans began flocking to her, all wielding their weapons furiously. Kikpona caught sight of Atoru, his horns doing their deadly work swiftly, cutting down the enemy like a scythe cuts the wheat. The big black bull bellowed furiously, his normal calmness completely gone as he fought.

Kikpona ran toward the advancing second battalion of enemies. This time, it was a pack of huge lobo wolves, their fangs bared and glistening. Saliva dripped from their mouths, and their eyes glowed red in their anger.

Kikpona slammed her spearhead into the chest of a leaping wolf. She jerked the weapon back and struck another wolf across the head with the shaft.

By this time, the army of Utomia was under control. Now that their Queen was with them, their courage was restored. They charged the oncoming battalions with a ferocity that surprised even Kikpona.

A scarce two hours after the whole battle had begun, the smoke began to clear. Bodies lay everywhere, both Ichodian and Utomian. The surviving Utomians began burying their fellow warriors with care and reverence, and Kikpona gave a special order to bury the Ichodian dead as well. Though they had been led astray, Kikpona still wished to respect their valor.

There were many well known Utomian warriors that had been killed. Atoru's half brother, Kitoru, had been killed by the arrows of a Darkshin Archer. The Darkshin's were a human race, and they were known for their deadly poison arrows. A Darkshin Arrow never missed its mark.

But Kikpona had new ideas as to how the Utomian armies could better meet their enemy and prove victorious in battle.

She found Atoru and pulled him aside. "Atoru, I want to bring my mother to Utomia. She is in grave danger as long she stays with Jarlir. If we can get her out of there, it may give us something to bargain with, because Jathren will never agree to stay without his mother there."

Atoru nodded in agreement. "I understand, my Queen. I will send out a few of our most trusted warriors to bring her to you."

Jarlir stood behind his table, arms braced against the wood, his eyes flashing in anger.

"What are you talking about, Ipotar? We were defeated? How can we be defeated by a girl that doesn't know what she's doing? Don't make me lose confidence in you, General!" he shouted at the lobo wolf that stood before him.

Ipotar lowered his head. "I'm sorry, my Lord. They were failing until she came. She fought beside them. I've never seen such skill with a weapon."

Jarlir slammed his fist down on the table so hard that the books stacked on top of it slid to the floor.

"I will not accept failure, Ipotar. You are banished from Ichoda and the Army of this city. Leave at once."

The wolf's eyes narrowed in anger. "I was a fool, Jarlir, to believe that you were the ruler we had all been waiting for. Now I see my error. I am going to join with Kikpona, because she is truly the Chosen One."

Jarlir's mouth tightened. "If you choose to join her, you will be hunted down, and killed without mercy, do you understand me?"

Ipotar nodded slowly. "If my fate is such, I cannot run from it. I will face whatever comes to me without fear."

With that, the big wolf turned and left the room. Jarlir watched him leave, and then sank down in his chair. He couldn't understand it. He was losing supporters left and right. Why? He really didn't know.

"Guard!" he called out. A leopard appeared in the doorway. King Jarlir looked at the guard closely.

"General Ipotar is leaving the palace this very moment. Kill him," he ordered. The leopard looked surprised, but she turned and left the room instantly to fulfill her king's order.

Jarlir sat back in his chair, and heard the sounds of a brief scuffle outside his windows. He didn't get up to see what was happening because he already knew.

Kikpona was a curse to him. He wished he had killed her when he'd had the chance, because now, she would be the one killing him. If she ever got close enough, Jarlir knew he was as good as a dead man. She would never show him mercy. He had shown her none.

Elaria gazed out the window of her bedchamber. Far below, in the arena, the old sword smith, Keporu, was teaching Jathren the ways of weaponry. The young boy was holding his brand new sword that his father had had made for him. Elaria shuddered. She remembered Kikpona's first sparring lessons. She had been a natural with a sword, but didn't like handling it.

And when she had found that spear, it was like magic when she used it. She could bring down the largest beast in Ichoda in a span of a few minutes.

Elaria shook her head. Why did she keep having thoughts of her dead daughter? She had other things to worry about right now. Jarlir had been acting very strange lately. He had sent an army into the jungle secretly, and only one third of the number he had sent out had returned. Elaria couldn't imagine what could possibly have arisen in the Western parts of Leyowan that her husband was so afraid of.

Elaria sighed as a soft knock came at her door. She turned to see a familiar face standing in the doorway. A black bull stood there, his face decorated by a single white star.

"Atoru?" Elaria whispered in total shock. "You're still alive? What, why are you here?" she asked, her eyes wide.

Atoru bowed respectfully. "I bring news from my mistress, Lady Opawani. She requests the pleasure of your company in her palace in the Jungle City of Utomia. Come quickly, we must get you out of here. Jarlir is planning your murder even as we speak."

Elaria shook her head, trying to clear her whirling mind. Who was Lady Opawani? The word "opah-wanee" meant forbidden. Was this mysterious Lady friendly towards her? And how had Atoru met her? The questions kept coming.

"I will come, Atoru. But how do I know your intentions are wise and good towards me? I have not even heard mention of your name since… Kikpona's death."

Her words echoed quietly in the stone room. She saw Atoru's eyes take on an understanding look.

"My Queen, I have never lost my loyalty to you. It is Jarlir that I oppose, not you. You were the mother of my best friend in calfhood."

Elaria nodded. She quickly put a second dress in a satchel, and followed Atoru out of the room. Using the back stairwell, they went down to the back of the palace quickly and quietly.

Atoru opened the tiny door in the wall for the Queen. She stepped out, and suddenly looked over towards the arena where her son still swung his weapon around, laughing and smiling all the while.

"I cannot leave him here alone, Atoru. He is all I have left of Kikpona's memory. I cannot live without him."

Atoru nodded understandingly. "Do not worry for Jathren, my Queen. He will be watched constantly by our spies. If the least threat should come to him, we will snatch him away and bring him to you."

Elaria swallowed hard, and nodded. Atoru lay down and motioned for her to ride astride his broad back. She climbed gracefully onto him, and held onto his long white horns.

"Who is Lady Opawani?" she asked as soon as they were out of sight of the castle. Atoru said nothing. Elaria repeated the question a little louder.

Atoru finally stopped. "Lady Opawani is the Queen of Utomia, the Jungle city to the west. She is a kind and fair ruler who lives to honor the memory of the Chosen One."

98

Elaria gasped. "The Chosen One? You mean Kikpona?" she asked. Atoru nodded, and continued along the barely seen path that they were traveling.

.~.~.~.~.~.~.

Kikpona paced back and forth in her bedchamber, restlessly waiting for the arrival of her mother. She had not seen Elaria for ten years, and wondered if her mother would even remember her face. She was sure that the Queen couldn't have forgotten her that easily. But still...

A shout came from outside the palace. Morgo came running in.

"She is here, Kikpona," he said quietly. She sighed and closed her eyes. Suddenly, she was startled by a soft touch on her shoulder. Opening her eyes, she saw Morgo standing inches from her, his eyes deeply penetrating hers.

"Do not worry, my Queen. She will remember the girl she knew so long ago. I am sure of it."

Kikpona pushed away from him and nodded. "I'm sure she will, Morgo."

The hurt in his eyes felt like a stab to Kikpona's heart. He stepped back into the doorway, and looked away.

"Well, I guess I'll...wait outside then," he said softly, and left. Kikpona felt her heart tear in two. How could she make him understand that she just couldn't love him right now? She had the responsibility of an entire country burdening her shoulders.

She shook her head and reached for her red velvet cape. Tying the strings to her shoulder flaps, she let it flow down in a long scarlet train behind her. She reached up and let down her hair. The red strands enveloped her in a river of beauty. She smiled. Perhaps she now would look like the Queen she had always imagined she'd be.

She picked up the Twisted Crown, and set it on top of her head. The weight of the crown reminded her of her status as Queen. She felt important. And she was ready to see her mother.

.~.~.~.~.~.~.

Meanwhile, outside, Atoru had brought a small throne for Elaria. The Queen sat down in it, her face the picture of dignity and elegance.

"You will now meet your benefactress, the great Queen of Utomia. She wishes you to have audience with her."

Elaria felt slightly nervous. Who was this Queen that her subjects should speak so highly of her? Would she be kind to Elaria, or had this been simply a trap to lull her into a sense of security and safety?

Elaria had no more time to think about it, because the trumpeters began blowing their instruments, and the town crier stood tall and began to speak.

"Presenting her Royal Majesty, Queen of Leyowan, the Chosen Ruler of her people, Queen Kikpona!"

Elaria felt her heart stop as she heard the crier's words about Kikpona. And then her daughter appeared... red hair flying in the breeze, velvet cape streaming out behind her, steel gray eyes fastening on her mother. Elaria flew from her seat into her daughter's arms.

"You're alive! I cannot believe this blessing," Elaria sobbed into Kikpona's shoulder. Kikpona herself was having a hard time keeping the tears back. The people and animals cheered and roared. Their approval of the reunion was deafening.

Quetoro stepped forward from behind the throne. "Welcome to Utomia, Queen Elaria," he said. Elaria stared at him.

"Quetoro? My daughter's tutor? I thought you to be dead also! What a day of wonder this is!" she cried as she threw her arms around the red stallion's neck. The great old horse bent his head around to encircle his former Queen.

"I will always remember your kindness to me in my younger years, my Lady. It is with great joy that I am united with you again. And to see the look in your eyes at your daughter's presentation..." he paused as his voice broke.

Kikpona gazed into her mother's eyes. Elaria sniffed and quietly brushed the tears from her face.

"It is with a warm heart that I welcome you to my city, Mother. Welcome to Utomia," Kikpona said softly with a smile. Elaria smiled back, and the two women went into the palace amid the cheers of the Utomians.

.~.~.~.~.~.~.

Jarlir burst into his wife's room. "Elaria! Come here, woman, I wish to speak to you!" he yelled gruffly. There was no answer.

"Elaria!" he shouted again. Silence was his only answer. In a fury now, Jarlir angrily stomped about her chamber, looking for her. When she failed to appear, his rage turned into suspicion.

"Bolek!" he yelled down the hallway. The leader of the Elite Warrior Panthers seemed to appear out of nowhere.

"Yes, my lord?" the gigantic cat purred demurely. Jarlir felt irritated. Something about Bolek had always made him anxious. It wasn't that he distrusted the Warrior; he was just so extremely laid back and seemed almost careless at times.

"Queen Elaria is not outside, nor is she in her apartments. Find her," the furious king shouted. Bolek bowed and walked away, his strides long and relaxed. Jarlir boiled silently.

"I was assuming that my command was to be understood as finding her sometime *soon*!" Jarlir called after the panther. There was no answer.

Jarlir put a hand to his forehead. Where had Elaria gone?

.~.~.~.~.~.~.

Meanwhile, Kikpona and Elaria were strolling leisurely about the palace garden, looking at all the beautiful plants that grew there. Elaria smiled at her daughter.

"It gives me joy beyond words to learn that you still live. My heart ached every day for you when Jarlir told me you had died."

Kikpona looked surprised. "He what?" she said. Elaria faced her with a grim expression. A tear meandered down her face.

"He told me that you were overcome by grief and depression, and that you took your own life soon after arriving in the Dungeon."

Kikpona's eyes hardened angrily. Elaria stepped back a pace at the hidden rage she saw underneath the face of her daughter. Kikpona looked at her mother.

"I was beaten. I was given the amount of lashes that my so called father would sentence a murderer to."

Elaria's eyes filled with sympathy. "Oh, my dear. Were you terribly scarred? It's a miracle you even lived."

Kikpona laughed softly. "I'm made of harder steel than you might think, Mother. Besides, my father's blood courses through me. I must be somewhat powerful and strong."

Now it was Elaria's turn to laugh. "I would hardly describe Jarlir as being strong and powerful, Kikpona!" she said with a smile. But the smile faded as she saw that Kikpona's expression remained emotionless.

"That was not the father I was referring to, Mother."

Elaria stiffened suddenly, and turned away. Kikpona watched her silently. Her mother's shoulders were tense and straight, and her hair curved around her neck in a satiny black cloud.

"Forgive me for neglecting my duty, Kikpona. I should've told you where you had really come from. But Jarlir threatened your life if I told you. He said that if I so much as breathed his name, he would kill you. I couldn't let him do that. So I kept silence. It is good that Quetoro has told you."

Kikpona frowned. "Yes, but how is it that you know that it was Quetoro and not another who told me?" she asked, curious. Elaria looked over her shoulder at her daughter.

"Do not take me for a fool, Daughter. The only living beings that have knowledge of your ancestry are Jarlir and Quetoro, and I."

Kikpona shook her head. "Cyus also knows does he not?" she asked. Elaria managed a weak laugh.

"Cyus is dead, Kikpona. And if he were not, still he would be ignorant. I never told him of my pregnancy."

Kikpona smiled softly. "Nay, Mother. Perhaps not. But we will talk of other things now. I have not been idle these ten years. I built an empire that stretches to the borders of Hakasye. I know every movement of Jarlir the moment he makes it. The very palace in Ichoda is teeming with my spies, and in his foolishness Jarlir has even promoted one of them to the rank of Elite Warrior of the Black Panthers."

Elaria gasped. "Bolek the Panther? He is your spy?" she asked in amazement. Kikpona nodded in satisfaction.

"Yes, one of my best. He has been with me for eight years now. I sent him to the palace to do exactly what he did; get under Jarlir's mask of security and lull him into trust. Bolek knows Jarlir's every strategy and movement; he even knows the placement of several hidden Elite squads of Warriors. Aye, he is invaluable to Utomia's knowledge of that tyrant that Leyowan calls King."

Elaria closed her eyes. "May his end come swiftly. Yet I somehow do not wish him dead. As arrogant and selfish as he is, he seems lost. I wish I could've reached him and made him see his errors, but alas! He would not listen."

Kikpona laughed. "No, Mother. Jarlir is never going to change. Accept that, because it is solid truth in my eyes. He is a tyrant and a dark lord. Leyowan cries with injustice under his reign, and I am here to put a stop to it…forever. I have come to silence the cries of my people."

Elaria did not speak.

Suddenly, someone cleared their throat behind the two women. Kikpona turned to see Quetoro standing there.

"Forgive my interruption, Majesty, but there is a spy waiting to report to you in your study. May I require your immediate attention for a short time? I believe the matter to be urgent…"

Kikpona nodded, and followed Quetoro into her study. Bolek stood before her, and he bowed low to the ground.

"My Queen, Jarlir knows your identity. He has sworn an oath to bring you to justice. He has the city crawling with spies."

Kikpona's eyes narrowed. She saw Elaria come to the door and lean against the frame to listen.

"Search them out. Find them. I don't care how you do it, or who it is. You bring them to me alive."

.~.~.~.~.~.~.

Within three days, Jarlir had revealed every spy in Utomia to Bolek. The Black Panther pretended grave interest in the placement of these spies. He warned the King that too few spies could give few reports. Jarlir agreed to send more spies. Bolek nearly chuckled at the King's ignorance.

It seemed as though things were moving toward Kikpona's favor after all.

8

Kikpona laughed as Bolek told her of King Jarlir's openness with him. The King was sure to tell him all, Bolek stated proudly. Kikpona nodded in approval of his work.

"Truly you are one of my best spies, Bolek. It is time I rewarded you for your bravery and loyalty to me and the kingdom of Utomia. Without you, much information would never reach my ears."

Bolek bowed low. "It is with great joy that I accept simply your approval, my Queen. I will serve you until the day I die."

Kikpona stood, and took a crown made of twisted oak branches, made in the likeness of her own crown. Placing it on his head, she raised her hand in a solemn blessing over him.

"Bolek, I give you a new name, so that the people may know of your loyalty to me and my kingdom. May the Great One smile upon you, Bolek the Light seeker."

Bolek smiled his appreciation. "Long may I serve you, Majesty."

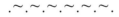

Kikpona walked the grounds alone that evening. Her mother had complained of a severe headache and had retired to her apartments shortly after dinner. Kikpona put her hand on one of the ancient trees in the garden.

She turned at the sound of a light footstep and saw Morgo standing there.

"My Queen, forgive my intrusion. My sister tells me that you wanted to speak with me the day Jarlir attacked Utomia. We never started the conversation."

Kikpona felt her blood run cold with anxiety. She hadn't expected to speak with him now. And she certainly didn't know what to say.

"Ahhhh.....thank you....I just wanted to say that I'm sorry for acting a bit....well, unsociable to you lately. It came to more than just your attention, I think. Quetoro especially said I was in a foul mood many times."

Morgo smiled. "Do not worry, my Lady. I'm sure you had a very good reason. Jarlir has been an annoyance for some time now."

Kikpona nodded. "Aye," she said. Slowly her tense shoulders began to relax.

"Morgo..." she began, but couldn't finish. He looked into her eyes, and she saw a question mirrored in his own.

"Kikpona, forgive me. But I must know your heart. Do you still feel the same as you did towards me when we talked before? Reject me again, and I shall let this subject be sent to the grave. But I must know."

Kikpona sighed. "Morgo, I have never felt that way towards you. I merely wanted to believe myself not to be in love, but alas! It was all in vain. My heart tells me to be true

108

to it, but my mind tells me that now is not the time. Jarlir will attack again soon, and this time we must be prepared. I just don't have the time for love, Morgo. But if I did, my heart would be yours."

Morgo stared at her in complete silence. He had expected another rejection. But now his eyes filled with hope.

"Perhaps, when all this is over..." he said softly. Kikpona nodded in agreement.

"Yes. When Jarlir is defeated and his armies sent crawling for the borders, then perhaps we shall talk again."

Morgo stepped towards her, and tipped up her chin. Gently, he placed the softest kiss on her lips. Kikpona closed her eyes. When they drew back from each other, both had shining eyes.

"I love you, Queen Kikpona of Utomia," Morgo said breathlessly. Kikpona's eyes filled with tears of joy.

"And Queen Kikpona of Utomia loves Lord Morgo of Halesbra back."

The midnight stars twinkled brightly as the two lovers shared another kiss.

Quetoro walked silently down the path in the jungle trees. The cool breeze blew gently into his face, lifting his forelock slightly. Unaware that he was being followed, he went down to the riverbank and slipped silently into the refreshing water.

He swam around for several minutes before his instincts warned him of a deadly presence. He looked at the opposite bank, and saw nothing. But turning to face the small shore he had entered the water in, he saw two eyes staring at him from the trees. The creature growled menacingly. Lips were raised to expose long yellowed fangs.

Quetoro felt his blood run cold. He knew what it was that stood in the trees. Hardly believing it possible, Quetoro swallowed hard. The Liger of Uytopia was nothing more than a myth to most Leyowanians. The huge beast was the progeny of a Siberian Tiger and a Lioness. The Liger was a non-speaking beast. Not only that, but he was a cold blooded killer.

The red stallion knew his only chance was to face the beast. If he were to flee, the huge animal would simply chase him until Quetoro ran out of breath and had to slow down.

The Liger slowly advanced towards the water, his slitted eyes never blinking. Quetoro lunged towards the bank, his churning hooves sending water flying up in sheets. The Liger leaped forward, landing full in the face of the big stallion. Into the water they went, the cat hissing and slashing with tooth and claw, and Quetoro pounding with his hooves and biting with his big teeth.

.~.~.~.~.~.~.

Vanddai, who was the gatehouse guard that night, leaped from her stool when she heard a loud splashing and the noise of fighting down by the river. She shouted down to the group of archers down below, and leapt from the gate to the back of her horse, Lumere. The black mare charged towards the river, with the archers following closely behind.

Reaching the water, the group saw a two animals fighting furiously in the water. One of them was Quetoro.

When the Liger saw the archers aiming for him, he lunged out of the water and went running up the opposite bank, but not before one of the arrows had reached his shoulder. He screamed, a wailing, haunted sound, sending shudders through the archers. Vanddai ran into the bloody water, reaching Quetoro's side just as the stallion collapsed. She called Lumere and hooked ropes to the mare's saddle. The other ends were secured around Quetoro's mutilated body.

Lumere used all of her strength to get the big stallion out of the water. Vanddai turned on one of the archers.

"Don't just stand there gawking! One of you run and get Baka the healer, and another of you go straight to Kikpona and get her down here, NOW!" she shouted at them. They sprang into action, running back towards the city.

.~.~.~.~.~.~.

Kikpona lay against Morgo, her head cradled against his chest. The big blankets of her bed were pulled up around them. The Queen was awake, and she looked at Morgo. She reached up and caressed the side of his face with a gentle forefinger.

Suddenly, a loud knock sounded at the door. Morgo leapt from the bed and grabbed for his shirt and breeches. Kikpona quickly wrapped a robe around herself and opened the door a crack.

"Who dares interrupt my sleep at this hour of the night?" she demanded. She saw a young man outside, his bow identifying him as an archer.

"Please, my Queen! Quetoro, your Chief Advisor, has been attacked! He is in mortal danger! We suspect the creature that attacked him to be the Liger of Uytopia! Please come quickly, my Lady! Lord Quetoro fades!"

Kikpona raced out the door with Morgo behind her. They ran all the way down to the river, and were met by a sight that nearly made the young Queen sick to her stomach.

The red stallion lay with his head cradled in Vanddai's arms. He was covered with the most hideous gashes Kikpona had ever seen. His eyes were dull and his breathing was labored.

Vanddai's hands and her shirt were covered with his blood. Kikpona let out a sharp cry and dropped to her knees beside Quetoro. Pushing Vanddai aside, she gently cradled his head against her.

"Quetoro, please do not leave me alone here. I need you. Utomia needs you. Don't go, Quetoro!" she sobbed into his coarse mane.

112

The stallion's lips moved in the softest of whispers. Kikpona had to lean down to hear his words.

"Kikpona, my Queen. You...are...the joy of your people....I fade ...all things must pass..."

Kikpona shook her head as Baka the Healer rushed up. She stood and placed her hands on the woman's shoulders.

"Save him, and I will exalt you high above your station with the richest rewards Utomia has to offer. I will shower you with gold."

Baka nodded. "I am going to do the best I can, my Lady. But I would do it for naught, for Quetoro is the friend of our people. He is very wise and Utomia needs him to survive."

Kikpona smiled gratefully through her tears as Baka knelt beside the tortured stallion.

Kikpona turned to Vanddai. "Where is the Liger?" she said ominously. Her eyes were steel hard. Vanddai looked away.

"He escaped on the west bank, my lady."

Kikpona's eyes narrowed in anger. "He was allowed to escape?" she said venomously. Vanddai didn't meet her gaze, but scuffed the toe of her boot in the soft dirt.

"I am disappointed in you, Vanddai. You didn't even follow him."

Vanddai's head came up, her eyes sparking. "Do not accuse me, Queen Kikpona. I arrived on the scene and the Liger left. How was I supposed to follow him in the dead of night? He would've murdered me and my archers without the batting of an eyelash, and it would not be only Quetoro that would be lying on the ground in pain, if not death!"

Kikpona's anger dimmed slightly. "I'm sorry, Vanddai. I just wish I could do something. It aches my heart to stand here in silence while Quetoro's attacker goes freely about the jungle unscathed."

Vanddai shook her head. "In the morning I will take Morgo and Makkiu with me and we will hunt down this beast. I shall not return to Utomia until its life's blood stains my sword."

Kikpona sighed. "I shall go with you."

Immediately Vanddai objected. "But my Queen, in all due respect, you should not put yourself in the path of unnecessary danger! You are the Queen of Utomia, soon to be Ruler of Leyowan. You need to protect yourself, not place yourself directly in harm's way!"

Kikpona looked down at Quetoro, whose breathing was shallow and labored.

"I must avenge this evil deed, Vanddai. My closest advisor and friend lies at death's door because of that beast, and I want to see its death with my own eyes. It shall be my spear that strikes through the heart of the Liger of Uytopia."

Morning rose, and the bustle of early morning street life began. But for Kikpona and Vanddai, the morning was one of anxiety and dread of the task that lay before them. Kikpona vowed not to rest until the would-be killer of Quetoro had been found and put to death.

Quetoro himself hung to life by a mere thread. Baka the healer swore she'd never seen such a strong will to live, yet the stallion's wounds were very severe. The Liger's claws and teeth were very foul and dirty, thus the wounds created by them were infected and swollen.

Kikpona had stayed by his side the whole night, talking to him when he was awake, and watching vigilantly over him while he rested. Vanddai also had been very watchful of the old stallion, trying to nourish him with herbal broths from the palace cook, who was a special friend of Quetoro.

Baka worked as hard as she could, cleaning the cuts out with cleansing herbs and poultices every hour, and rubbing the surrounding skin with a soothing leaf salve that took out some of the pain.

By midday, Baka pronounced the verdict. If Quetoro's progress was the same as it had been during the night and morning, he would live. The relief was evident in the faces of all who heard the announcement. Kikpona immediately went out to the city to tell the worried people who waited to hear the news.

She stepped out onto the balcony and looked over the concerned faces she saw below her.

"People of Utomia, Quetoro will live!"

The cheers broke out as the people hugged each other happily. The great Advisor of their beloved Queen would live to see the defeat of Jarlir.

115

.~.~.~.~.~.~.

Kikpona brought her spear into Quetoro's room. The stallion paused from eating his meal to look up at her. The Queen was dressed for war, her armor and helm polished and shining. Her spear was gripped tightly in her right hand.

"Quetoro, I must ask your blessing before I go."

The stallion looked at her worriedly and motioned Baka to take the bowl of oat mash away.

"My Lady, please reconsider. The Liger is not an enemy that will bother us again, I think, and to risk your life when there is so much depending on you right now is foolhardy. Please do not go, for I fear for your life."

Kikpona smiled reassuringly. "I shall be well protected, Lord Quetoro. Vanddai and Morgo will not let anything happen to me. And I am determined to see your attacker beneath the earth. That beast should have been destroyed years ago. He has been a terror to the cities around him for decades."

Quetoro sighed deeply. "If you are so determined to go, I suppose I cannot change your mind. But take this word of warning. Look where you do not expect him to be and you will find him. The Liger may be a non-speaking animal, but he is very cunning and dangerous. He will follow behind you as you search for him, and if you find his lair, he will attack you from the place you least expect it. Watch for him where you think he will not be."

116

Kikpona bowed in respect. "Your wisdom is beyond compare, Lord Quetoro. I thank you for your words; I shall keep them in mind as we seek him out."

Quetoro smiled. "I give you all the blessings I may as God has bestowed them on me. As my life was spared, may he also spare you."

9

Morgo, Kikpona, Vanddai and the cheetah Makkiu marched across the river to the bank where the Liger had last been seen. Weapons drawn and ready for battle at any instant, the four Warriors went quietly through the jungle. They had decided on a smaller group to go after the Liger since they would be able to travel faster and more quietly.

Kikpona led the way for some time before they found their first sign of the beast. It was the ever observant Morgo who found the track. He stopped to examine the footprint in the soft mud.

"My Lady!" he exclaimed softly. Kikpona and Vanddai returned to him, and looked down at the imprint, the long claw marks shockingly visible. A shudder ran through the Queen. The print was huge, twice the size of her own footprint.

"Is it him?" she asked, though she already knew the answer. Morgo's nod simply confirmed it. Makkiu placed a paw over one of the long claw prints.

"He is here," the cheetah whispered quietly. The cheetah's back bristled and his hackles rose. Kikpona's eyes immediately scanned the area for any sign of the beast. Seeing none, she crouched down beside Morgo. But she knew why Makkiu had suspicions. Kikpona's keen senses had picked up a strange foul odor on the gentle breeze.

"Makkiu, where is he?" she asked in a soft whisper. The cheetah raised his nose to the air, and sniffed.

"West....that way," he said and motioned towards a thick outcrop of brush. Kikpona gripped her spear tightly, and swallowed when she saw a slight movement in the bushes. The wind was not strong enough to move the branches that much.

"Yes, Makkiu, I believe we have found him."

With that, Morgo promptly pulled his longbow from the straps holding it to his back, and strung a poison arrow from the string. Vanddai's two slender swords made an appearance. Makkiu's fur began to raise even farther, his bristles up and stiff, his hackles raised to expose his shiny white fangs.

Kikpona spoke to the brush. "Show yourself, you cowardly beast!"

Two slitted eyes appeared through the branches, and a loud growl sounded, echoing through the trees. All the defenders felt a cold chill run through their bones.

The Liger's growl scaled up to a wail, a haunted scream that made Kikpona reach up and cover her ears.

Morgo drew back his bow. The Liger saw the movement and leaped. Morgo released the arrow and the poison dart found the Liger's chest. The beast roared and drew its claws across Morgo's arm.

Vanddai brought her sword down on the back of the Liger. The cat's roar changed to an outraged bellow. Kikpona twirled her spear and threw it into the shoulder of the beast.

120

The Liger, now fatally wounded, growled fiercely, its eyes shining menacingly with hate. Kikpona shuddered at the look in the beast's eyes. Collapsing on the ground, the Liger glared at Kikpona, its slitted eyes dimming slightly. And to the astonishment of all the Warriors, the beast spoke for the first and last time.

"Hyuma...keol...kalamu," he bubbled angrily, and closed his eyes in death. Kikpona stared at the body of the beast.

"He spoke! Vanddai, what did he say?" she demanded. The other woman looked just as confused as her Queen.

"I...do not know, my Lady. It sounded like some form of Cat Speech, but a much older and ancient tongue than is normally used."

It was then that Kikpona noticed the face of Makkiu. The cheetah's eyes were wide with amazement, and his hackles were down.

"Hyumakeol?!" he gasped. Kikpona knelt beside him.

"Makkiu what is it?" she asked worriedly. The cheetah's behavior was very strange. The cat looked at her with agonized eyes.

"It is almost too horrible to say...it is an old curse in the Cat Speech. The very worst curse there is in our language. He said; May the heavens fall upon you for the deeds of your family."

Kikpona frowned. "What does that have to do with me?" she asked, still confused. Morgo and Vanddai looked equally puzzled. But Makkiu explained.

121

"Many years ago, the Liger was tortured by your father for nothing more than being a non-speaking half-breed, but he escaped. Ever since then he has been tormenting the cities around Ichoda as a revenge on your father's horrible treatment of him."

Kikpona stared. "And so he singled me out because I am from Jarlir's family? Because I am his...daughter?" she asked. It made sense when she thought about it.

Makkiu nodded solemnly. Suddenly Kikpona felt tears sting her eyes. This beast that she had just killed was merely reaping revenge for such a terrible early life that her father was responsible for. For being tortured and mutilated simply because he did not speak and was the product of two breeds. Though his revenge may not have been the right thing, she still should have tried to reason with him.

"I know what we are going to do. Leave the body of the Liger on the palace steps in Ichoda. Let us see if Jarlir shows any remorse," she said. Morgo frowned.

"How are we to get the carcass through the ring of guards Jarlir has posted there?" he asked.

Kikpona smiled. "There is a caravan going into Ichoda from Bailin tomorrow. Perhaps we should be an unannounced caravan from Terar in the East? Jarlir would never suspect it. But we will surround the city just in case."

Morgo grinned. "How about you let Kero and I take the caravan? We did a bit of disguise work before we came to you. Let the masters work their trade," he said smiling.

122

Morgo never called Kero by her new name, because he claimed that Vanddai was not her real name.

Kikpona smiled at him. "If you wish the task, I give it to you. I trust you will make quick work of such an easy occupation."

Morgo nodded confidently, and Vanddai looked just as pleased with having something to do. Kikpona looked down at Makkiu, who was still listening to the conversation with a touch of pain haunting his eyes.

.~.~.~.~.~.~.~.

Morgo stripped off his shirt and gently peeled the sleeve away from the gaping wounds created by the Liger's claws. Vanddai pressed a leaf poultice against them gently to draw out the infection.

Kikpona stood behind Morgo and massaged his shoulders. "You're tense, Lord Morgo. You have knots in your muscles everywhere. What is troubling you so?" Kikpona asked.

Vanddai's eyes slowly looked up to watch her brother's face. Morgo didn't answer for a long moment, and then he looked at Vanddai meaningfully.

"I will tell you on the road back to Utomia."

And so it was that when they set out, Makkiu and Vanddai went ahead some ways to give the pair behind a chance to have a private conversation.

"I love you, Kikpona," Morgo said. Kikpona laughed softly, her eyes sparkling with merriment.

"I know you do, Morgo. You've told me before."

Morgo shook his head. "Yes but I cannot keep settling for half of you. I want all of you. We have sinned, and I cannot feel right about it until I marry you."

Kikpona stared at him. "You feel the same way I do? I hoped so. I want all of you too, Morgo, but we have sinned. Have you asked forgiveness in the temple?" she asked quietly. Morgo nodded.

"A thousand times. But my heart keeps leading me back to you. I need you, Kikpona. As a wife. I care not that you are Queen of Utomia, Leyowan or the whole world. I want to be your husband. You don't even have to make me king if you do not wish it."

Kikpona sighed, confused as to what to say. "I..." she started and then stopped. Morgo suddenly circled in front of her and knelt down.

"Kikpona of Leyowan, will you marry me?" he asked quietly.

Kikpona's eyes filled with tears of love and joy. "But Morgo, Jarlir has not been defeated..." she was stopped by his fingers pressing gently against her lips.

"Don't say it. For this moment let us be the only two people in the world. What does your heart tell you?"

Kikpona blinked the tears away. "Yes, Lord Morgo, I will marry you."

.~.~.~.~.~.~.~.

Morgo came running back into the city with Kikpona in his arms. She was laughing and telling him to put her down. But he ran up to the dais that housed Kikpona's ceremonial throne, and set her down.

"People of Utomia gather round!" he shouted. A large crowd had soon flocked around the dais.

Morgo's eyes were shining. "We have defeated the Liger of Uytopia, and Queen Kikpona has agreed to become my wife!" he said. The crowd's astonishment was plain, but suddenly the whole city became engulfed in excitement. The people and animals cheered for Morgo's achievement.

Morgo took Kikpona's hand and led her into the palace. He knocked on the door to Elaria's room. The Queen Mother opened the door and looked out expectantly at them.

"Yes, what is it?" she asked. Morgo smiled breathlessly and bowed.

"Your daughter has agreed to marry me, my Lady! I wish for your blessing upon our new life together."

Elaria's eyes widened in surprise. She glanced at Kikpona, but her doubts were silenced. Her daughter's face glowed as if she had swallowed the sun. Elaria smiled at the pair of them.

"I am very pleased for you both. Accept my most heartfelt blessing on your union."

Morgo felt like jumping for joy. He squeezed Kikpona's hand. She smiled up at him with tears in her eyes.

125

"When shall we have the ceremony?" she asked quietly. Morgo sighed thoughtfully.

"Soon, perhaps on the first day of autumn. That would be a good time."

Morgo went out the door to tell Vanddai. Kikpona fell into her mother's waiting arms.

"Am I foolish to believe such a wonderful thing possible, Mother? Is it too much to hope for such a blessing?" she asked. Elaria did not answer for a long moment.

"My dearest daughter, it seems like a lifetime since I first saw you. You were such a sweet-faced little thing; with your red hair barely fuzz over the top of your head. But you were mine, all mine, and I loved you from the minute I saw you. You are so much like your father, and you remind me of him every time I see you."

Kikpona listened quietly to her mother's words, full of love and happiness. Elaria finally continued.

"Now you are a woman. A strong, powerful woman with a kingdom at your fingertips. It is as I had always hoped. But I knew that someday a young man would capture your heart. It is not unlike my story...but there is a consideration."

Kikpona looked up at Elaria with her eyes searching those of her mother's. Her face spoke a silent question. Elaria put her hand against her daughter's cheek.

"What if Jarlir defeats your armies? What if all you fear most comes to pass? If you marry Morgo, Jarlir will see him as a way to get to you, and would stop at nothing to kill him."

126

Kikpona's hand flew to her mouth. "He wouldn't kill Morgo!" she exclaimed, as if trying to convince herself.

"Sometimes when we love someone, we have to put our own feelings away, and do what is best for that person. It may be hard at first, but when you've lived with it for a while, it is a better choice in the long run," Elaria said.

Kikpona's eyes filled with tears, and she broke down into sobs of despair. Vanddai came into the room, and stopped when she saw Kikpona and Elaria.

"Oh, my Queen! What troubles you so?" Vanddai asked softly, swiftly crossing the room and placing a hand on Kikpona's back. She knelt down beside her Queen and began to gently rub Kikpona's shoulder. Elaria smiled at her.

"I...want to marry him....Mother....he loves me..." Kikpona gasped out between sobs. Vanddai looked down as she realized what Kikpona was talking about. Elaria hugged her daughter to her chest and whispered into the red hair.

"I know he does, sweetheart. I'm sure of it. When he looks at you, his eyes tell you much that his lips do not say. He is a wonderful match for you. But do you really want to put him in danger?"

Vanddai stood up and spoke to Elaria. "My Lady, please! My brother would never wish such a grief on the Queen! He knows the dangers, and has accepted them. Do not burden the heart of our Queen any more than it already is."

Elaria's glare sent shivers down Vanddai's spine. "Do not tell me how to deal with my own daughter!" she said. Kikpona drew back from her mother.

"Mother! Vanddai was only trying to help."

To both the younger women's surprise, Elaria's eyes misted over. She looked away out the window.

"Kikpona, I know of these things. My heart was given to a man once. And he was taken from me. I do not wish the same thing to happen to you. I do not wish to see your heart shattered like a wave upon the rocks of the shore."

Elaria stood and left the room. Vanddai looked down at Kikpona with sad eyes.

"Your mother is right, my Queen. But I believe that Morgo cares not of your father's evil nature. He loves you, and told you so in front of the entire city. Marry him, for he can take care of himself. Besides, even if he couldn't, I am never far from my brother in times of danger."

Kikpona smiled up at Vanddai. "You are a very good friend, Vanddai. I thank you for your support and your wise words."

Vanddai nodded loyally. "They are always waiting for you if you should ever need them again."

.~.~.~.~.~.~.

Morgo and Vanddai completed their task efficiently. They delivered the Liger in a huge coffin to the palace steps and left strict instructions with the maid that it was for the King's eyes alone.

128

When Jarlir unclasped the lid of the coffin and opened it, he jumped back in terror. The lifeless stare of the Liger was even more haunting and fearsome than when he had been alive. The King grabbed the arm of the maid and shook her.

"Who left this here? What was his name?" he questioned her roughly. The maid's wide eyed stare quickly became more frightened as she answered her infuriated king.

"It was two people, m'lord! But their faces were covered and they didn't leave any names!"

Jarlir released her and pulled the lid back over the coffin. He signaled to a couple of guards, and instructed them to bury it somewhere far away in the jungle. Shaking his head, he went back inside the palace to compose himself.

Out in the arena, Jarlir smiled at Jathren. The young boy was exhibiting his skills with a sword for his father. His instructor had told Jarlir that Jathren was very natural with a weapon and showed great promise.

"Very good, my son!" the king called across the arena sand. The boy stopped and looked at him. He came over to his father.

"When is Mother coming home?" the young boy questioned sadly. Jarlir sighed.

"I don't know, Jathren. We are trying to find her. But your Mother was very angry with me."

Jathren's lower lip quivered slightly. "Why was Mother mad at you, Father?" he asked. Jarlir shook his head.

"For something I did not do, Jathren. Come now, we must go to the hall for supper."

Together, father and son went inside the palace.

.~.~.~.~.~.~.

On the first day of autumn, all of Utomia gathered in the meadow outside the city. It was the day of the greatest marriage in history. Lord Morgo of Halesbra was marrying their great Queen, Kikpona of Leyowan.

The Queen approached the stone altar, her white dress flowing out behind her, making her red hair look like a flame against the light fabric. Morgo caught his breath. She was beautiful beyond words. He suddenly felt a hard lump in his throat. He was marrying the woman of his dreams.

She stepped close to him and he took her hand. They faced the priest together, waiting for him to begin the ceremony.

Softly, before the entire city of Utomia, the Queen and her Lord said their vows, swearing their faithfulness and love to each other. The silence was deafening as the two exchanged rings. Kikpona gasped at sight of the silver band that Morgo placed on her finger. The silver was accented with twisted designs, matching her crown. An onyx and a ruby sat side by side, embedded into the silver.

The priest raised his hands over them.

"Upon this day you have entered into the holiest of unions. Keep the heart of the other well, be faithful, be fruitful and multiply, and love each other until the end of this world."

Kikpona blushed and she and Morgo turned to face their subjects, amid roars of approval. They left the altar and walked into a small hut that had been set up for them to spend their first night as husband and wife in.

The crowd dispersed, leaving Elaria and Vanddai to watch Morgo shut the door of the hut and close the windows.

"And so it begins," Elaria said.

The hut was elaborately decorated. Heavy velvet drapes hung over the windows, and thick rugs covered the boarded floor completely. The large bed was adorned with silken blankets and a thick feather mattress. Rose petals lay everywhere, adding a romantic touch.

Kikpona sat on the bed, smiling at Morgo, who stoked up the fire. The chill of the night was beginning to creep into the hut. Kikpona stood up and crossed the tiny room. Leaning over his shoulder, she whispered in his ear.

"Come to bed, love. I grow cold with the night's chill."

Morgo laughed at her, and took her hand. Pressing it to his lips, he kissed it. Kikpona's eyes shone with love. He jumped up and grabbed her up in his arms. Spinning her around, he held her tight. She laughed aloud.

Never had two people been so much in love. Morgo and Kikpona had a loyalty to each other that was unmatched by any…save perhaps Elaria and Cyus.

Lying in their bed later that night, Kikpona was deep in thought. Morgo was half asleep, but Kikpona's troubled dreams kept her awake.

"Morgo, love," she whispered quietly. His eyes opened.

"What…what is it?" he asked drowsily. She laughed and playfully swatted his arm.

"Our first night together and you are falling asleep? For shame, Lord Morgo!" she scolded him teasingly. Morgo's mouth curved up into a smile. Kikpona moved over to lie across his stomach. Morgo sputtered.

"Ow! You're heavy!" he said. Kikpona smiled and shook her head in amusement of his antics. He patted her knee.

"So what were you thinking about?" he asked her. Kikpona sighed.

"I want to find my father," she said softly. Morgo stared at her in surprise.

"Lord Cyus? But Kikpona…isn't he dead?" he asked. Kikpona shrugged, and shook her head at the same time.

"I don't know. No one has heard of him for many years, but in my heart I believe he is alive," she said. Morgo sighed.

"Well, let's think about it tomorrow because right now, since you woke me up, we now have another matter that needs discussing."

He smiled playfully and pulled her closer to him. Laughing, she threw her arms around his neck as he kissed her passionately.

10

Kikpona yawned and stretched. Looking out the window, she saw the sun streaming through the trees, its warm light chasing the night's chill from her bones. Reaching over to the other side of the bed, she felt only blankets. She looked around the hut but did not see Morgo.

"Morgo?" she said quietly. He wouldn't have just left her alone...would he? As if on cue, the door opened and Morgo entered, carrying a covered silver bowl that was steaming out of the cracks.

"Break the fast with me, my love," he said with a smile. Kikpona sighed in relief.

"I thought you had left me already," she said. Morgo chuckled and shook his head.

"What a notion, Kikpona. I was simply getting breakfast, and making arrangements to send Makkiu to look for your father," he said with a smile. She laughed and accepted the bowl of sweet porridge that he handed her. Sitting down on the bed with her, Morgo began eating.

"Morgo, what if we have children?" Kikpona asked innocently. Morgo spit his porridge back into the bowl, and coughed several times in succession. Putting the food away, he looked at her.

"What if we have children? I would love to have a whole palace full of children, but I believe we should hope that it

135

will not happen until Jarlir is defeated. Jarlir is on the move even as we speak, and you being pregnant would not be a very good deterrent. In fact, he would be more likely to attack because he would want to destroy the child before it was even born!" Morgo's voice had risen quite a bit.

Kikpona's eyes filled with tears. Instantly Morgo was sorry he had snapped at her. He wrapped his strong arms around her shoulders and kissed her hair.

"I'm sorry, my love. I just don't want you to get hurt. You are my wife, and it's my duty to protect you."

Kikpona nodded. "I know. It is so hard, Morgo. Everything I want cannot happen because it is too dangerous. My mother even tried to convince me not to marry you because of the risks on your life."

Morgo sighed. "I had thought of that before I asked you. But I can't wait for you. If my fate is to die in this war, then nothing I do is going to change that."

Kikpona stroked his stubbly cheek. "I am your fate, Lord Morgo."

Morgo smiled down at her, and smoothed a wayward lock of red hair away from her eyes. Kikpona's eyes closed as she let the moment warm her heart. Her love for her husband overpowered her fear of Jarlir.

"I want to find my father, Morgo. I believe he is alive."

Morgo sighed again, and looked down at his wife. "Kikpona, what would that accomplish? He probably remarried and has other children. He does not even know about you."

136

Kikpona's jaw was set stubbornly. "Well, I wish to change that. He is my father, and I cannot run from that fact forever. I want to know where I came from, Morgo. Surely you can understand that," she said. Morgo nodded.

"Yes, I understand that. Makkiu has gone to Morbia to look for him."

Kikpona gasped and stared at him. "Morbia? My father is in Morbia? But that place is...evil..." she whispered. Morbia was the neighboring country of Leyowan, and was infested with jackals, hyenas, and all manner of lawless, blood shedding beasts. Morbia was known for its evil nature and didn't take kindly to newcomers. Especially not from Leyowan.

If Cyus was truly in Morbia, Kikpona knew it was doubtful whether or not they would ever find him. If the Morbians had not killed him, he was probably hiding in some desolate place.

Morgo looked rather worried about the whole situation. He was nervous about sending Warriors to Morbia, because he didn't want to lose any soldiers when they were so near to battle with Jarlir and his Ichodian armies.

Jathren flipped through the pages of the dusty old book. His tutor, the elderly beaver Kiunee, gazed at him reproachfully.

"Young Master, you do not learn by simply reading a few of the words. You must recite the entire history of the Ancients, so instead of trying to cheat and get past it, why don't you try applying yourself for once. My, but you are so restless."

Jathren shook his head. "I miss my mother, Master Kiunee. I do not understand why she left! What did my father do that made her so angry?" he asked. The beaver pushed his spectacles up farther on his nose, and shook his head.

"That is a matter better left alone, young Prince. Your mother and father did not ever get along well, and that is all you need to know."

Jathren sighed and returned to his book. He read in silence for several minutes before looking up at Kiunee.

"Kiunee, what is all this about a Chosen One? The Ancients go on and on about it. From what I have read, it is a woman. I've never heard of a *woman* ruler..."

Kiunee started. He had been instructed very clearly by Jarlir never to breathe a word about Kikpona.

"Well….it is very likely she has not even been born yet."

Jathren shook his head vigorously. "Nay, Master. It says that she was to be born in the Year of the Red Rain, when the Morbians first attacked from our western borders…"

Kiunee took the book from the Prince and put it back on the shelf with the other history books.

"We've had a long enough lesson. You may be excused to go play in the palace yard, Prince Jathren," said the old beaver hurriedly. But Jathren merely narrowed his eyes.

"Why do you do that? Every time I mention the Prophecy about the Chosen One, everyone gets so scared like I said something wrong and you all just try to change the subject. Why?"

Kiunee said nothing, but simply sighed deeply. Jathren waited patiently for the beaver to speak. Finally the tutor looked up at his charge, a determined look in his eyes.

"It is time you knew, Young One. Perhaps I shall tell you, but you must swear on your mother's blood that you will never repeat what I am about to tell you. Do you swear?" Kiunee said sternly. Jathren breathlessly nodded. He knew that this would be a good story.

"Come, tell me!" he said eagerly. Kiunee shook his head.

"Nay, Prince. Not here. If your father hears me speak her name, he will kill me. He has made it a law that her name is never to be spoken by any tongue in Leyowan. Violation of that law is punishable by death."

Jathren frowned. "Why?" he asked curiously. Kiunee simply shrugged and reached for his ancient blue cloak.

"Come, let us go for a walk," the beaver said. Together they left the palace and went into the woods behind the city. An ancient gate stood against the face of the mountain. Jathren had often seen the gate and wondered what it led to. But no one had ever told him.

Kiunee slowly opened one of the huge iron doors. Inside, the smell was nauseating. Jathren covered his nose.

"What is this place? It reeks of blood," he said, shaking his head in disgust. Kiunee led him down a wide flight of stone stairs. Jathren heard faint screams from down long hallways on either side of the main hall that they were walking down.

"Kiunee?" he asked, frightened. The beaver motioned for his charge to be quiet and opened a barred door to the right. Inside, Jathren stared at all the torture instruments that lay on tables, on the floor and propped up against the walls. Chains hung from the ceiling in one corner.

"A torture chamber!" Jathren exclaimed. He had read about such places in his books, but had never imagined what they looked like. He shuddered at the dried blood that decorated most of the items.

Kiunee led him to the corner that had the chains hanging from above them. He sat down on the stone floor and Jathren followed suit.

"Almost twenty-seven years ago, a woman and a man fell in love…"

Kiunee proceeded to tell the story of Elaria's affair with Cyus. He told of how she become pregnant and how the evil king she was married to had banished the lover of his Queen and never told the child her true identity. Kiunee did not, however, use any names.

"And so it came to pass, eleven years ago, shortly before you were born, the girl hid her true identity under a suit of

140

armor and entered the Great Tournament. She defeated her opponent, but when she revealed herself to her father, the evil king, he was very angry and banished her to this very dungeon. The floor you sit upon is stained with her blood, for she was beaten almost to death."

Jathren quickly moved, and gagged when he saw the red stains on the floor he'd just been sitting on. Kiunee continued.

"But she escaped with the help of her old tutor, Quetoro, the great Hupeg Warhorse…"

Jathren broke in. "A Hupeg Warhorse! Kiunee, do such great animals truly exist? I have read about them in my books… but have never seen one."

Kiunee pushed his spectacles back up on his nose. "Aye, my Prince. Quetoro is truly a Warhorse. His stature and strength is unequaled by any other of his race. But back to the story… Quetoro had been banished to the dungeon years before by the evil king for something he did not do. After her beating, the girl's best friend and bodyguard, Atoru the Black Calf, rescued her with the help of Quetoro and they disappeared into the jungle. We have not heard of them since."

Kiunee did not mention that Kikpona lived in the city of Utomia.

Jathren frowned in confusion. "What does that prophecy have to do with my family, that my father has made it punishable by death to even speak of it?" he asked. Kiunee looked at the floor.

141

"My Prince, the Chosen One is your half sister. She is the daughter of your mother and a man named Cyus. The king is your father."

Jathren's mouth dropped open. "My...sis...sister?" he stammered in total shock. Kiunee nodded. Jathren stared at the stains on the floor. With a hesitant finger, he touched the red spot.

"My sister. I have a sister. My mother said something about a sister a long while ago, before she left. My sister is the child that my mother had with that man she loved before my father?"

Kiunee shook his head. "Your mother never loved your father, Jathren. She hated him."

Jathren suddenly understood. "That's why she left. She wanted to get away from my father...where did she go?" he asked. Kiunee smiled.

"She is presumably with your sister, Jathren."

The young boy looked again at the chains. "What...what is my sister's name, Kiunee?" he asked softly. Kiunee waited a long moment before he responded.

"Your sister's name is Kikpona."

Two months after Kikpona and Morgo's marriage, the Queen had gone to visit Baka the Healer, because she had been experiencing some severe sickness.

Now, Kikpona's eyes shifted uncomfortably from the gaze of the Healer. The woman looked sympathetic, and it was too much for Kikpona to bear. She stood, thanked Baka, and went outside. Breathing deeply, she inhaled the scents of the city…baked goods, spices, leather… she felt like she was going to be sick.

Going to the meadow, she fell on her knees before the stone altar and her hands went together.

"Great One, you have the power to change the course of the future, and to give life whenever you see fit. Please, help me with this new crisis that has arisen. Help me explain to Morgo…I fear for him."

"Why do you fear for your own husband, my Queen?" said a voice quietly. Kikpona looked behind her to see Atoru's familiar face looking at her worriedly.

"Oh, Atoru… forgive me, I have neglected you of late. Please accept my apologies."

The bull sighed. "Do not worry yourself about it, my Lady. Quetoro and I have kept each other company in your absence. His wounds have healed, and though he will carry his scars and his lameness for the rest of his life, he is in high spirits. It is a miracle that he even lived to tell the story."

Kikpona smiled through her tears. "I am eternally grateful that God spared his life. I could not rule this kingdom without his advice and friendship. Or yours."

Atoru's eyes filled with loyalty and gratitude. "Many thanks, my Lady. Why is it that you fear for Lord Morgo, so much so that you came here to pray for help?" he asked

143

quietly. Kikpona sighed. She had hoped that Atoru would drop the subject.

"It is a personal matter, old friend," she said softly. Atoru shook his horns.

"Since when have you withheld personal matters from me, my Queen?" he asked, a sad edge to his voice. Kikpona rose and placed her hand on the white star that sat in the center of Atoru's forehead.

"I know I have been distant from you these days. What I am about to tell you is for your ears only, you will repeat it to no one."

Atoru stared at her in surprise, but nodded solemnly. Kikpona's hand dropped to her side, and her eyes closed.

"I am with child, Atoru," she said. The bull's mouth dropped open slightly. His eyes widened, and he began to speak, but he said nothing. Finally, he spoke to her.

"Lord Morgo does not know?" he asked. Kikpona shook her head, her fists clenching at her sides.

"I have told him nothing of this. Jarlir still has not been silenced. He would seek to destroy my children. Morgo knows this."

Atoru sighed deeply. "Tell him, my Queen. More harm will come of it if you wait."

Kikpona nodded silently, and smiled at Atoru. The black bull looked down, obviously troubled at this news.

"Do not fear for me, old friend. I will tell him tonight."

.~.~.~.~.~.~.

Morgo opened the door to the bedchamber, and set his sword against the wall, and threw his cloak next to it. He saw Kikpona braiding her hair, sitting on a soft cushion on the floor.

"How was your day, my love?" he asked her softly. Kikpona did not answer. Morgo crossed the room and knelt down beside his wife.

"I asked you a question, Kikpona," he said, a little louder. She looked up at him. A scared light lit her eyes, and she smiled hesitantly.

"It was...fine," she stammered. Morgo frowned. He saw her quickly look away from him. He was now very worried about her. Kikpona never acted like this.

"Kikpona, what's wrong?" he asked. She didn't answer for a moment, and then she slowly lifted her eyes to his face. She swallowed hard, and quickly spoke.

"Morgo...I... I carry your child."

The words were spoken quickly, and immediately after she said them, Kikpona looked away, tears filling her eyes.

Morgo was silent, but his eyes said much. A shocked light filled them, but just as suddenly as it came, it vanished.

"I had hoped for more time. But if we are meant to be parents now, I am overjoyed to be the father of your child."

Kikpona looked at him, and smiled. "You don't know how happy I am to hear you say that."

Morgo caressed the side of her face with a gentle fingertip. "Actually, maybe it's a good thing. It might keep

145

you from putting too much of a strain on yourself. And also it will keep you from participating in all the fighting."

Kikpona's eyes gleamed with mischief. "Perhaps," she said devilishly. Morgo looked sternly at her.

"Not perhaps, it will."

Kikpona put on a slightly pouting face. Morgo grinned and shook his head in amusement.

"Come, let us dine and celebrate. It is far past the time of the evening meal."

11

Jarlir looked over his army, his eyes scanning the thick mass of soldiers, all fully armored. Those who could bear arms held a weapon of some sort. The steers had poison caps on their horns, and the Darkshins were well equipped with their deadly arrows.

All the beasts and humans stood together, awaiting the command of their king. Jarlir smiled evilly. At last, his army was ready. But he was not quite about to send his entire force to Utomia. He would start by sending a battalion of about 3000 soldiers into the city to stir up Kikpona's anger.

"Separate yourselves into battalions!" the new general, Lesoru, who was a strong blacksmith, shouted at the army. Immediately the groups shifted into battalions. Jarlir smiled.

"The first battalion attacks the city of Utomia tomorrow. I want fifty Darkshin archers in that group, as well as one hundred ten of the poison capped steers. General Lesoru, you decide the rest."

The army cheered in anticipation of a battle. The beasts roared and whinnied and bellowed.

Jarlir turned and was confronted by Jathren. "Father, let me accompany your army into battle. I want to fight."

Jarlir laughed, his eyes mocking his son. "Fight? You? Jathren, you are the Prince of Ichoda. You do not fight in battles. You should be keeping to your studies."

Jathren's eyes darkened. "Why are we going to war, Father? Who is the enemy?"

Jarlir hesitated. "It is a jungle city, and there is a man there that pretends to call himself Lord of Leyowan. I am simply destroying his city and putting him to death for treason."

Jathren shrugged. "Then why not let me fight..." he stopped his words when he saw his father's eyes take on an enraged light. Jathren turned and left the balcony. Jarlir shook his head. He would have to tie a tighter rope on that boy. Jathren was beginning to ask too many questions.

At midnight that very same evening, Jathren stood before the armory doors, the full moon illuminating the dark sky above him. He slowly pushed one of them open and stepped inside. Dust fogged his vision, as the older armory had not been visited for many years. The new armory was farther from the palace, and that was where the army had been outfitted.

Jathren lit a lantern, and looked around at all the ancient weapons and armor. He gently touched a dull spear with his forefinger.

"Needing somethin', are ye?" came a soft voice from the shadows. Jathren whirled around, his fingers tightening on the lantern. He saw an old man, shriveled and withered with age, gazing curiously at him out of one eye. The other eye was covered by a black patch.

"Aye, sir. I need to be suited up in armor. I fight on the morrow, and I do not know what I need for the battle."

The old man smiled, revealing a toothless mouth. "I think I might be able to help ye, son. Hanre am I called. Hanre the Old, for I have walked this earth for ninety and nine years. Aye! And so I have."

Jathren blinked in surprise, finding it hard to imagine anyone being that old. He bowed respect. Hanre quickly pulled out a chain mail shirt from a shelf. He held it out to Jathren. The chain mail was so tightly woven that Jathren knew it would almost be impossible to force any weapon through it. He slipped into the shirt, and looked up at Hanre.

"It fits!" he exclaimed in surprise. Hanre nodded, his one eye twinkling merrily.

"Aye, and so it does, at that. Quite well, indeed, indeed!" said Hanre, chuckling gleefully. Jathren felt a warm smile come to his face at the old man's excitement. Obviously Hanre did not receive many visitors.

"Hanre, how long have you been in this armory? Do you stay here alone, all the time?" Jathren asked quietly.

149

Hanre sighed deeply. "I have been in this 'ere armory for seventy years. And yes, alone I have been all those years. I've never married nor have I any chil'ren. If ye don't mind my askin', who might ye be, Young Master?"

Jathren smiled and straightened his shoulders. "I am Prince Jathren of Ichoda, and my father is King Jarlir of Leyowan."

Hanre nodded, his eye twinkling again. "Well, bless my eye! Prince Jathren? I've heard of you, me boy. So, back to this 'ere suitin' up business...what be yer preferred weapon?"

Jathren felt his heart race in excitement. He looked over all the weapons, and his eye fell on a large broadsword.

"That one," he said, pointing to the blade. Hanre's eyes lit up. He slowly shuffled across the room and drew the sword from its holder.

"A good choice ye have made, Prince. This be the Broadsword of Gamwren the Wise. A great warrior was Gamwren! Aye, one of the greatest of all times, he was."

Jathren's interest was piqued. "Tell me about him, please Hanre! I love the stories of warriors and their heroic deeds."

Hanre winked at him. "As I did also, when I was but a young boy. Well then, make ye'self comf'table."

Jathren settled himself on the floor, and waited eagerly for the story to begin. Hanre sat on a chair, deep in thought, as if recalling the story from the depth of the past.

"Well, Gamwren were a young lad when 'is father passed on. 'Is mother was so grieved by 'er husbands passin' that she died o' a broken 'eart. Gamwren knew that the only thing 'e could do was join the army. Had nowhere else to go, y'see. So join the army he did. And he was the bravest of all the soldiers. I know, because I was there when he served our kingdom."

Jathren listened, scarcely daring to draw breath lest the story end too quickly. He looked up at Hanre.

"What happened?" the boy asked. Hanre jerked as though he'd been woken from a deep sleep.

"Oh, I'm sorry, me lad. I must've drifted off to sleep. Now let me see, where I was...oh yes! So Gamwren was the bravest of all the Warriors in the kingdom. His heroism in battle and in everyday life was amazin' to all 'is fellow soldiers, and that be includin' me. But one day, one o' his fellows got mighty jealous on account o' Gamwren's popularity, I guess ye could say. Stabbed the mighty Gamwren in the 'eart while he be sleepin', and we couldn't save him. Died the very next mornin'. But afore he passed, he looked at me and said, "Hanre, ye be brave for Leyowan, ye hear?" And then he was gone, just like that."

Jathren's eyes misted over. "What an act of complete cowardice and hate! How could anyone murder someone else just because they were popular and brave and truly a heroic person?" he asked incredulously.

Hanre smiled sadly. "Men be a dangerous breed, Young Master. Jealousy is the root of the deepest hatred. So it was

151

with Gamwren's murderer. But that lowlife got what was comin' to him. Got hanged, he did."

Jathren nodded in approval. "Good. People like that should not be allowed to remain alive."

Hanre frowned disapprovingly on the boy. "Do not be so hasty to end life, Prince Jathren. There ain' nothing glorious about death. I have killed men, and I watched men die."

Prince Jathren sat deep in thought. "Forgive me, Lord Hanre. I am ignorant to the ways of war. But my father marches on the city of Utomia tomorrow. He is angry with the King of that city. I don't know who he is, but apparently he has done something to anger my father. I wish to march with them, and fight for my country. But my father does not wish me to come."

Hanre's one eye sparkled with amusement. "And so ye're going to stowaway with the army? Ye be remindin' me o' meself when I was a young'n."

Jathren grinned, and looked down at the sword in his hand. He gripped its handle tightly, and swung it around in a wide arc. The blade cut through the air lightly, making a soft swooshing sound.

"Well, let's suit ye up, lad. Ye can't go to battle with naught but a sword," Hanre said, and scuttled off towards the suits of armor, Jathren following closely behind him.

.~.~.~.~.~.~.

152

Vanddai walked briskly through the palace hallways. Her eyes were narrowed, and a worried crease lined her brow. Pushing open the door to Kikpona's private chambers, she stopped in front of the chair where her Queen sat.

"My lady, we must prepare the army for war. Papilu and Makkiu just came back with the scouting report. A large force marches on our walls even as we speak! I've already alerted Atoru and Morgo, and they are getting the soldiers ready. I wanted to tell you."

Kikpona pushed herself up from the chair, and faced Vanddai with a grim expression on her face.

"Let me get ready, and I will meet you and Atoru outside the palace in the span of half an hour. How far is Jarlir from here? How much time do we have, Vanddai?"

Vanddai looked at her Queen worriedly. "Majesty, you cannot fight with us! Not in your condition! Morgo will have my head if I allow you to fight. Your job is to focus on planning strategies."

Kikpona's eyes hardened. "Do not tell me what I can and cannot do. If I wish to fight in this battle, I will. Morgo may be my husband, but I am Queen of Leyowan," she said harshly.

Vanddai lowered her eyes. "And because you are Queen of Leyowan, you need to take care of yourself and not put yourself into any kind of danger. You know Jarlir wishes you dead. Do not make it easier for him to fulfill his wish. Please, Highness."

Kikpona now regretted her thoughtless words. "You are right, Vanddai. As wise as ever, and loyal. How ungrateful I am."

Vanddai smiled and bowed, leaving the room. Kikpona sighed and leaned against the table.

"But I am still Queen of Leyowan."

Morgo looked over the grim faces of his soldiers. He was commanding the battalion of elephants from Pernog, who had recently moved his tribe up into the mountains, and also a group of mounted spearmen. The horses snorted and stomped, their blood growing hotter and hotter as they readied themselves for the coming battle.

"As your captain, I am proud to command you," said Morgo. "Let us show Jarlir that he is not welcome in Utomia!"

The warriors began to stomp their feet, making a thundering noise. The elephants kept up a steady rhythm as they moved into the trees to meet the oncoming enemy.

Vanddai watched her brother disappear into the forest before turning to her own group. She was mounted on Lumere, and the black mare pranced about eagerly. Vanddai silently put her war helm on her head, and tightened the chin strap.

"You heard my brother. Repay Jarlir for his evil doings!" she shouted. Lumere charged after Morgo's group. The herd of horses galloped behind the leading pair. The stampeding herd's pounding hooves shook the earth as they raced through the trees.

Unseen to either of the previous captains, a third Warrior mounted a white stallion, watching after the proceeding groups.

"My Queen, please reconsider," the stallion pleaded with his rider. The woman looked down at him sternly.

"Hasero, I am the Queen of Leyowan. I am not going to sit in the palace and twiddle my thumbs all day because I carry a child. The battle will keep up my strength and my child's as well," she said recklessly.

Hasero lowered his head submissively and said no more. His worry was evident in his eyes, and Kikpona frowned. She mounted the horse and sent him into the forest.

But she was not unseen to one captain. Atoru the Black Bull saw the mysterious figure disappear, and shook his head in frustration. He knew exactly who the rider was. The Queen would ride with them to battle. Atoru shook his head and led his group of steers and bulls silently into the jungle.

.~.~.~.~.~.~.

King Jarlir's general, Lesoru, held up his hand, calling for a halt. His small force of Ichodians were in a thickly wooded part of the jungle. He dismounted from his bay stallion Kiu. Kneeling down in the dirt, he traced the footprint with his finger.

"What do you make of it, Kiu?" he asked gruffly. The stallion studied the print.

"It is fresh, my lord. Very fresh. Scarcely a few minutes ago, I would say. And it is a cat's foot. See the slight claw marks? But it is not a large cat like a lion or a tiger. I would say cheetah, perhaps."

General Lesoru nodded. "A messenger. Well, it looks as though we might have company sooner than we thought. Tell the soldiers to prepare for combat."

Kiu trotted back through the lines, alerting the group. Lesoru straightened and peered up through the branches of the trees. He saw nothing out of the ordinary, but something felt....

An arrow whistled through the branches of a tree and plummeted down towards the general. The weapon hit Lesoru square in the chest, and he fell to the ground with a cry.

"General!" Kiu raced back to his master. The bay stallion turned Lesoru over with his nose, and saw the veil of death over the general's eyes.

"Darkshin archers, ready!" called Kiu. Now that Lesoru was dead, he had to take over the command of the army.

The archers knelt down, stringing their bows with their deadly poisoned arrows. Suddenly, there was the sound of many hooves pounding the earth, and Vanddai's horse battalion thundered through the brush and was upon the Ichodians before the startled army had a chance to react.

156

Vanddai was thrown from Lumere's back as the mare reared to dodge a Darkshin arrow. She scrambled up and drew her swords, whirling them over her head, and bringing them down on the archer that had loosed the arrow. Her weapons twirled and slashed, dropping more and more of the archers as she furiously fought.

Morgo was soon on the scene with his elephants. The huge animals went right to work with their sharpened tusks and huge feet. Morgo caught sight of Vanddai making a swift end of a large tiger.

He grinned at her and pulled out his double-bladed war axe. Letting out a loud war cry, he charged into the furious battle, his cloak billowing out behind him.

Horses fell to the remaining Darkshins' arrows. Vanddai ran right into the group, and began cutting them down. But one of the archers set his sights on her and strung his bow. He drew back, ready to make a killing shot, when a spear ran him through from behind. He screamed and fell forward. Kikpona jerked her spear from the body, and whirled it over her head. She saw a mounted warrior go running for Morgo, who was busy fighting a steer.

Using all of her strength, she hurled her spear straight and true. The warrior's horse fell on top of him, killing both of them. Kikpona ran forward and retrieved her spear. Morgo saw her and frowned. Kikpona looked away and quickly left for a different area of the battle.

Morgo suddenly knew. He had seen the lock of red hair that had been exposed under the war helm as Kikpona had run away from him. His anger boiled over. He jerked his weapon from his opponent's body and ran after her.

.~.~.~.~.~.~.

Vanddai faced a huge warrior. The man was at least six and a half feet tall if not more, and his huge arms were thickly muscled. He held a heavy war hammer in one hand, and a spear in the other. Vanddai felt a twinge of doubt. Could she defeat this giant?

She shook her head. She had to. She flipped her swords around in her hands. The giant spat into the dirt.

"What's your name girl, tell me so that I may carve it into your corpse!" the giant growled. Vanddai swallowed hard.

"I am Kero-Vanddai. I am a Lady of Utomia. And I do not fear you," Vanddai said, her voice cold and full of contempt. The warrior laughed loudly.

"I am Atrobius, King Jarlir's champion warrior. I have killed many, many soldiers. You should fear me, Kero-Vanddai, for I will kill you also. You have my word on that."

Vanddai dodged a lightning fast jab of Atrobius's spear. She whirled and brought her sword down on his spear, snapping the shaft in two. Atrobius roared and dropped the useless weapon, twirling his war hammer. Drawing a dagger from his belt, he held it up. Blood coated the short blade.

158

"All the great warriors I have killed have been killed with this dagger, Kero-Vanddai. Fear it, for it is your doom also!" he shouted insanely.

Vanddai somersaulted under the war hammer just as it came down, meaning to crush her skull. She vaulted to her feet and made a quick jab with her left sword, drawing a long gash across Atrobius' leg.

"Aaaarrrrggh!!!!" the giant roared, and reached down, grabbing the two swords that Vanddai held and throwing them into the trees. Vanddai slipped her own knife from a hidden compartment in her breastplate. She gulped when she saw Atrobius smile evilly.

"You're mine now, Lady of Utomia. Say your prayers!"

Vanddai ducked under the swing of the war hammer. When she straightened, she blocked the giant's dagger with her own knife. But Atrobius was the stronger of the pair, and he began to push forward, catching Vanddai off balance. She fell backwards onto the bloodstained dirt.

Atrobius put a hand on her stomach, keeping her down. She struggled wildly, vainly attempting to get up. The giant pressed his dagger against her throat. Vanddai's eyes suddenly filled with a fierce determination to live, and she sank her knife into Atrobius's dagger arm. He jerked back, and she rolled out from underneath him.

A steer charged up to her and shook his horns menacingly. She threw her knife at him, and it lodged in his chest. The steer fell to the ground, and Vanddai saw one of her swords hanging off a bush barely ten feet away. She made a run for it.

A huge arm came in and grabbed her, pulling her back. Vanddai turned just in time to see Atrobius's evil smile, and then his dagger plunged through her armor.

Her cry of pain was heard throughout the battlefield. Morgo recognized the voice and raced towards his sister. But he was not the only one racing to Vanddai's rescue. Kikpona had also heard the cry, and she was running for all she was worth.

Vanddai gasped for breath, and Atrobius slowly drew the dagger back, twisting it as he did so. Vanddai grabbed her stomach, and her eyes got wide as she struggled for breath. Atrobius leaned close to her ear.

"I told you I would kill you, did I not? I gave you my word. And I always keep it."

.~.~.~.~.~.~.

Kikpona saw Vanddai double over. Red hair streaming out behind her, Kikpona raced forward, brandishing her sword in a wild fury. She brought it down on Atrobius' shoulder, and then shoved him back into Morgo's battle axe. The giant fell dead. Kikpona knelt beside Vanddai, and looked down at the gaping wound.

"Vanddai! Speak to me, please!" Kikpona pleaded, her voice barely above a whisper. The other woman's eyes were half-closed as she opened her mouth slightly.

160

"You have my loyalty, Queen Kikpona. Like a sister you have been to me since I arrived in Utomia. I should have told you this before."

Morgo cradled his sister's head in his lap, and stroked his dirt and blood covered fingers gently down her cheek. Tears rolled from his eyes and dripped down onto Vanddai's face.

"It is nothing, Morgo. I will not... die. I am made of sterner stuff than that! Please, do not weep for me!"

Kikpona stood and shouted for a healer. Atoru came running up, bringing with him a tall man. The healer dropped to his knees and slowly pulled the bloodstained chainmail away from the wound.

Vanddai's teeth gritted harshly. Morgo reached down and took his sister's hand.

"No, sister. You will not die. I will not allow it," he said fiercely. Vanddai smiled shakily and squeezed his hand.

Kikpona stood next to Atoru, her face ashen with fear. Morgo did not look at her. Kikpona knew that her husband was angry with her for fighting. But right now Vanddai needed them, and they would not argue in front of her.

Makkiu came bounding up to Atoru, and bowed swiftly. Atoru looked down at the messenger and nodded, motioning him to speak.

"General, another battalion advances! They are spearmen and a few of the Jungle Raiders march with them, as well as mounted warriors."

Atoru looked at Kikpona. "My Queen?" he asked, seeking her opinion. Kikpona looked down at Vanddai, whose face was twisted in pain as the healer worked.

"Morgo, take your sister back to Utomia and see that she is made comfortable in the hands of Baka the Healer. I will lead…"

Morgo was shaking his head violently. "No. I am not going to leave you here alone to fight the Ichodians. Vanddai will be well cared for, and she will live. I am not going to stay with her only to find out that you were killed because I did not stay."

Vanddai nodded in agreement. "Fear not for me, my Queen. I will be fine. It only distresses me that I cannot fight beside you."

Kikpona reached down and patted Vanddai's shoulder. Smiling, she gave the other woman an encouraging look.

"Do not worry about it, Vanddai. After today you have already proved yourself a hundred times over. You will be rewarded for your bravery."

Vanddai said nothing more as the healer gave her an herb to make her sleep. He motioned for a litter to be brought, and carefully Vanddai's mounted soldiers lifted her onto the soft cushions. Hurrying back towards Utomia, the litter soon disappeared from sight.

Morgo turned to his wife. "I would be furious with you, except that I know I would have done the same thing had I been in your situation. I will not leave your side for the rest of this battle, and may I be struck down should a single scratch be made on your skin."

Kikpona kissed him quickly and smiled at him. "Do not worry, my love. All will be well."

12

Jathren's nervousness began building as his battalion moved into the forested valley. He sat astride a great bay stallion called Yuro. The big horse had said nothing as Jathren had told him of his true identity, and had promised to keep it a secret.

But now, Jathren wondered if Hanre had been right. The old man had warned him that battle sounded more glorious than it was. Jathren's hands began trembling as he gripped the black mane of his mount. Yuro turned his head to the side slightly.

"My Prince? Are you ill?" he asked concernedly. Jathren quickly shook his head in denial.

"Nay...not ill. This is my first battle, and I... fear what is to come."

Yuro nodded. "So it was with me when I first galloped into the battle of Espoda with Toru the Black Bull. I was afraid of death then. But now it is just another part of life for me. We all must pass on someday, and better to die in battle for your country than to die at a worthless old age."

Jathren pondered the stallion's words. They made sense to him. But he wasn't sure if he would rather die in battle than in old age... But of course, he was only eleven years old. He had his whole life ahead of him. Yuro was middle aged and starting to slow down a bit as his youth began slipping away.

Jathren had no more time to think on the subject, however, because a great war whooping sounded from up ahead. Instantly the Ichodians were in a line of battle formation. Yuro spoke quickly to the young prince.

"Stay with me, and I will protect you. Watch your back and be wary at all times. Do not attack first, let the enemy come to you and wear himself out."

Jathren nodded shakily. He drew his broadsword and tried to steady his hands. They shook violently now, and his mind whirled with all the things he had been taught.

Horses, mounted archers, and foot soldiers of Utomia suddenly began pouring out of the trees toward the line of Ichodians. The two armies clashed with ferocity. Tooth and claw, weapon and shield were wielded mercilessly against the enemy.

Jathren found himself flying through the air as Yuro jumped over the body of an elephant. The young prince fell off the side of the horse, crashing to the ground heavily. He quickly stood and ducked as an arrow whizzed past his ear. Thoroughly shaken, he steadied himself. He was not going to do any good if he was so afraid.

Yuro found him again and shouted at the prince to follow him. The horse and the boy rushed to another place in the battlefield where the fighting was less fierce. Jathren brandished his sword as a spearman came running for him. He dodged the spear's shaft and brought his blade up into the Utomian's stomach. The man fell.

166

Jathren felt a rush of adrenaline as his will to survive began taking effect. He whirled and dropped another spearman, and then felled a mighty buffalo wolf.

Yuro was right beside him, hooves flying, teeth flashing as he fought his opponents. Jathren felt a rush of pride run through him.

He was the brother of a Chosen Queen, and he would fight bravely and he would show his father the meaning of courage!

Jathren rushed into a clearing and saw two heavily armored humans slashing his comrades down like wheat in the harvest. One of these two saw him and strode purposefully forward.

Jathren's newfound bravery wavered. This soldier appeared to be a great warrior, skilled in battle and killing. Jathren felt grateful for the protective helmet that covered his face, hiding his fear.

The warrior flipped his spear around in his hand then up over his head. The shaft whizzed by Jathren's head. He stumbled backwards, and heard the warrior laugh.

"Are you afraid, soldier? Aye and so you should be, for I am one to be feared. Behold, Kikpona of Leyowan!" the warrior said, and whipped her helmet from her head. Jathren stared as dark reddish hair was revealed and sparking blue eyes stared at him ominously. It was his sister!

Jathren dropped his sword in amazement, and Kikpona smiled smugly, thinking she had frightened him into surrender. But the young boy turned and ran from the scene, his legs traveling faster and faster.

Kikpona gazed in disgust after the boy. She did not know that he was her brother. Shaking her head with repulsion at the young soldier's lack of courage, she returned to the battle.

.~.~.~.~.~.~.

Yuro found Jathren huddled beneath a tree. The big stallion began to speak, but was silenced when he saw the tearstains on Jathren's cheeks. The young prince sat there and shivered, even though it was not cold. Yuro's eyes surveyed the boy worriedly. He had no idea what had happened to make his prince so frightened.

"She's real. She's alive."

Jathren's lips had moved in an almost silent whisper. Yuro cocked his head to the side in confusion.

"Who is real, my Prince? What has distressed you so?" the stallion asked gently, not wanting to startle the boy. Jathren turned agonized eyes up to the big horse.

"My sister. Kikpona is my sister."

Yuro's mouth dropped in astonishment. "Who has told you, my Prince? Tell me their name that I may reveal them to the King!"

Jathren started. "No! You cannot. I will never betray the one who told me. But why is it such a terrible thing that I know this? My mother told me once that to so much as

168

whisper my sister's name was high treason and was punishable by death. Now I know what she did that made my father hate her, but I do not understand why he hates her for it. She did nothing wrong, she merely told him the truth. Is the truth now despised? Is doing right now treason?"

Yuro was amazed at the wisdom of his young prince. This mere boy knew so much more than many of the Elders did. It made him doubt his own loyalties. Had Jarlir really become so hardened? And exactly why was Kikpona so despised?

Yuro shook his head. "I cannot rightly answer that, my Prince. All that I knew once seems to be casting doubt into my mind. Perhaps I am wrong to fight for your father. Perhaps I should look for a more deserving place to lay my loyalties."

Jathren shrugged his thin shoulders, a lock of his unruly red hair flopping down over his eyes. "I don't know what to think anymore, Yuro. My father says he loves me and that he is trying to build me an empire to rule. But do I have rights to this empire? I do not even wish to be King. My sister wants to rule. She has the power and courage to rule. So why shouldn't she?"

Yuro looked away. "Your father doesn't want her in power because she is the symbol of a love that he could never have. He wanted Elaria but he could never really have her because she had already given away her heart."

Jathren sighed, closing his eyes. "There is so much bloodshed, Yuro. So many innocent people are dying because

169

of my father's jealousy. And he acts as though it is their duty
to die for him. That they should do so without question,
without a reason. How ashamed I am to be his son."

Yuro had nothing to say at that. The words had been so
deeply heartfelt. Jathren really was ashamed of his father's
greed and jealousy. Yuro felt a deep pride stirring within him.
He knelt down on his knees, his black mane falling down over
his face.

"Whatever your heritage, you are destined for greatness.
You have the heart of a lion, and the courage of an eagle. You
are truly a royal Prince, and I give you my loyalty, be it ever
so humble. Command me as you see fit."

Jathren stared at the horse in surprise. "But, Yuro! If my
father knows you broke your oath to him to give your loyalty
to me, he will kill you! In his opinion, loyalty to me rather
than him is as treasonous as it is to be loyal to Kikpona!"

Yuro's dark eyes surveyed him solemnly. "But is my
choice where I will put my loyalty. And now I give it to you."

Jathren's eyes misted again. "I will forever treasure your
loyalty, Yuro. And since you have so willingly bestowed your
honor upon me, I will also do the same to you. I give you a
new name. From henceforth you shall be called Yuro the
Loyal. And I choose you as my brother-friend."

Yuro stood. "May honor and glory shower you with
their blessings, Highness. I am honored beyond measure. I
will serve you proudly."

.~.~.~.~.~.~.

Kikpona watched with growing pride as her army chased Jarlir's battalions to the edge of the forest. The defeated Ichodians fled back to their city, looking rather like whipped dogs with their tails between their legs.

Her eyes turned suddenly to the death and horror that lay all around her. Dying Ichodians and Utomians groaned in pain. Healers darted back and forth, trying to save as many lives as they could. Kikpona had given orders that all the wounded Ichodians were to be tended and then brought to Utomia, where they would be looked after until they were well enough to transport to the dungeons to await their trials.

Kikpona knelt beside a young Utomian steer, whose red coat was stained crimson. She saw a long sword slash running from his neck to his shoulder. Another cut scored his side.

"Bravely you fought today. You will be honored when you have been tended and your wounds healed," Kikpona whispered to the groaning calf. His eyes turned to her, bright with pain. Kikpona shouted for one of the healers. He scurried over quickly.

"Give me a bag," she ordered. He handed her one of the bags he had strapped to his shoulder. The bag was used by the healers. It contained many herbs, bandages, and poultices.

Kikpona took it and motioned him away, back to his other patient. She took out a cloth and soaked it with her water filled pouch. Dabbing gently at his wound, she wiped away the blood and dirt. The wounded steer stretched out his neck, his breathing shallow. Kikpona pressed a poultice over

171

his neck wound, staunching the flow of blood. She made him eat the root of a Trymn plant, known for its ability to ease pain.

The steer took it gratefully. "God shower his blessings on you, my Queen," he rasped.

A dark presence appeared beside the Queen. Without glancing up, she knew it was Atoru. The black bull made a distressed sound in his throat.

"Many have died today. We suffered great casualties, my Queen. The Ichodians also have lost many. But we lost more."

Kikpona closed her eyes. "Let us tend to the wounded, Atoru. We cannot help those who are dead."

The black bull bowed and walked off to assist the litter-bearers who were transporting the wounded back to the city. Kikpona smiled down at the red calf.

"What is your name, soldier?" she asked him gently. He looked up at her.

"I am Lylu of Jertoma, Revered One. My brothers still fight for Jarlir. It grieves me to know now that it was one of them who made this mark upon me."

Kikpona felt a lump rise in her throat. Before she could stop it, a choking sob wrenched itself from her. She threw her hand up to cover her eyes as she began to cry heavily.

Lylu was greatly alarmed. "Please, my Queen! Do not trouble yourself about it. I should not have told you. Forgive me," he pleaded weakly. Kikpona shook her head.

172

"It...is not...you..." she said brokenly. Gathering the contents of her healer's bag, she called for a litter to be brought. She swallowed her tears, and tried to smile reassuringly at Lylu.

"They are going to take you back to the city. I will see you again soon, Lylu of Jertoma."

The calf watched her worriedly as the big oxen lifted him up to the litter. He never took his eyes off of her until she vanished from his sight behind the trees.

Kikpona straightened her shoulders. Her back ached suddenly. She stretched a bit, and then moved on to a big wolf that had been struck by a war axe.

.~.~.~.~.~.~.

When all the wounded had been removed from the battlefield and taken back to Utomia so they could recover from their injuries, Kikpona stood alone in the middle of the clearing. Tears fell freely from her eyes as she looked over all of her fallen subjects. Horses, steers, wolves, leopards, lions, humans... they had all died willingly for her. They would never see the defeat of Jarlir. They would never see the peace that would come to the country.

She sat down in the dirt and covered her face with her hands. What had she done? Had she brought her people to this...for nothing?

Doubts encircled her mind, torturing her with visions of a dark future. Would her beloved city fall? Would her people beg for mercy before Jarlir's merciless greed?

A vision of Utomia in flames, human and animal alike forced to flee from their homes screaming in fear, came to Kikpona's eyes. She gasped and covered her face with her hands. What had she done?

.~.~.~.~.~.~.

Jarlir paced the floor. Jathren had been missing the entire day. But the King did not have to ask where his son had gone. Fury filled Jarlir at the very idea that his son had dared to disobey him...no, deliberately defy his command.

The infuriated king stomped about his bedchamber, his long robes flowing out behind him like a scarlet flag. He stopped at the window, and saw the exhausted battalions of Ichodians returning from the forest. His eyes dimmed with anger when he saw they brought only a few Utomian prisoners. One of them looked familiar... Jarlir's face hardened when he saw Bolek the Black Panther among the Utomian captives.

How dare he! So his chief Raider was a spy! Jarlir felt hate rising toward Kikpona with the very thought. So she thought she could just send in a cunning spy and learn all about his movements, did she? Well he would show her what he thought of that.

He turned and stomped down the stairwell to the door. He flung it open and stood staring at the prisoners. Bolek did not look up at the enraged king. Instead, his panther eyes closed. He knew very well what lay in store for him.

Jarlir stepped up to the panther's side. Looking down at the big cat, the king spoke angrily. "I called you my Elite Raider. And this is how you repay me? With treachery. I trusted you, and you deceived me!"

The cat said nothing, his eyes still closed. Jarlir felt his temper rising still more. "Speak, and defend yourself! For this will be your only chance to do so!"

Bolek's eyes opened. He looked up at the king. His eyes were filled with hatred.

"You are destroying your people. Even your own son despises you. I fight for one who gives us the promise of peace and unity, something we have not had as your subjects. Not ever! You kill hundreds just to feed your own lust for revenge on a woman who has never done anything to harm you. She only claimed what was hers, and you scorned her, mocked her in front of Ichoda itself, beat her within an inch of her life, and threatened her with death!"

The entire courtyard was silent after the panther's outburst of fury. Bolek gazed up at the king.

"If death awaits me for what you consider as treason, so be it. At least I will have died for a cause that I believe in. I remain loyal to the One Queen. She has been faithful to me with promises that she has kept."

Jarlir's hands clenched into fists. He motioned for a guard to come forward. Looking down at his former Elite Warrior he spoke menacingly.

"Take Bolek the Betrayer to the common square and chain him to the stocks. Have the people throw their rotten food at him for three days. Let them mock him and taunt him. Divest him of his dignity, and show him how we treat traitors in Ichoda. Give him only a trickle of water and no food. On the third day, we will turn him loose in the arena with some of our warriors, that they will make sport of him and then kill him. Then we will see how deep his loyalty runs!"

.~.~.~.~.~.~.

Flames roared up behind the city walls. Houses crumbled to dust before the fire. Humans and animals milled about in the streets, looking for a way to escape the furnace. All around them were Jarlir's army, taunting them and blocking all the escape routes. The Utomians suddenly realized it was their fate to perish in the flames. Turning agonized eyes to their Queen, their hurt and betrayal coursed through her.

"NO!"

Kikpona screamed and sat up. She looked around her in confusion. There were no flames, no dying Utomians. Frowning, she saw only her bedchamber walls. Morgo was not there. The door to her room opened and Quetoro hurried in.

"My Queen! What is wrong?" he asked. Kikpona looked up at him, and her eyes ran over his scars.

"Do not fear for me, Kikpona. I am well enough healed. What troubles you, child? Let me help you."

Kikpona felt herself relaxing to the familiar voice of the old stallion. She tried to give him a shaky smile through her tears.

"It was a dream. That is all. A very bad dream."

Quetoro stood patiently, waiting for her to continue. Kikpona closed her eyes. "I saw Utomia falling to flames. And my people...dying."

The big stallion lowered his head slightly. Kikpona looked at him. He was acting strangely quiet. Finally, however, the stallion spoke.

"Perhaps God has given you a vision to see what will happen to your people if you should fail."

Kikpona caught her breath. "Quetoro?" she whispered in horror. That couldn't be true!

"It is well that you know this. But you will not fail. You are a mighty Queen. God has favored you thus far. And I believe he will continue to do so."

Kikpona sighed. "But, Quetoro, what if I do fail?" she asked quietly. The possibility was almost too terrifying to think of. Quetoro shook his head.

"Nay, my Queen. Do not even consider it. Do not believe that you will fail. For in doing so, you will make failure all that much more probable."

Kikpona knew that Quetoro was right. The old stallion's words made sense to her. Her fist closed on her blanket, her knuckles whitening. Being Queen was so hard for her. She loved her people and believed in her cause. But was this all really worth it?

Quetoro sensed her inner turmoil. "My Queen, please do not keep your feelings from me. I am your Advisor, but more than that, I am your friend. I want to help you, but I cannot do that if you always shut yourself away and hide your feelings from me."

Kikpona closed her eyes tightly. "I feel so helpless, Quetoro. I don't know what to do anymore," she said. Opening her eyes, she looked up at the stallion. "I feel death all around me. So many of my people are dying, and now that I have started this war with Jarlir, I cannot end it until one of us is dead. Jarlir will never let me go free after all this. So I cannot even surrender."

Quetoro's eyes widened to show his astonishment. "Surrender? My Queen! How can you even speak such a word? Surrender to Jarlir, and all your people that have been killed will have died for nothing. Do you want their deaths to be in vain? Did they die for a cause that will never come to pass?"

Kikpona shook her head. "No, Quetoro. I will not let that happen." Determination filled her and her eyes hardened.

"I will not let that happen. Where is Morgo?"

The red stallion sighed. "He is with his sister. She was in much pain tonight, and he went to comfort her."

Kikpona nodded. "Thank you, Quetoro."

"I'm always here for you, my Queen," the old stallion replied with a smile.

13

Kikpona thoughtfully chewed a bite of watermelon. Beside her, Morgo watched his wife carefully. She had been so quiet the past two days since the battle. No word had come to them about the Utomian prisoners, and they were all worried.

"Kikpona..."

The Queen looked over at him. "What is it, my love?" she asked him quietly. Morgo looked down at his plate.

"What is wrong? You've been so quiet and sad lately. It troubles me. Please tell me. I hate it when you hide your feelings from me."

Kikpona laughed. Morgo stared at her, his eyes darkening with hurt.

"Why do you laugh? I am not playing with you, Kikpona. Why do you laugh at me? I am merely concerned for you. Is that such a terrible crime? Please, enlighten me!"

Kikpona's laughter died. "Forgive me, Morgo. I was not laughing at your words. I was simply amused because only just yesterday, Quetoro said the exact same words to me. I am just trying to think on the best way to rule my people. Forgive me if I seem distressed."

Morgo nodded slowly, still only half convinced. His eyes traveled down to her slightly noticeable pregnant belly.

"I am worried for you. I don't want you to become distressed."

Kikpona reached across the table and squeezed his hand. She smiled reassuringly at him. "Do not fear for our child, Morgo. I will protect him with my life."

Morgo's eyes brightened a little. "I know you would, my love."

Kikpona watched him closely. "How is Kero?" she asked him quietly. Morgo looked up. He had not heard her use his sister's old name since they had changed it to Vanddai.

"My sister recovers well. But Baka has told me that there was a lot of infection. She will always be pained at times by the wound, even when it heals. The blade that marked her was a Juilorien dagger, the kind that causes terrible infections and painful scars. The same kind that marked her face."

Kikpona shuddered. "I will visit her after our meal is finished. I have not seen her since the battle."

Morgo's face became suddenly pained, and he stood and left the dining hall. Kikpona sat watching after him. She frowned. Why was Morgo now hiding his thoughts and fears from *her*?

.~.~.~.~.~.~.

"Greetings, Brave One," Kikpona said from the doorway of Vanddai's room. The wounded woman's eyes fluttered open swiftly at the sound of her sister-in-law's voice. She struggled to sit up, and Kikpona moved quickly to her

182

bedside. Laying a hand on Vanddai's shoulder, she stopped her.

"Please, Vanddai, do not strain yourself. I am merely here to tell you the news of what is happening."

Vanddai smiled, and shakily wiped sweat from her forehead. She reached for an iron cup, and drank slowly. Kikpona got a damp cloth and dabbed at her sister-in-law's face.

Vanddai spoke. "My thanks, Sister. Tell me what is happening."

Kikpona put the cloth back in the basin and sighed as she sat down on a cushion beside the bed. "Well, we defeated Jarlir's army. But I'm sure you already have been told that by Morgo."

Vanddai nodded. "Tell me about yourself. How have you been lately? You are beginning to be noticeable," she said, nodding at Kikpona's abdomen.

Kikpona chuckled and shook her head in amusement. "Everyone has been telling me so. Frankly, I hadn't even noticed. But I must admit I will be very glad to see this little one. I haven't even been pregnant for five months and already I am tired of carrying him around."

Vanddai laughed. Kikpona stretched, dulling the ache in her back. She patted Vanddai's arm.

"Now you must focus on regaining your strength. I need you to help me defeat Jarlir, and you can't do that until you are well again."

Vanddai gripped Kikpona's hand. "I will not fail you, my Queen."

The words were spoken with such a fierce determination that Kikpona only stared at the other woman. Then her eyes softened with a smile. She nodded slowly.

"I know you won't, Kero-Vanddai."

On the third day after the battle, Makkiu the cheetah bolted through the city gates and into the palace courtyard. His sides heaved as he gasped for breath. Kikpona quickly came out to meet him.

"Makkiu! What is it, what's wrong?" she asked him worriedly. The cheetah breathed heavily.

"My Queen, Bolek the Shadow Slayer has been sentenced to death by King Jarlir for treason! He is to die today in the arena!"

Kikpona gasped in dismay. "Makkiu, find Atoru and tell him to assemble seventy of our best Warriors. We must save Bolek!"

Bolek trudged weakly out to the arena sand. The crowds around him were jeering. In their opinion, death was too good for a traitor of his kind. The panther stopped in the center of the arena. He saw the group of his Jungle Raiders waiting outside the opposite side of the fence.

Jarlir's command to the former soldiers of Bolek had been cruel and unsympathetic. Bolek's own fighters were to cut him down mercilessly. Jarlir's anger toward the spy was unappeasable. Bolek had not even tried to defend himself at the trial. Jarlir had no mercy to spare for traitors.

Bolek stood, his black coat dulled somewhat from the malnourishment of the past three days. His eyes never left those of his Raiders. His muscled body was ready to make a last stand. The odds were heavily against him. There were twelve Raiders standing ready at the gate.

Bolek turned to the king sitting up high above him in the palace balcony. Jarlir's smug smile made the panther feel sick to his stomach. What kind of a king was this?

Drums rolled and the gate on the far side of the arena was slowly opened to allow the Raiders to enter. Bolek's eyes still never left those of the other panthers. They avoided his gaze as they formed a circle around him. Bolek felt shame rising up in him. He had trained these Raiders. They had followed him without question, and were proud to serve under him. Now it would be they who brought the great Warrior down.

The drums stopped. King Jarlir rose from his throne on the balcony and raised his hand. Bolek did not look.

When the hand dropped, all of the Raiders lunged for Bolek. The proud Warrior flung out his sharpened claws and

185

bared his teeth. When the Raiders reached him, he ripped and slashed wildly, quickly felling two of the traitors.

The rest backed off after their wild first attack, leaving Bolek covered in long, bleeding cuts. The big panther hissed at them, his ears flattened, his tail whipping back and forth.

The Raiders charged again. Bolek tried valiantly to defend himself, but there were too many of them. He slowly fell, still swiping with his claws, his last resort to try and free himself.

Jarlir called the Raiders off. They retreated from the bloodstained figure lying in the sand.

Bolek's eyes were clouding fast. His body was ripped and mutilated. His blood poured onto the sand. Feeling his death drawing nearer, and nearer, Bolek raised his head with a great effort to speak one last time.

Kikpona's group of Warriors stopped atop the hill before the great city of Ichoda. From her lofty rise, Kikpona could see the arena…and what was in it. She saw the body of Bolek lying there in the sand. And faintly, she heard his voice.

"People of Ichoda…I lie here before you….no traitor. This king…you serve has no…place on the throne…of this country…God bless the true queen…Kikpona!" he shouted. Then, the great Black Panther stretched out on the sand, and breathed his last.

Kikpona gasped. Tears poured from her eyes, blinding her. Dismounting from Quetoro's back, she knelt down on the ground and smeared her face with dirt.

"Oh wretched day! How bravely hath the Great One fallen!" she cried out, her voice filled with despair. The warriors hung their heads and their hands went to their foreheads in a salute to their fallen Captain. Quetoro's eyes misted as he watched the soldiers of Jarlir drag the body away to leave in the forest borders.

"My Queen, we must retrieve the body for a proper burial," Quetoro said gently to the grieving Kikpona. The Queen's eyes rose to those of her Advisor's.

"Quetoro...he's dead. Bolek, who was the Mightiest Warrior of all of us. His courage surpassed that of the bravest in my army. He died for me!"

The red stallion nodded silently. Kikpona burst into tears again. She so badly wanted to go back in time and save her brave warrior. But she had arrived moments too late. She had failed him, and he had paid for it with his life. Guilt fairly overwhelmed the Queen's heart. But she knew what she had to do.

"Quetoro, we must bring him home, to Utomia. He will receive a hero's burial, as is his due. Let us...let us go and find him."

.~.~.~.~.~.~.

A grim procession it was that marched through the iron gates of Utomia. Four steers bore upon their backs a huge platform. On the top of the platform was a small table, draped in black and silver, the colors of the Jungle Raiders.

Lying amidst the cloth was Bolek. The panther's eyes were closed in a peaceful expression. The body of the great warrior was carried into the city. On each side of the street the Utomians gathered, mourning for their warrior.

Quetoro, Atoru, and Kikpona brought up the rear of the procession. They stopped in the grassy clearing that was the burial ground of all the heroes that had died in battle for Kikpona's cause. The Queen had declared it a sacred graveyard of those that had fallen for their Queen and it was considered by the people a very holy place.

And so, with all the dignity due a royal being, Bolek was solemnly buried in the burial grounds beside his fellow Utomians.

Kikpona was the last to leave. She stood looking down at the fresh mound of dirt, and felt pride swell up in her.

"I am proud to have subjects such as you, Bolek the Shadow Slayer," she whispered quietly. The wind blew her hair, gently swirling it about her face as she turned to go back to the palace.

.~.~.~.~.~.~.

Jathren sat silently on Yuro's back. The two of them had been living out in the forest for a few days now, and Jathren knew what he had to do. He and the big bay stallion stood on a hill overlooking Utomia.

Yuro looked over his shoulder at his young rider. "My Prince? Are you sure that this is the road you wish to take? Your sister may not receive you well. She harbors great anger towards your father. And rightly so. But still, this may be a mistake."

Jathren sighed. His eyes surveyed the great stone walls of the city, his sister's kingdom. The huge iron gates dominated the west wall of Utomia, which were the only entrance to the city. Other secret paths out of the city were also known to a select few, but they were to be used only in greatest need.

The young prince nodded to his questioning warrior.

"Yes, Yuro. This is the road I must take. My mother is there, as well as my sister. I cannot flee from my own kin. Or at least, some of my own kin. My father may be another matter."

Yuro huffed wearily. "I agree, my Prince. I think it would be best if you did not return to Ichoda. Let your father's anger cool for a time."

Jathren silently agreed. He watched the caravans slowly traveling in and out of the city gates. There were wagons full of lumber, iron, jewels, prisoners, food, and refugees.

His sister certainly had a very successful trade market, or so it would seem, Jathren thought to himself. The city itself looked very rich.

Yuro began the slow descent down into the valley. Jathren's eyes never left the city walls. He watched the guards endlessly walking back and forth above the gate, and the powerful catapults that sat atop the walls in case of invasion by the Ichodians.

Reaching the gate, the two weary travelers passed underneath the huge stone arch. Jathren sat atop Yuro's back, his eyes drinking in all of his surroundings. The city was more grand and beautiful than he could have ever imagined. The architecture was incredible. Stone columns lined the broad street, each one with strange runes and symbols on them. Statues of heroes sat proudly between the columns. There were horses, steers, wolves, panthers, and humans, each statue a testament to the great deeds of the hero.

To the right of the road was a paved avenue that ran between two groves of sycamore trees. At the end of the avenue was a palace, grander and larger than the one in Ichoda. Jathren stared at the immense building.

Even the double doors leading into the palace were uniquely carved and beautiful sculptures sat on each side of the entrance. Broad stone steps led up to the doors.

Yuro looked around him in admiration. "Your sister certainly has a taste for grandeur, my Prince."

Jathren wholeheartedly agreed. "Look at those statues. Are they not made from red marble?" he asked the stallion in excitement. Yuro nodded.

Two guards stepped down from the broad steps to stand in front of the two travelers. Jathren dismounted and waited for them to speak. The taller of the two men looked at him suspiciously.

"Ye are no Utomian, or me eyes are failin' me! Who are ye? State yer business 'ere quickly, afore I drag ye to yonder dungeon fer a spy!"

Jathren's blue eyes fastened on the guard. His good nature was dimmed slightly by the disrespectful tone the guard had used with him. The young Prince's eyes hardened and the guard flinched.

"I ahh....meant ye no harm, lad. Jes' tell me quick like, who ye are and what yer business is here."

Jathren spoke calmly. "I am simply a traveler. I bear no ill will with her Majesty. I can assure you that I am no spy of Ichoda. My name is Jori, and this is my companion, Nanothar. We were caught in the midst of the great battle that waged here merely a few days ago. We have barely escaped with our lives."

The guard still looked unconvinced. "Be that as it may, laddie, I've no way o' tellin' whether ye be friend or foe. The Queen doesn't take kindly to spies..." his voice trailed off as Yuro stepped forward.

"My good man, my companion has already stated that we are not spies. We merely wish to pay our respects to your Great Lady."

The guard sighed and gave in. "All right, all right. I 'spose 'tis no harm done to let ye in. Queen Kikpona will have yer 'eads if ye be any but who ye say. Go on in, then, if ye've a mind to," he said.

191

Yuro nodded gratefully at the guard and led the way up to the double doors, which were opened for them. Once inside, they were confronted by a large black bull, who wore a gold chain about his neck and had a commanding air about him. Jathren knew that this must be the great General of Utomia, Atoru the Black Bull. The army leader's strategic genius was known all over Leyowan.

"Who are you?" the bull questioned them, his dark eyes surveying them coldly. He didn't like the idea of strangers coming to see Kikpona before they had been properly questioned.

"I am Jathren of Ichoda, Prince of Leyowan, brother of Kikpona."

Atoru stepped back in shock. Now that the boy had revealed his true name, the black bull saw Kikpona's face mirrored in that of the young Prince. Truly, Jathren was his sister's brother.

"Please forgive my insolence, my lord. Let me take you to your sister."

Atoru's thoughts whirled as he led the pair down the hallway. How had Jathren managed to escape from the lair of that fox, Jarlir? What would Kikpona say when she finally laid eyes on her younger sibling?

Atoru pushed open the door of the Great Hall. Before him, seated upon her cedar throne, sat the Queen of Utomia, her glory radiating from the dais on which she sat. Her throne was encrusted with ruby and onyx stones, made in twisted patterns to match her crown. She was in deep conversation

192

with Quetoro, who stood at her right side, when the trio entered the great room.

"Presenting his Royal Highness, Prince Jathren of Leyowan, brother to her Royal Majesty, the Radiant One, Queen Kikpona of Utomia!" Atoru's booming voice announced. Kikpona jerked around, her eyes sparking. She saw her younger brother for the first time, and a great emotion filled her.

Rising from her throne, she stepped down the stairs to the bottom of the dais. She strode forward, her long blue skirts trailing behind her. Quetoro hurried after her stiffly.

Kikpona stopped before the prince, who stood trembling under her fierce gaze. The Queen's eyes never left his.

After a long moment of torturous silence, Kikpona's eyes filled with tears, and her face softened. She opened her arms, and Jathren fled to them like a little boy. He did not even know his sister, yet her strong arms around him were like a safe haven from all of his troubles.

"My baby brother, Jathren! Oh what joy the sight of your face brings to me! How have I longed for this moment to come!" the Queen murmured into Jathren's ear.

Those who stood in the hall kept total silence, watching with awe this happy union of brother and sister, who loved each other as only siblings can, without having ever seen one another.

Finally, Kikpona stepped back from Jathren, and put her bejeweled hands on the sides of his face. Smiling, she nodded.

193

"Yes. You are most truly a brother of mine. If it weren't for your age, you could very well have been mistaken for my twin."

Turning slightly, the Queen looked at Atoru. "Bring our mother here. She will wish to see her son after so many months have passed. It has been almost a whole year since she has laid eyes upon him."

Atoru hurried to obey, vanishing out the oak doors. Jathren squeezed Kikpona's hand.

"My sister, please be generous to my faithful companion. His name is Yuro, and he has sworn loyalty to me, and protected me during the battle with no thought to his own safety."

Kikpona looked at Jathren sharply. "The battle?" she said suspiciously. Jathren bit his lip, but his sister's face gave no room for small talk. Jathren looked down at his boots.

"Remember the little boy who ran from you when you threatened him on the battlefield?" he asked quietly. The Queen stared openly at him.

"You? You were the little boy? Oh, Jathren, forgive me! I did not know that it was you! I never would have frightened you so!"

Jathren wiped tears away from his eyes impatiently. Shaking his head, he reassured his sister.

"Do not trouble yourself, sister. I will not speak of it again."

Before Kikpona could speak, a side door burst open to reveal Elaria. The Queen Mother was dressed in a simple blue
194

robe, a light silver circlet nestled in her black hair. Her eyes were misty as she looked at her son. Jathren gave a small cry and ran to her. Elaria reached for him and pulled him close to her.

"My son…" she whispered into the red curls. Whispering praise to God, she looked up at Kikpona, who stood there, watching.

"Of all the joys a mother can receive, this truly is the greatest of them all. Now both my children are here with me again. May God be eternally praised for his gracious mercy upon me!"

14

While Jathren, Elaria and Kikpona had their happy reunion, Jarlir sat simmering in his palace study room. He gripped the edges of the scroll he was reading with such ferocity that the parchment began to tear.

Luluk, the badger, trembled slightly as he stood before Jarlir. It was he that had the fearsome task of reporting the knowledge of Jathren's whereabouts to the temperamental king.

Jarlir dismissed the courier with a flick of his wrist. The badger scurried out the door so fast that he tripped over his own paws. Jarlir took a deep breath to calm his fury, and yelled out the door.

"Jahere! Get in here!"

The stout bull rumbled into the room, his large hooves shaking the floorboards as he lumbered in.

"Yes, my lord?" he asked, expressionless. Jarlir's rage mounted. Would any of his subjects show emotion in front of him? They all wore blank faces and acted as though it were troublesome to serve him. He stood up, and pointed at the new head General.

"Jahere, I have had enough of this small talk with Utomia. Take the army, give them as much armor and as many weapons as you can, and ready them for war. I am going to crush Kikpona, once and for all!"

By the last few words, Jarlir's voice had risen to a shout. Jahere bowed deeply and strode from the room to do his master's bidding. He left the palace and walked to the army camp. His three commanders, who were all battle-scarred steers, came up to him obediently.

"What does the king wish us to do?" one of them asked. Jahere sighed. He had known that Jarlir would give the command sooner or later. But now that it was here, he found himself doubting the strength of the Ichodian army. He knew that Utomia was well fortified and teeming with supporters of Queen Kikpona. They would not hesitate to fight for her. And the defense of their home city would make them even more dangerous.

Jahere thoughtfully surveyed his soldiers. They were all lazy and bored with waiting. They had anticipated a battle long ago. But now, they doubted whether or not their king would even send them to the gates of Utomia.

"My lord?" one of the commanders spoke again. Jahere snapped his attention back to the present.

"Well, my commanders, it is time again to prove your worth. King Jarlir orders the entire army to march on Utomia. Only a few personal bodyguards are to remain to protect his Majesty."

The steers' faces brightened at the prospect of fighting. The second commander, Drasus, spoke up.

198

"When do we leave, General?" he asked eagerly. Jahere smiled.

"In a month or two, when the army has been suited up and is ready for war. Then we will break Kikpona's golden city."

.~.~.~.~.~.~.

Three months later, on a sunny morning in Ichoda, Jarlir woke and stood. He walked to his bedchamber window, overlooking the army. He smiled in evil anticipation of the destruction that was to come. His personal attendant, the wolf Abeku, came to stand beside him. Of all of the Ichodians, none was more devoted to the tyrant king than the old wolf. Abeku hated the Utomians, because they had killed all three of his bachelor sons.

"So it begins, my lord. The destruction of the one whom you hate," the old wolf said maliciously. Jarlir nodded.

"Aye, my friend. So it begins. My heart will rest easy once the Pretender is dead. She has brought nothing but irritation to me since her mother's maid first placed her in my arms in her hour of birth. And now she has dared to turn my own son against me."

Abeku frowned. "What will you do with the Prince, my lord? And what of your wife, Queen Elaria?"

Jarlir's voice sounded like a snarl. "She is no longer my wife, nor my Queen. She has deserted me and made her allegiance known. And as for my son, I will make him my slave, for he too, has abandoned me."

Abeku fell silent, the King's angry words whirling about his mind.

Kikpona clasped her two hands to her belly. A strange spasm of pain gripped her. She gasped involuntarily, and frowned in confusion. The child was not due for another three weeks!

The Queen rose from the table where she had been eating her midday meal, and called hoarsely.

"Guard! Someone help!"

Quetoro burst in from one of the doors. He saw the Queen shudder and sink back to her chair. He called for another guard, and raced for Kikpona.

"My Queen! What is wrong?" he asked, knowing full well what it was that ailed his queen.

Kikpona drew a deep breath and pulled herself up again. "Quetoro, I think... I think that the child does not wish to wait any longer to be born. Bring me my mother and Baka the Healer."

Quetoro turned to the guard that had just come running into the room and repeated the command. The tall man hurried off.

The big stallion moved his scarred body towards the Queen, and let her support herself by holding onto his mane. Kikpona smiled gratefully up at him.

"Your loyalty and kindness will forever be honored, my friend," she told him quietly, just as Elaria and Baka came flying into the room. Elaria gasped and quickly grabbed her daughter's arm. Baka supported Kikpona from the other side, and together, the two women managed to help the Queen out of the dining hall and into her bedchamber.

Quetoro, seeing that there was no more he could do to help the Queen, hurried out of the palace to find Lord Morgo. It didn't take long. Morgo was inspecting the city walls with Atoru, discussing the defenses of the city.

"My lord!" Quetoro's urgent tone broke Morgo's conversation. He and Atoru turned to face the red stallion.

"What is it, Quetoro? What is wrong?" Atoru asked worriedly. The old stallion motioned towards the palace.

"Lord Morgo, you must go to the Queen. Your child is being born." he said calmly. Atoru's eyes widened. Morgo suddenly became panicky.

"What? But that is impossible! The child is not due for three weeks yet, Quetoro! Are you sure?" he asked. The red stallion nodded solemnly at the frenzied man.

"Yes, my lord. I have seen it with my own eyes. You must go to her."

Without another word, Morgo took off at a run for the palace. Atoru looked up at the red stallion.

"I cannot believe it, Quetoro. It seems like yesterday that you and I rescued her from the Dungeon in Ichoda. She was merely a girl then. Now she is having a child of her own."

Quetoro nodded in agreement. "It is almost unbelievable. Pray that she has no trouble. Utomia is nothing without her Queen."

.~.~.~.~.~.~.

Baka rose from where she knelt beside the Queen's bed. She lifted the tightly wrapped bundle from beside Kikpona.

"Your daughter, my lord," she said to Morgo before placing the tiny baby in her father's arms. Morgo felt a hard lump rising in his throat, choking off his breath. He gazed down at the angelic face of his daughter, and gently touched one of the tiny hands with a gentle forefinger.

"Morgo," said a quiet voice from the bed. Morgo looked down into his wife's eyes. Kikpona smiled weakly at him. Though she was exhausted, her face shone with pride.

"Kikpona, my love, she is beautiful. Just like her mother," Morgo told the Queen lovingly. He knelt down to her side and reached out, caressing the side of her face with his calloused hand. Kikpona closed her eyes. Momentarily, the troubles of her country slipped from her mind, and she felt peaceful.

The small cry of the baby brought her out of her reverie of happiness. She looked up at the puckered face of the child.

"Well, well. We are going to have our hands full with you, I think. Yes, most definitely," Kikpona murmured to her baby girl. Morgo placed the bundle in the crook of Kikpona's arm.

"What shall we name her? We hadn't expected her quite yet, so I am at loss for a good name. It should be a name worthy of the Princess of Utomia," Morgo commented proudly. Kikpona surveyed her newborn.

"I think I will call her Kona. The name of the Northern Star."

Morgo nodded his approval. A quiet knock sounded on the oak door. Baka opened it, and Atoru and Quetoro's faces peered around the corner. Kikpona laughed at their undisguised curiosity.

"Come in, my friends. You have nothing to fear, I am well and so is the Princess of Leyowan."

Atoru gave a mighty sigh of relief. "May God be praised! A Princess for Utomia!"

Elaria took the baby from Kikpona and brought her over to Atoru and Quetoro. The two friends gazed with wonder at the bright blue eyes, and the soft golden hair. She was a tiny replica of Kikpona.

"My Queen! You have given us the image of you!" exclaimed Atoru in wonder. Kikpona laughed.

"Aye, so it would seem, friend Atoru."

Elaria and Morgo took Princess Kona to the palace balcony. Morgo looked down over the crowd gathered there. Every citizen of the city had come to hear the news. People sat crowded onto rooftops, and animals squeezed into alleyways, just to be able to hear.

Morgo lifted his daughter high above him, showing her to the Utomians.

"Utomia, I give you your Princess…"

The rest of his words were drowned out by the deafening roar of the huge crowd.

.~.~.~.~.~.~.

Jahere called for a halt. He listened carefully. To his surprise, he heard a distant thundering, as though thousands of animals and people were cheering, all at once.

"Humph, must be having some sort of festival. Well now, ain't that grand. We'll catch them unawares. Gives us a bit of an advantage, I'd say," he commented to Drasus and Hemni, his third commander. Both steers bobbed their heads up and down.

"Aye, General. 'Tis a fine day for a party. Too bad we'll have to crash it, eh?" Hemni observed dryly. The steer was a veteran of war, his hide covered in scars from long ago battles.

Jahere chuckled deep in his throat. "Too bad, indeed. We'll give those Utomians something to cheer about, all right. We'll march their little Queen through the streets of her own city, chained and in rags."

Hemni roared with laughter. Drasus remained silent. He was listening again. The sound of rapid hoof beats thundered from behind the battalion.

"General, sir, I hear..."

Jahere shook his horns. "Don't think me a deaf bull, Drasus. I hear it also. Could it be a messenger from Ichoda?" he wondered out loud.

Their questions were soon answered. Galloping up to the army General was a big bay horse, and on his back sat the king of Ichoda, Jarlir himself.

Jahere bowed deeply as the king dismounted and dismissed the horse. He surveyed the battalion, and then his eyes traveled to the left and right, scanning the huge army, which was spread out for at least a mile in each direction. Thousands had flocked to answer his call of war.

"General, how far are we from the city?" the king asked. Jahere bowed again.

"Merely two miles, Your Majesty. We hope to break upon Utomia by nightfall, and camp at the border. Then at daybreak tomorrow we will attack."

Jarlir nodded thoughtfully. "It is good. I am pleased with this plan. I want to see Kikpona's humiliation with my own two eyes. I want to see her beloved city crumble into the dust. I want to watch as her iron gates fall!"

Jahere was slightly taken aback by the malice and hate in his King's tone of voice. Jarlir obviously had absolutely no love for his stepdaughter. Jahere could hardly blame him. To be usurped by someone you held dear? The outrage of it all, Jahere thought to himself.

"Your wish is my command, Majesty. The army will follow you to the very end, no matter what comes out of those gates."

.~.~.~.~.~.~.

Kikpona slowly swallowed the chicken broth that her mother had brought her to eat. She glanced over to where her daughter slept peacefully in her basket. Motherly pride swept through the Queen.

"You will one day rule a powerful empire, Kona. I'm building it for you," Kikpona said softly. The baby did not stir. Soft sighs came from the tiny body as she slept. Kikpona smiled.

Soft footsteps announced the presence of another being. Kikpona glanced towards the doorway to see Makkiu the cheetah.

"Makkiu! Come in, my old friend! What news do you bring me? It has been many weeks since I have seen you!"

The cheetah bowed deeply. "May the Queen live forever! Great joy is mine to see your Majesty in good health. I am greatly relieved to be home. I have been scouting in Morbia these past three months."

"Morbia? Did you find my father? Is he well?" she asked curiously, her interest piqued.

Makkiu did not answer for a long minute. Finally he lifted his eyes to look her in the face. "My Queen, your father is alive."

Kikpona gasped. "Oh! Where is he? Did you find him, Makkiu?"

"Yes, my Queen. I spoke to him myself. He is wary to return to Leyowan. He fears for Queen Elaria's life and yours as well."

Kikpona felt tears running down her cheeks. Her father was alive. Her father was alive! Hopeless joy filled her. She smiled at Makkiu through her tears.

"I wish you to return to Morbia, Makkiu. I want you to bring my father here."

"My Queen, there is another matter which requires your wisdom. It is the other reason why your father cannot return," Makkiu responded.

"Speak, Makkiu. Tell me."

"Morbia is assembling an army. Orluc, the great Bear, is preparing to invade Leyowan, civil war or no."

Kikpona scowled. "He should know better. Since when have the Morbians succeeded in invading this country? They have never defeated us in battle!"

Makkiu trembled slightly in distress. "My Queen, the army Orluc commands is far greater than any army I have ever seen in my life. They number... more than forty thousand strong."

An icy chill crept up Kikpona's spine. "Forty thousand?" she whispered in shock. "Does Jarlir know of this?" she asked quietly. Makkiu nodded slowly.

"Aye, I spoke with one of his messengers. He will tell the Imposter of the news. The messenger was an old friend of mine, and one that owed me a favor from the past. I instructed him to tell Jarlir, and Jarlir alone. I do not know what else I could have done."

Kikpona shook her head. "No. You have done well. Jarlir should know of this. It seems as though the only way we can save Leyowan is if we...become allies."

Makkiu started. "Surely there is some other way! My Queen, Jarlir wishes to kill you!"

Kikpona looked thoughtful. "I know this. But Jarlir will not risk invasion of the Morbians just to secure my death. There will be time for us to war later. Right now, this country is in deadly danger. If the Morbians succeed in their intentions, Leyowan will become a land of death and darkness.

Makkiu, bring me Atoru, Morgo, and Quetoro. Bring Vanddai also, if she is feeling well enough to come to me."

Makkiu bowed low. "It shall be as you wish, Majesty," he said, and turned to go. Kikpona stopped him.

"Wait. Makkiu, after you have summoned them, go and rest. You have done your Queen greater service this day than ever before. Your courage and loyalty will not be easily forgotten. From henceforth you shall be known as Makkiu the Swift."

Makkiu's eyes misted. "You do me great honor, your Majesty. I would serve no one but you. May I die in your service, my Queen."

With that, the cheetah vanished out the door. Kikpona leaned back against her pillows and set the bowl of broth down on her bedside stand. Closing her eyes, she sighed and tried to clear her head.

First Jarlir, now Morbia. Could her country possibly be more in danger? If Jarlir refused to become allies with Utomia, Leyowan would surely fall to the servants of darkness. And Orluc was no fool. He would strike hard, and hit Leyowan where it would hurt the most.

And that would be to destroy Leyowan's rulers. Kikpona, Jarlir, and even Jathren and Elaria would be foremost in the Morbian General's mind as threats. And that would put their lives in danger. Kikpona knew she had to get her mother and brother out of the country. She would send them to the friendly neighboring country of Nenamene. They would be safe there until the Morbians were defeated.

Kikpona looked over at her still sleeping daughter. Yes, Kona would also have to be taken out of Leyowan. Kikpona would never let Orluc get his filthy clutches on her precious child. Never.

Morgo entered the room, followed by Quetoro and Atoru. Kikpona smiled gratefully at them.

"I'm sorry that I couldn't have given you more warning, but a most urgent matter has risen, one that will not wait to be discussed. Is Vanddai coming?" she asked.

Morgo nodded solemnly. "She will be along shortly."

Kikpona pushed herself up farther. "Please forgive my undignified state. I would get up…"

Quetoro shook his head. "No, Your Majesty. None of us condemn you for resting. You have just had a child. Of course you should be in bed."

Kikpona smiled gratefully at him. Her eyes swept the three standing before her.

"My dear friends, Utomia would be lost without you to guide her Queen. And Morgo, you have been a better husband than I could have ever dreamed of having. I want you all to know how much you mean to me, each one of you."

Concern now lined all three faces. Atoru spoke up first.

"My Queen, what troubles you? You speak as though death is soon to be our fate. Please do not fear to speak openly with us."

Kikpona nodded solemnly. "I do not fear any of you. My mind is troubled with a dream that I have had every night for the past six days. Every time my eyes close, it begins afresh. I do not trust dreams, but this one seems to have come to me for a reason. It concerns the outcome of the war with Morbia."

Morgo stared at his wife. "Morbia? But we are fighting Jarlir…" his voice faded as he saw the steel hard look creep into Kikpona's eyes. He said nothing more.

"Yes, so we were. But Orluc, the Master of the hordes of Darkness, has chosen this opportune time to invade Leyowan, while she is divided in civil war. He could not have chosen a better time to attack. Makkiu has just reported to me that the strength with which Orluc marches numbers more than forty thousand."

A dark silence hovered over the room. All three commanders were speechless at this horrible news. Finally Quetoro spoke.

"May the darkest curses of this earth fall upon Orluc the Destroyer. Many a dark day has passed in this country because of that foul creature."

Kikpona looked curiously at the old stallion. "Quetoro, you have seen him?" she asked in surprise. Atoru and Morgo also looked at the big horse. Quetoro bowed his head slightly.

"Yes, my Queen. He is wicked and bold. He will strike soon. Orluc does not give his enemies the time to retaliate. He kills mercilessly, there is none left alive. The Master of Darkness shows no pity, torturing his captives..." the horse's voice trailed off.

Atoru, Morgo, and Kikpona were all watching him. Kikpona suddenly realized something.

"You told Jarlir that you had come from a dark past when you applied for the post of being my tutor. You said that you wanted to forget what you had been, what had happened to you... Quetoro?"

The old horse's body shook with emotion. For the first time, Kikpona saw her loyal friend completely and wholly in

211

despair. A dark, haunted look passed into Quetoro's dark eyes, masking his normal bright cheerfulness. Kikpona reached up to the bedpost and stood up, leaning on the wall for support. Reaching out, she placed one hand gently over the red horse's forehead.

Quetoro jerked, as though he had come out of a trance. His muscles slowly relaxed under Kikpona's reassuring touch. Kikpona focused on transmitting her love and comfort through her hand to the horse. The room was silent as Quetoro fought the fears within his own mind.

After several long minutes, the haunted look left Quetoro's eyes, and his head came back up. Looking at Kikpona, he murmured, "You have a true gift, my Queen."

Kikpona smiled. "I never hesitate to help a troubled friend. You would have done the same for me. Now, it is time for you to speak and for me to listen."

Atoru slowly bent his knees as he lowered himself down to the floor with a grunt. Morgo sat down in one of Kikpona's armchairs. Before Quetoro had begun, a quiet knock sounded at the door. Vanddai came in, her dark hair neatly plaited into an ebony braid that hung down to her hips. Her smile vanished as she surveyed the grim faces of the room's four occupants.

"Have I brought the rainclouds with me, my friends?" she joked, attempting to lighten the mood. Morgo and Kikpona laughed.

"No, Vanddai. You have brought sunshine with you, as you always do. How could something as dreary and unpleasant as rain be mentioned when you are with us?"

Vanddai smiled and bowed to Kikpona. "Many thanks for your kind words. I am sure that a poor wretch such as me does not deserve the compassion of a queen as great as yourself," she murmured smoothly. Morgo shook his head in amusement.

"Ever the court jester, my dear sister. Please, be seated with us."

Kikpona quickly told Vanddai what had happened, and Quetoro finally began to tell his story.

15

"When I was only a yearling, my sire, my dam, I, and my four brothers lived at the border of Leyowan and Morbia. We had never thought ourselves in any danger, and we lived a peaceful and happy life. My sire was a simple merchant, and we were sometimes allowed to travel with him when he would go to different cities, selling the wagonload of fancy carpets he bought during the year."

"Well, it was on such a trip when I learned that life wasn't always how you wanted it to be. My sire had chosen me to go with him to Ichoda. We got to the city in fine fettle, and sold all of our wares. My sire made a very large amount of money those three days, and we were in a hurry to get home, for with such a sum we could live in pleasure for the rest of that year."

"When we got in sight of our home, which was a humble stable-like lodge, we saw the column of smoke rising high up above it. My four brothers were lying slain outside the building. My sire told me to stay where I was, and I did, being so frightened that I could hardly lift my legs."

Quetoro stopped for a breath. Kikpona pushed a pan of water toward him. He took a long drink, and then returned to his story.

"My sire raced down to the clearing, and immediately threescore of those servants of darkness had ambushed him.

215

Four archers shot him down. I remember feeling numb with shock that my sire was lying dead. Then I saw the sight that has haunted me since that very day."

"My sweet, gentle dam was standing before Orluc, covered in burns that she had suffered from the fire, sobbing uncontrollably over the loss of my sire and four brothers. She begged him to let her go, to bury her mate and sons. Orluc laughed at her. He dragged her over to the burning lodge, and shoved her inside, just as it collapsed on top of her."

Four gasps of horror sounded from the room. Quetoro's eyes were haunted again. One tear rolled down the left side of his face. His ears flattened down to his head.

"I felt a rage build up inside me. I could not keep hidden. I leapt from behind the bushes and charged Orluc. Three arrows found me, but I kept running, scarcely even noticing them in my hatred."

Quetoro shuddered. "Orluc himself forged the mighty weapon he carries. It is a huge scimitar, a blade so strong that no iron we of Leyowan possess can break through it. He drew the sword, and shouted for me to come to him, that he would break me into tiny pieces and feed them to his hyenas."

"I kept running, determined to kill him for murdering my family and destroying my home. He let me come within a foot of him, and then he caught me and threw me into a boulder. Coming up to me, he cut a mark in my hide, and said, 'This is so you remember me, little horse. I killed your family, but I will let you live, because then you will have to live with their memory the rest of your life.'"

216

Silence filled the bedchamber. Not one eye was dry in that room. Even the tough general Atoru had tears pouring down his cheeks, his kind heart unbelieving that such a cruel act could possibly be committed. Atoru had seen death plenty of times, but such brutal slaughter and torture?

Kikpona covered her face in her hands. "And now Orluc wants to destroy us all. How can we defeat such a monster?" she said helplessly. Morgo patted her hand, and kissed her hair.

"No matter what evil should invade this country, I will protect you until my last breath," Morgo said gently.

Vanddai stiffly stood, holding a hand to her stomach. "So shall I, you have Vanddai's word of honor on that!" she said forcefully.

"Mine as well!" Atoru stated firmly.

Kikpona's eyes glistened as her friends swore their loyalty to her. She swiped a hand across her face. Stepping back, she tried to sit back down on her bed, but a wave of nausea and weakness swept over her, and she began to fall.

Instantly, Morgo was behind her, catching her in his strong arms.

"Rest easy, my love. You have exerted yourself too much. You should be resting right now. See, now you have awoken our daughter."

Kikpona shook her head and leaned back against the pillows. Vanddai picked up the wailing Kona from the cradle and snuggled her niece against her. The babe instantly quieted. Kikpona looked at Quetoro again. The stallion was watching her wordlessly.

"Quetoro, you said that Orluc cut a mark in your hide. Where is it?" she asked softly. Quetoro lowered his head. When he spoke, his voice was almost a whisper.

"When you were young, I told you a great tale of a battle, in which I was horribly scarred on my face. I said that it had been made by a chance happening in the midst of the fighting."

Kikpona gasped. "That was made by Orluc's blade?" she asked. Quetoro's head nodded slightly. The light from the window shone on the scar running from the tip of his right ear, across his face, and down to the left side of his nose.

"How I wish that it had been made in a battle. But alas! I am cursed to carry that mark of evil upon me until the day I go to my eternal rest. A memory etched into my very being of that awful day."

Kikpona smiled reassuringly at her old friend. "Quetoro, never say that you are cursed. I am grateful to God himself that Orluc chose to spare you that day. Had he not, I would not be here right now. I would have been killed in that terrible dungeon."

Atoru hung his head. His sudden embarrassment did not go unnoticed by his Queen.

"Atoru, why do you look so sad?" she asked him. The black bull whispered his answer.

"It would've been a tribute to my fear and worthlessness had Quetoro never come to your rescue. I was worried about

218

saving my own self, with no thought to the danger that confronted you. How dim-witted I was!"

Kikpona was shaking her head. "Atoru, you showed great bravery by coming to my rescue that day. Do not trouble yourself over what could've happened, because it didn't. I am here, and I am very much alive and well. So do not condemn yourself for something you never did."

Atoru's eyes brightened gratefully. "My thanks, great Queen."

Kikpona turned to Morgo again. "My love, we must discuss options for dealing with the Morbian invasion."

Morgo sat down again, and was accompanied by the others. Vanddai laid the now sleeping Kona back in her velvet lined cradle. Quetoro's eyes were now hardened with the thought of revenge.

"We must catch him unprepared. We must make him think that we will be easy to subdue. That is the only way to defeat Orluc, by using his confidence against him."

Kikpona wholeheartedly agreed with Quetoro. The old stallion's words made perfect sense. But Morgo pointed something else out.

"True, Quetoro, he is overly confident, which could be a detriment to him. But how are we going to appear submissive without risking the lives of those in Utomia with royal blood? Doubtless Orluc's first thought will be to destroy Leyowan's rulers, to dishearten her people. That places Elaria, Jathren, Kikpona, and Kona in deathly danger."

Vanddai spoke up. "I think we should send Jathren, Elaria and Kona immediately to another country for safekeeping. We cannot afford to lose even one royal. This tells me that we should probably remove…the Queen as well."

Kikpona sat bolt upright. Her steel gray eyes flashed and sparked in anger.

"I will not leave this country until Orluc murders me with his own claws. I am not going to leave my people to fend for themselves against his mighty armies. Never!" she stated forcefully.

Morgo laid a reassuring hand on her arm. "Do not worry yourself about it, Kikpona. No one is going to make you leave. I for one would be uneasy to try it myself!" he said teasingly.

Kikpona huffed quietly. "Good. I hope you all agree with my very wise husband. Friend or no, the first human or beast that tries to force me out of my country will be as good as dead."

There was a dark unspoken warning belying the Queen's calm tone. It was very clear to all those present that Kikpona was definitely and without doubt not going to be pushed around. Quetoro cleared his throat.

"I agree with Vanddai. It is essential to move those royals that we can," he paused and looked closely at Kikpona, "To safer and more secure areas. Kona especially. There is the possibility that our beloved Queen will not survive this war.

If that forbidden thing should happen, Kona is the last link we have to the royalty of Leyowan. She must be kept safe."

There were murmurs of agreement from around the room. Morgo stood up and addressed the others.

"I think we should wait to make further decisions until we know Jarlir's intentions toward the alliance between Ichoda and Utomia. I think we should offer to hold council with him, under strict surveillance by bodyguards from both sides. It is essential that we reach an agreement with him to survive this war."

Vanddai stood and walked to the doorway. "I agree, brother. I must go to my chamber and rest now. My queen, should you need me at any time, you have only to call my name and I will come to you."

One by one the other three filed out into the hallway after her, all of them grim faced and silent, thinking hard about the news Kikpona had confronted them with.

"NO! I will NOT leave Utomia!"

Kikpona sighed as she faced her infuriated younger brother. Jathren had objected to her command as soon as she had gotten the words out of her mouth. Now, the queen was at her wit's end.

"Jathren, calm down. You are acting like a toddling child. Stop trying my patience! You will do what I tell you to. And it is my wish that you go with our mother to Nenamene

221

for safety. You are barely eleven years old! You cannot fight in this war. No matter what you may think, you are not a warrior yet!"

Jathren's face was hard as stone. "You cannot make me go. I will not go. I will fight beside you. Utomia is as much my home as yours. Besides, I am Prince of Leyowan, and you cannot order me around," he said.

That was the wrong thing to say to an already irritated Kikpona. She turned on him with all the fury of a female tigress protecting her young.

"Do not *dare* challenge me, Jathren! Prince or not, you are still my younger brother and you are *not* my equal! You may be Prince, but I am Queen! You will do as I say if I must drag you to the border myself!"

With that, Kikpona whirled and disappeared into her bedchamber, slamming the door behind her. Jathren sank to the floor, tears of anger coursing down his cheeks. He balled his fist and slammed it against the wall.

A dark presence appeared behind him, and lowered itself down with a heavy grunt. Jathren recognized the form of Atoru. The big bull sighed wearily.

"My Prince, do not condemn your sister. She carries a very heavy burden, being the ruler of a country. Orluc and his armies are nothing to be confident about. They very well could destroy this city, brick by brick. And if they do, we are all dead beasts. Our very lives depend on Kikpona's decisions. She knows this, and it troubles her exceedingly."

Jathren shook his head. "But why must I go to Nenamene? I don't want to go; I want to fight with the Utomians! It is as much my right as it is my sister's!"

Atoru's head lowered slightly. "There is the blood of many warriors coursing through your veins. But think of it this way. Your sister would protect you throughout the battle. And in doing so, she would not be able to protect herself. Would you be able to forgive yourself if by fulfilling your own desires, you secured your sister's death?"

Jathren had not thought of this. He scuffed the stone floor with his boot, his eyes fixed on his hands.

"She wouldn't die for me...would she?" he asked quietly. Atoru saw the tiny tear that ran down the young Prince's cheek. It was obvious that Jathren could not comprehend such love.

"Aye, my Prince. She would, and willingly, without as much as a second thought. She loves you very much. You are her only brother, and she would give her life to protect you. Just as I would give my life to protect her."

Atoru watched the young boy's face. Jathren was deep in thought, his mind whirling as he contemplated the big bull's words. Finally, the prince turned towards Atoru and smiled.

"I understand, Atoru. I was just being selfish. Besides, there will be plenty of other battles when I am older and stronger. And my mother will need me to help protect Baby Kona. I'm her uncle, you know. It is my duty to see that she is well taken care of."

Atoru smiled broadly. "So it is, my Prince," he said.
Then the bull's face grew more solemn as he looked Jathren
in the eye.

"You have much wisdom for your youthful years, Prince
Jathren of Leyowan. Your sister is very proud of you. And she
has every right to be. You are a true son of Utomia."

Atoru stood up and left the Great Hall, leaving the
young prince staring after him in surprise. Jathren felt
warmed clear to his toes by the powerful General's approval.
Atoru did not waste compliments, and Jathren knew it. The
boy stood up and quietly knocked on his sister's bedchamber
door. He knew that he had a sincere apology to make.

.~.~.~.~.~.~.

King Jarlir silently sipped wine from a silver goblet. The
noise outside his tent was bothering him. He sat in his
wooden chair moodily, chewing on a bit of meat that had
been brought to him for the evening meal.

His messenger had arrived last night, relaying the
dreadful news of Orluc's invasion. When asked how he had
obtained this information, the messenger had simply stated
that it had come from a reliable source. Jarlir had been irked
by that, but had chosen to press no further.

Now, he fought within himself. He knew full well what
Kikpona would ask. He was only waiting for her to send a
messenger. But how was he to answer?

224

Furious that his personal war with his stepdaughter had been interrupted by Orluc's invasion, Jarlir slammed his fist down on the table. The food on the silver plate in front of him jumped into the air at the impact.

"Your Majesty?" a voice inquired doubtfully from the entrance flap of the tent. Jarlir looked up, startled. General Jahere stood there, his eyes full of concern.

"Is something troubling you, Majesty?" the bull asked. Jarlir closed his eyes and shook his head, gritting his teeth.

"No, General. What do you want?"

"My lord, there is a messenger from the Pretender waiting to speak to you outside."

Jarlir sighed. "I knew she would send one sooner or later. Send him in, and do him no harm until I have heard his message."

Jahere disappeared behind the tent flap, but was back a moment later with a tall cheetah. Jarlir surveyed the messenger coldly.

"You have been sent to give me a message. Relay it, and do it quickly. I would like nothing better than to impale your head on a spike outside my camp, so do not try my patience."

Makkiu's eyes darkened in anger. "I bear no loyalty to you. Your command means naught to me. But I will speak, only because my Queen has bidden me to do so."

Jarlir breathed heavily, his rage building up inside him. He nodded curtly to the defiant messenger. Makkiu spoke quickly.

"My queen wishes to hold council with you. She says that in order to defeat Orluc and his Morbian army, we must become…allies… with you, however unpleasant that may be to both parties. She asks that you and she be allowed to meet together tomorrow at the midday meal. She will provide food and wine. Only two guards each of your choice will accompany you both. This meeting is to be conducted in the good faith that neither of you will try to capture or injure the other."

Makkiu finished, his eyes sparking with disgust at his own message. It was clear that the cheetah wanted nothing to do with Jarlir, and that it made him extremely uncomfortable just to be in the Ichodian lord's tent.

Jarlir sat, his eyes studying the messenger. He glanced at Jahere, who obviously wanted to rip the cheetah into tiny pieces. The king put his head in his hands resignedly.

"Tell your queen that I agree to the arrangement on one condition. I want a hostage to hold as an assurance of her good will towards me. Someone that means something to her. I will supply her with a hostage also, if she so desires. If she so much as raises a dagger to strike me, I will slay the hostage with no mercy."

Makkiu bristled. "The queen will not enjoy the demands of an Imposter. But I shall relay this message to her without delay; you may be assured of that."

Jahere stepped forward, shaking his horns menacingly. "Watch how you address His Highness! King Jarlir is no imposter! Kikpona is nothing but a false queen, a woman with an inflated opinion of herself!"

Makkiu snarled furiously. "If I were you, Insolent One, I would curb my tongue before it was cut out of your mouth!"

Jarlir stood up from his chair. "ENOUGH!"

The two animals were silent, their rage kept unspoken behind the barriers of their minds. Jarlir addressed both of them.

"Jahere, stay here with me. Messenger, get out of my sight before I skin the hide from your back!"

Makkiu needed no second invitation to leave. He spat on the ground and bounded out of the tent. Jahere started after him, and then stopped himself. Breathing heavily and trying to keep his fury under control, he turned to face his king. Jarlir cleared his throat.

"Do not touch the messenger. There will be time for that later. Once Orluc is defeated we can go back to our war with Kikpona. And then, I promise you, the cheetah will be struck down by your horns alone. For now, we must contain our intentions towards Utomia and her queen. There is a bigger danger in Leyowan now than Kikpona's uprising."

Jahere nodded, calm returning to him. "Aye, Majesty. I will overcome my anger. What would you have me do?" he asked.

Jarlir sat back down. "The only thing we can do is wait. So we will wait until tomorrow, and then I will hear what Kikpona has to say."

.~.~.~.~.~.~.

Jarlir awoke the next morning to hear a great scuffling outside. He hurriedly dressed and stepped out of the tent. He saw soldiers mocking and throwing dirt at the hostage that Kikpona had sent. It was Atoru. Jarlir could not believe his eyes. Kikpona had sent her favorite General, her best friend, to Jarlir's mercy.

"Leave him alone!"

The command cut through the air like a knife, silencing the soldiers and causing them to scurry away, out of their king's path. Jarlir stopped in front of the big bull. Atoru met his gaze evenly, not flickering so much as an eyelash.

"Well met, Atoru, son of Toru the Black Bull. As always you prove your worth and bravery."

"Do not seek to flatter me, Jarlir. I do not fear you, nor shall I fear you ever. I am loyal to one Queen. And one Queen alone. Thus I am here by her request only."

Jarlir straightened stiffly, his eyes flashing momentarily, and then his anger disappeared behind his emotionless face. He took a deep breath before answering the General of Utomia.

"Aye that is true, Atoru. I seek no flattery towards you. Jahere! Take this noble beast to my tent. See that he is fed and given drink. And see that he is treated well, and undisturbed."

Jahere said nothing. He stepped forward, and the red bull faced the black. The two animals stared long and hard at each other. Jahere felt slightly intimidated by the larger size

228

and power of the other bull. He stood tall and inclined his head slightly. Atoru did the same, and the two bulls disappeared into the tent.

Jarlir looked around and quickly chose two bodyguards. "Hhuru, Nenkin! Come with me."

The two wolves left their battalion and followed Jarlir towards Utomia. When they reached the hillock overlooking the city, they saw a large pavilion set up on the grassy field in front of Utomia's gates.

Jarlir walked toward it, his eyes warily glancing in the direction of the wall top. He swallowed nervously. It would be very easy for archers to pick him off without so much as aiming.

Quickly he entered the pavilion, and found himself face to face with his mortal enemy. Kikpona stood eye to eye with her stepfather, her hatred barely concealed. But she was ever courteous.

"Please be seated, Jarlir. I'm sure your long march has wearied you."

"Yes Kikpona, it has."

Jarlir seated himself, watching Kikpona. Begrudgingly he admitted to himself that she had grown very beautiful, and the essence of her power radiated from her. She seated herself down on an ornately carved throne, and motioned the wine-bearer forward. The man quickly poured Kikpona's goblet full, and then did the same for Jarlir's.

Kikpona raised her glass. "To good health and victory," she said, her blue eyes watching Jarlir's every move. He raised his own goblet.

"Aye, to good health and victory," he echoed. Kikpona snapped her fingers, and Vanddai and Morgo stepped up from behind the throne to guard her. Jarlir found himself staring at Morgo. The young man's muscled arms and powerful build were very intimidating.

Jarlir cleared his throat nervously. "I can see that you harbor no love for me, as you once did."

Kikpona was up out of her throne, fury shining from her eyes. Her hands balled into white fists, and her arms trembled from exerting every ounce of self-control that she possessed. Nenkin and Hhuru stepped protectively in front of their king, unsure what the queen was going to do.

"How dare you insult me! You have caused me more pain than I ever thought capable of *anyone*! You of all people would have the nerve to rub salt on an old wound that should never have been struck in the first place!"

Jarlir felt his hands grow clammy under the tongue lashing that Kikpona was giving him. But his eyes grew colder and fiercer. For a long moment, the pavilion was silent. Jarlir finally decided to speak.

"Very well. Since I can see that a temporary alliance is vital to the survival of this nation, I agree to whatever terms you may require. However, the moment that Orluc and his armies are destroyed, our war will continue."

230

Kikpona gritted her teeth furiously. "So be it. My terms are simple. You will not kill any of my soldiers, you will not command my army, and you will do no harm to my advisors, family, or close friends. Am I understood? Break the agreement, and I will see to it personally that your head is dislodged from your shoulders!"

Jarlir scowled darkly as he stood up. "Do not seek to frighten me with threats, Kikpona. I am no weakling that seeks to honor you. No, quite the opposite. When Orluc is defeated, I will break you," the king replied, the last sentence spoken so maliciously that a hush fell over the pavilion.

Jarlir flicked his wrist at the two wolves and left the tent. The wolves glanced menacingly over their shoulders as they followed him, snarling and growling.

Kikpona sank back onto the throne. Morgo placed a hand on her shoulder, his reassurance calming her. Vanddai was shaking her head in complete disgust of the king of Ichoda.

"Who does he think he is? How that man ever became the king of such a prominent city as Ichoda, I will never understand. How could those people follow a man like that? He is a bloodthirsty rebel who wants the whole world to bow down to him as if he were a god," Vanddai said, and spat on the ground in contempt.

Morgo was grim-faced. "If he ever talks to you like that again, I will be the one doing the breaking!"

Kikpona smiled up at him, and then at Vanddai. "I don't know what I would do without the two of you to support me.

231

I'm starting to feel the effects of his hatred. My heart grows heavier each day."

Morgo gripped her hand tightly. "Don't let him control you, my love. Jarlir wants to burden you with his malice. Don't let him do it!"

Kikpona's head dropped slightly as a tear squeezed from her eyelid. Morgo swiftly knelt beside her and wiped the drop from her cheek with his thumb.

Vanddai, who had been silent for a long moment, suddenly bolted out of the pavilion. Kikpona stared after her in complete surprise, wondering what on earth her sister-in-law was doing. There was a *thwack!* And then a low groan from outside…

A second later, Vanddai dragged the limp form of Nenkin into the tent. She dropped him unceremoniously on the floor.

"This one was eavesdropping on our conversation. The other wolf was too, but he got away. I couldn't strike both of them at the same time," Vanddai said angrily. Morgo noticed that his sister was breathing heavily, exhausted from her effort. It was clear that she had not fully recovered from her old wound yet.

Vanddai eased herself down into a chair, and placed a hand on her stomach. Grimacing, she motioned to the flask of wine sitting on the table. Morgo gave it to her, concern lining his face.

"Kero, are you…" he began.

Vanddai shook her head. "No, brother. I am fine. Just weary."

Morgo looked unconvinced, but Kikpona came to Vanddai's rescue. She stood up and sighed.

"I think we should return to the city. There is nothing further to do here, and I need to rest, and Kona will be hungry by now. Besides, I need to clear my head and think about what I am going to do. Oh, and Morgo…" she looked at him meaningfully. "Make sure Atoru returns safely. If anything should happen to him, I…"

Morgo nodded understandingly. He and Vanddai took Nenkin out of the tent, and handed his unconscious form over to the guards. Kikpona heard Morgo telling the guards to lock the wolf away until he could be questioned.

Kikpona walked briskly back to her city. She just wanted some time to herself, to think about what to do next. Also, she wanted her daughter. Kona always brought joy to her mother, no matter how dreary and bleak the day had been.

.~.~.~.~.~.~.

Atoru made his way back to Utomia. The mocking shouts and jeers of the Ichodian army still rang in his ears. They had scorned him and even spat on him as he had passed through them to the outskirts of the encampment. And Jarlir had allowed it.

The big bull had borne it all with the nobility of a king. He had not so much allowed his tormentors a glance. It had taken all of his willpower not to cut the soldiers to ribbons when they had begun prodding and poking his sides and legs with their spears and javelins.

Now, out of sight of the enemy, Atoru began loping slowly towards Utomia's big gates. His eyes were bloodshot red, and his fury was mounting by the second. Lunging through the gates, he ran behind the palace to his own quarters in the barracks. His horns slammed forcefully into a large sycamore tree growing beside the door.

Again he charged the sycamore, causing the whole tree to shudder violently. Large branches cracked and fell to the ground around him. He was unaware of the curious stares coming from his soldiers, watching from their barrack windows.

The big bull sank slowly to the ground, his eyes closing. He felt defeated, and worthless. He barely heard the soft footsteps that sounded behind him.

Kikpona was there, kneeling down beside her friend. Pulling his head onto her lap, she gently stroked the white star on Atoru's head, just as she had done when they were young. The bull's eyes did not open, but he spoke quietly.

"How did it come to this, my Queen? How did our country become so misled that we now mock and scorn our own brothers? That we spit upon them and treat them like slaves?"

Kikpona's eyes filled with sympathy. "Oh, Atoru. Was it like that?" she asked, her mind filling with anger toward her stepfather.

234

"Those that I knew and played with as a calf, now spit on me and call me all kinds of foul names, jabbing me with their javelins. The king that I served so faithfully before you were banished watched and laughed as though it were some sort of game."

Kikpona bowed her head. "It grieves me to hear this, my friend. Ever since we were young, you have been my eyes and ears. You have been more loyal to me than any other, and yet I subjected you to treatment that would've been fit for a common thief. How low have I fallen to submit my own friends to this?"

Kikpona stood up, preparing to leave, but Atoru stopped her and looked her straight in the eye.

"You did right, my Queen. Had you sent another, he would have been angry and attacked the Ichodians. You sent me because you knew that I would not. And I did not disappoint you, for I kept my anger to myself and said nothing, for I would not have brought shame to you were I offered all the kingdoms of Leyowan. You are the Queen, my lady. And you are a good queen, so do not deign to think otherwise. I will not allow it."

Kikpona's head came up slightly. "Thank you, Atoru. You are a true friend to me. None in the entire kingdom has been as loyal to me as you," she said quietly.

16

Orluc's armies halted just inside the border of Leyowan. The gigantic bear was leading his hordes fully armored. He held his heavy scimitar with a vise-like grip. Looking over the lush valley with greedy eyes, he turned to his advisor, a cunning, wickedly intelligent fox called Satnul.

"Well, Satnul, there lies the land of Leyowan. It will be fitting as my capitol, do you not think?"

The fox bowed low to his evil master and spoke. "Aye, lord. A very fitting capitol, indeed. What is your plan of action?"

The bear slowly swung his head from side to side, surveying the lush country before him with greedy eagerness. He turned and looked over his head at the army behind him. Thousands upon thousands were there, all heavily armed and ready to destroy what Leyowan had always loved. Her people.

"My plan is simple enough…destroy all in our path."

Kikpona held the torch in front of her, walking down the slimy stone steps into the prison. The darkness was almost stifling. She nodded curtly to the jailor, who bowed deeply.

237

Continuing down the long row of cells, Kikpona stopped in front of the one that housed the wolf spy from Jarlir, Nenkin. She held the torch towards the iron bars of the cage. The wolf's hate-filled eyes stared back at her maliciously.

"Have you come to try and torture information out of me, Great One?" the wolf asked sarcastically. Kikpona sighed wearily. She hated the anger that was between the two loyalties. She looked closely at Nenkin, her eyes sympathetic and soft.

"No, Nenkin. I will not harm you. I am not a barbarian who tortures my enemies for information. I am going to let you go free. Your choice will be whether to go back to your master, or stay and fight for me."

Nenkin's eyes widened. "Let me go? You would really do such a thing?"

Kikpona smiled slightly. "You'll find I'm not as evil as Jarlir. Perhaps it would do you good to consider your options carefully."

Nenkin snarled. "But if I stay here, your people will mock me and hate me until I am killed or die. I thank you, but I do not wish a life as full of agony such as that."

Kikpona shook her head. "Nenkin, I would never allow my people to harm you. It is your choice," she said. Turning to the jailor, she motioned for him to open the door of the cell. The jailor did so quickly, swinging the door wide open. Kikpona lifted her arms.

"You have a chance to kill me, Nenkin," she said, her blue eyes boring holes into Nenkin's skull. The wolf faltered slightly, but made no move to attack the queen. He was completely confused. Why was the Queen being so kind to him? It made no sense. Then Nenkin realized something. This Queen really wasn't evil. She had made no inclination to hurt or taunt him. Something that Jarlir would never have hesitated to do. He lifted his head, looked Kikpona in the eye, and then bowed.

"I am yours to command, Noble One," he said softly. "My lord Ipotar was right about you. Before Jarlir had him killed, he was planning to join your cause. He said you were much more of a ruler than Jarlir ever would be. And I think perhaps he was right in saying so."

Kikpona smiled again, her blue eyes losing their hard edge. "Then welcome to my city, Nenkin. I hope you will find your new home comfortable and accommodating. If any of my people harm you, report to me at once and they will be punished. Go to my General, Atoru, and report for duty, if you wish to join the army."

Nenkin bowed again and then left, going towards the barracks. Kikpona went back to the palace, and saw a long caravan lined up in front of the marble columns. Wounded people lay in the wagons, some silent, some groaning pitifully. Huge steers were hitched to the wagons haphazardly, as if they had been forced to leave in a hurry.

Kikpona raced towards them. She looked into one of the wagons, and her hand flew to her mouth. Three young children lay inside, two of them holding onto the third, whose face was covered in blood and deep cuts. Kikpona felt tears well up in her eyes. These were her people...

Morgo found her then, and steered her away from the wagons. One of the men was standing in front of the caravan, leaning heavily on a walking stick as a result of a tightly bandaged leg. He bowed low to Kikpona, and attempted to kneel. Kikpona quickly took him by the shoulders and lifted him up gently.

"No, no. Please do not worry yourself with courteousness. My good people, you have been through enough already. What happened?" she asked, her blue eyes full of sympathetic pain.

Tears rolled down the man's face as he began to relate the story to his queen shakily. "Oh, my lady! It is beyond my knowledge of words to fully relate this terrible thing to you in a way that would describe it well enough. A great bear came... leading hordes of evil beasts, over the hill behind our village. They struck without warning, killing all who were not lucky enough to escape their path. They burned our homes, and destroyed every building brick by brick. Only these few of us managed to escape. All the others...perished... my wife and child," he said, his voice breaking.

Kikpona stared at the man. "A great bear?" she asked, her voice trembling slightly. The man nodded silently, a tear slipping past his eyelid and dripping down his cheek. Kikpona staggered back into Morgo's waiting arms. She buried her face in her hands, despair filling her.

"I had hoped for more time. These poor people," she whispered to Morgo. He hugged her tightly and kissed the top of her head, reassuring her.

"Rest easy, my love. You knew this would happen sooner or later. We are as prepared for it now as we ever will be. My only sadness is that these poor people were not warned in time to escape the attack. So many deaths might have been prevented had they had ample warning."

The man standing before the Queen wrung his hands in distress, his eyes dark and troubled.

"Please forgive me, my lady. I should not have troubled you so. Forgive my foolishness, it was wrong of me," he said, his voice cracking on the last few words. Kikpona instantly went to him, and put her hands on his shoulders.

"No, my dear friend, do not place any blame on yourself. This is not your trouble. Right now, all you need is to clear your mind and get some rest," she said to him kindly.

Turning, she motioned to Quetoro. "Quetoro, please take these good people to the almshouse, and give them food and drink. Take Baka the Healer with you to look after those who are wounded. Make sure they are properly lodged, and give them whatever provisions and clothing they need. Let them rest."

Quetoro bowed low, and led the ragged group away. Kikpona looked meaningfully at Morgo.

"I want a council of war to be called, now. Assemble everyone in the Council Hall. We must have a plan of action, and soon." Kikpona straightened her shoulders and walked briskly into the palace.

.~.~.~.~.~.~.

Vanddai, Quetoro, Atoru, Morgo, Makkiu, and Kikpona were soon all seated in the gigantic Council Hall. The new building was enormous, and served many different purposes: the treasury, the armory, the barracks of the high ranked army officers, and finally, the actual Council Room itself. The walls were rough limestone, and decorative tiles inset with jewels adorned them. Scrolls and swirls were carved deep into the limestone, adding a touch of sophistication to the room. Tall marble columns rose up into the ceiling ominously, creating an aura of grandeur.

Scrolled benches were carved into the lower half of the walls, creating places for the High Council of Utomia to sit. And gracing the wall opposite the massive oaken doors, sat the Sovereign's Seat. The dark cedar wood throne was intricately carved in spiraled vines and flowers. Two carved wings supported the back.

Kikpona mounted the dais and sat down solemnly in the Sovereign's Seat. The others all took their places on the carved benches, except for Quetoro and Atoru, who stood in three sided stalls with cushioned floors.

A grim silence hovered over the room, creating a strained atmosphere. Kikpona sat with her head in her hands. Finally, she spoke, her voice echoing softly around the room.

"My friends, it is a dark day in the history of Leyowan. For the first time, Morbia has an army that could potentially destroy everything we know and love. Atoru, what is the army's status?"

The black bull stepped into the middle of the room. "My Queen, the army numbers nearly fifteen thousand strong. We have five thousand mounted warriors, nine thousand foot soldiers, and one thousand warriors of the sky," Atoru said proudly, referring to the birds of prey. Atoru cleared his throat and then continued.

"Our weapons are upgraded and strong, and our blacksmiths make more every day. We have just come into the possession of three large wooden rock catapults, and our wood craftsmen are replicating them. Is there anything else I need to tell you, my Queen?"

Kikpona sat silently, deep in thought. She shook her head absent-mindedly, dismissing the General back to his stall. She then turned to Quetoro.

"What can you tell me about Orluc's movements and position?" she asked. The red stallion motioned to an attendant. The man brought forward a small map table, and spread a large scroll over it, pinning down the edges so it would stay flat. Everyone gathered around the table as Quetoro spoke.

"Orluc entered Leyowan here, near Juntaro, the town that was attacked. From what our messengers can tell, he is somewhere between Juntaro and Ichoda, in this fifty mile stretch of desert. He will not stay there long, because feeding an army of that size in the desert is nearly impossible. We suspect that he will move into Ichoda from his current position, and take the city. I have sent messengers to the Ichodians to warn them, but I do not know if they will evacuate the city in time."

Kikpona nodded. "Aye, Jarlir's people can be stubborn. Surely they would not stay when the city is inevitably going to be attacked. I do not think even the Ichodians are that foolish."

Quetoro looked at her intently. "Still, you can never tell. We should begin readying Utomia for refugees. We must be able to house any groups of people and animals that seek refuge from Orluc."

Kikpona turned to Makkiu. "Get a group of builders ready and start work on some new huts. Make sure we have plenty of room to keep these people comfortable."

The cheetah bowed low and raced out the door. Morgo was studying the map intently.

"We can't let Orluc find Utomia. We have to meet him somewhere outside of the city. Perhaps... in the jungles between here and Ichoda. Then after we've destroyed part of his army, he will have a weaker force to attack Utomia with."

Atoru spoke quickly. "No, Lord! It is far too dangerous to meet him outside of our defenses. We would have no chance of victory. Between us, with the armies of both Ichoda and Utomia, we have only thirty-five thousand soldiers. Orluc has more every day. Our latest messenger brought back the number as being fifty thousand or more. He has added nearly ten thousand to his army. How can we triumph against such an army if we are out in the open with no defense?"

Morgo sighed. "I don't see what other choice we have. We cannot afford to lose Utomia to Orluc. If he takes the city, we will lose Leyowan."

Kikpona pressed a hand to her forehead. "I understand your point, Atoru, but Morgo's plan makes more sense. Plus, if we are going to lose this war, we have to give our families enough time to escape. If we are going to die, let it be to ensure their safety."

Quetoro nodded solemnly. "I am with you on that, my Queen. Let us fight like warriors, and make them remember us!"

Vanddai, who had kept silence the entire time, now spoke softly, her eyes downcast. "But if Orluc takes Leyowan, we will have died for nothing."

The tone of Vanddai's voice made everyone in the room look at her. Her face was pale, and her hands trembled slightly. Her eyes were dark and clouded. Kikpona put a hand on her sister-in-law's shoulder reassuringly.

"Vanddai, do not be troubled. I have the intention of sending you with my brother to guard Kona and the others who go to Nenamene. I want you to see to their safety," she said.

Vanddai retaliated instantly. Sparks lit her eyes as she replied, "Never! You are not going to send me away to guard the young and the old. I am going to battle with you, whether you wish it, or not!"

Morgo shook his head in amusement. "Don't push her, Kikpona. Vanddai is as stubborn as a mule. You won't change her mind now that it's made up. I would suggest giving in."

Vanddai smirked as she looked Kikpona in the eye. "You may think that I am crippled and unable to fight in this war. But I tell you, I will be standing right beside you to the very jaws of death, and beyond."

A cheer went up from those in the room at Vanddai's brave words. Quetoro caught Kikpona's gaze and smiled slightly at her, his dark eyes shining with approval.

.~.~.~.~.~.~.

Ichoda was deserted when Orluc came within sight of the city. The huge bear motioned to his wolf pack.

"Go into the city, and kill all in your path. I want no prisoners," he growled ominously, his beady eyes surveying the city evilly. Two hundred wolves leaped past their comrades and raced into the city. They dashed madly around, ripping through every house, every stable, searching for any left in the city.

246

Finally they reported back to Orluc, dragging with them one lone prisoner. It was a messenger cheetah, one that had warned the Ichodians to leave. The cheetah was injured, one of his hind legs dragging limply along behind him. The cheetah was flung down before Orluc, who surveyed him critically.

"Why do you linger here, cat?" the bear asked, his eyes locked on the cheetah's. The young cat bowed his head silently. Orluc stepped forward and slammed his claws into the cheetah's shoulder.

A howl of pain escaped the cat's lips as the deadly weapons of the bear dug into his skin. Orluc laughed mirthlessly.

"What is your name, and where are the Ichodians hiding? Tell me know, or die here."

The cheetah raised valiant eyes to his oppressor. "Deynru the Utomian will never betray his Queen!"

Orluc drew his battle blade with stunning ferocity and struck the cheetah down, killing him instantly. Sheathing his sword, the great bear looked at Satnul, whose hackles were drawn back in a fiendish grin.

"He said Queen, Satnul... what is this? You told me that the ruler of Leyowan was a man, not a woman!"

Satnul, ever cunning, bowed low. "Perhaps the king died, Great One, leaving his daughter to take the throne. I myself will find this Queen, and tell you where to find her. Does my lord honor me with such a mission?"

Orluc's gaze pierced the fox as he spoke. "Aye, I will give you this mission. But if you fail me..." the voice of the bear went lower and lower, ending the sentence in a deep growl. Satnul didn't have to hear any more. His master's intent was all too clear. It was succeed, or pay for it with his life.

Satnul bowed deeply and raced off into the woods, leaving the army and his master behind him. He knew that he had to find this Queen as quickly as possible, learn as much as he could in a few days, and return to Orluc without delay.

17

Kikpona walked among the workers, surveying the area of new and half finished huts. Quetoro walked beside her, his great red mane shifting slightly as he moved his head from side to side, inspecting the work.

"They have done well, Highness. We can accommodate many refugees now. We shouldn't have any trouble keeping them safe and sound."

Kikpona sighed wearily, rubbing a hand across her forehead. "Aye, Quetoro, the work goes well. But Jarlir is still a very eminent problem. He is now asking my permission to move his army into Utomia, to ensure the safety of his soldiers."

Quetoro snorted angrily. "Then let them build their own city. He cannot be allowed to travel within ours freely! He would use it against us as soon as Orluc is defeated."

Kikpona looked at him thoughtfully. "You say with certainty that Orluc will be defeated, Quetoro. How can you be so confident? We have barely over half of the army that he does, and our city is not built to withstand the heavy attack that Orluc will wreak upon it. Furthermore, our soldiers are growing more and more anxious. They have heard the tales of Orluc's merciless customs of war."

Quetoro's eyes darkened as he lowered his head. "That is so, Your Majesty. But I truly believe that we will defeat this evil. Any beast or man finds courage enough when defending his homeland against foes."

Raising her eyes to the majestic red stallion, Kikpona smiled gratefully at him. Further conversation was cut short as Makkiu came bounding up to them, panting.

"My Queen, the last messenger just came in from Ichoda, the one called Tymo. He said that one of our cheetahs was murdered by Orluc, the youngest of our messengers, Deynru. Tymo saw it with his own eyes. But Deynru did not betray us; he told Orluc nothing of Utomia or you."

Kikpona felt tears spring to her eyes. "But he was so young…alas, but such are the evil times we have fallen upon, Makkiu."

The big cat's eyes lowered. "Yes, Majesty. So he was. We all mourn his loss with great feeling. He was beloved by all."

Suddenly, a great trumpet blast rang out from the outer wall. Quetoro and Kikpona immediately set off in that direction. Another trumpet blast sounded, and then another.

Upon reaching the wall, Kikpona saw two big leopards standing on either side of a large fox, who looked around fearfully at the angry Utomians surrounding him. He saw Kikpona approaching and shrank back before her.

"Who are you, fox, and from whence do you come?" the Queen spoke with electrifying clarity. The fox suppressed a shudder. Orluc was powerful in a great evil way, but this Queen was equally powerful in a serene and radiant way.

"I am called Satnul, O Powerful One. I come from the armies of Orluc, where I was a prisoner in his camp. I escaped and found this city to warn you, and to tell you information about him which you may find helpful."

Kikpona knelt down in front of him, her scepter balanced inches from the fox's nose. Satnul swallowed hard, praying that his lie would work. Kikpona's dark sapphire eyes stared hard at Satnul's black ones. The Queen's eyes reminded Satnul of chips of blue ice, and he felt as though she was piercing his skull with them.

"Take him to the guardhouse. I will interrogate him later."

The leopards dragged Satnul towards the guardhouse. Quetoro looked at the Queen uneasily.

"My Queen, something tells me that this fox is not who he says he is. You would be very wise to keep your wits about you at all times when he is present. He very well could be a spy, sent to inspect our defenses and army strength."

Kikpona nodded silently. If Orluc had sent a spy, then how close exactly was he? The very thought made her shudder. Her next thought was very, very clear. *Get your family out of Leyowan.*

Kikpona straightened her shoulders and strode briskly towards the palace, her determination set firmly in place. She swept through the main hall and into the small hallway that led to her mother's room. She came to the chamber door, and knocked quietly. A familiar voice came from inside.

"Come in."

Kikpona opened the door and entered the bedchamber. She shut the oak door behind her softly, and turned to face her mother. Elaria sat at a small table, holding a copper mirror in her hand as her servant expertly wound strips of the older Queen's raven black tresses into a fancy braided crown on top of her head.

Elaria smiled at her daughter. "What is it that you have come to see me for, Kikpona?" she asked, her voice husky and soothing. Kikpona wanted nothing more than to be cradled against her mother as she had been when she was a young girl. Instead, she walked up to her mother's chair and knelt down, laying her face in Elaria's lap.

Surprised, Elaria stared at her daughter. Then her face softened, and she smoothed tendrils of the bright red hair back with her fingertips. The surge of motherly protection rushed over Elaria.

"You haven't done that since you were ten years old," she said, her voice breaking on the last words. Kikpona shook her head and sighed deeply.

"I don't know what to do, Mother. My kingdom is about to be attacked by the most powerful enemy Leyowan has ever known, and I am surrounded by spies and traitors. Other than those closest to me, I don't know who to trust anymore. And now I must send you, Jathren, and Kona away from here for your protection. I don't know if I will live through this war. What will happen if Orluc defeats us, and takes Leyowan?"

Elaria continued stroking her daughter's hair as she replied, "I don't know what will happen, Kikpona. And you know that I will stay here with you if you need me. I still haven't given up hope that one day Cyus will return."

A soft moan emitted from Kikpona's lips. "Mother, I had ordered Makkiu to bring him here, but then I had to revoke my command because of Orluc's arrival. I'm sorry."

Kikpona felt her mother tense. "You...you know of your father's whereabouts? Kikpona, please, tell me where he is!" Elaria begged. Kikpona sat up and looked at Elaria, her blue eyes soft and sad.

"He is in Morbia, Mother. The very lair of Orluc. He has been hidden there for many, many years. I should have told you sooner, but I was afraid that you would try and find him. Please promise me that you won't."

Elaria nodded silently, tears coursing down her face as she thought of her long lost lover. Her heart felt heavy with grief, yet light with the joy that Cyus still lived. This was more than she had hoped for. But now that she knew of his existence, she wanted to see him more than anything else.

Kikpona saw her mother's struggle. "Forgive me, Mother. I should not have told you yet. You will still go with Kona and Jathren to Nenemene?" Kikpona said, her eyes still locked on Elaria's green ones.

The Queen Mother nodded. "Yes, I will. But if you need me, all you have to do is send for me and I will return."

Kikpona smiled. "I know you will."

.~.~.~.~.~.~.

Kikpona watched as the long caravan slowly rumbled out of Utomia's gates. Jathren rode Yuro at the front of the procession. Kikpona had given her brother command of the expedition as a way of apology that she had to send him away.

Her eyes filled with tears as she saw her mother wave one last time from the back of a wagon. Baby Kona was snuggled into her grandmother's arms, swathed in blankets and soft furs. Kikpona watched as her daughter faded from view. A gentle hand squeezed her shoulder reassuringly.

"Don't worry, my love. Elaria and Jathren will take very good care of our daughter," Morgo said softly in Kikpona's ear. The queen sniffed and nodded, wiping away the tears that were streaming down her face. She turned to her husband and clung to him.

"What's going to happen, Morgo?" she asked, her voice soft and vulnerable. Morgo felt his heart melt as he caressed his wife's red hair lovingly.

"I don't know, Kikpona. But whatever does happen to us, we will be together. I will be with you to the very end. You know that. So don't worry."

Kikpona's eyes once again looked out over the wall of Utomia to where the end of the caravan was just vanishing into the jungle. A bay horse cantered out of the trees, and Kikpona recognized her brother's figure. The boy waved, and Yuro reared up. The Queen smiled and waved back, a chuckle rising in her throat as her brother galloped back into the jungle, the very image of a heroic knight.

"He's still so young, Morgo. I fear for him," the queen said quietly. Morgo sighed.

"Kikpona, everyone is going to be fine. They will all be safe in Nenamene. Trust me. Besides, don't you have an interrogation to complete?" asked Morgo with a twinkle in his eye. Kikpona nodded and went down the stone steps towards the ground. Morgo watched as she disappeared within the door to the dungeons.

.~.~.~.~.~.~.

Satnul lay quietly in his cell, but his head swiveled upwards at the sound of Kikpona entering the stone room. The Queen's radiance was not dimmed by the dreary interior of the prison, and her voice carried a heavy tone of authority.

"Tell me, Fox, what is your name? And why are you in my city?" Kikpona asked, her eyes gazing piercingly at the animal before her. Satnul stood up, his legs taking on a slight tremble at the ferocity of the Queen's gaze.

"Please, Your Majesty, I am naught but a humble traveler from the southern lands. I was captured by Orluc, and tortured, for he believed me to be from this country and thus hoped to gain information by me. I knew nothing, therefore I told him nothing. My name is Satnul."

Kikpona's eyes never left those of the fox. "Is that so? Do not think you can easily beguile me. I know that you are a servant of the Dark One. I should have you put to death for being a spy, but I am not that cruel. You will remain here until we have defeated Orluc, and then I will consider releasing you."

Satnul's eyes glittered with hate. "You speak of victory as though it were already in your grasp. Do not underestimate my master, for he is the most powerful ruler Morbia has ever known!" he spat out angrily. He was immensely surprised when Kikpona smiled.

"Ahhh...you realize, Fox, that you have just given yourself away. I did not know that you were a spy for the Dark One, but you have just spoken it with your own lying tongue."

The fox realized his mistake too late, and lunged for Kikpona, teeth bared. The Queen flicked her scepter and knocked him back into the cell, then turned and closed the barred door behind her. Satnul was left alone to lick his bruises and snarl with hatred.

.~.~.~.~.~.~.

Orluc's army kept moving slowly towards Utomia. They were now only about fifty miles away from Kikpona's forest city. The bear halted the hordes in a dense jungle where they would be concealed and have plenty of supplies at their disposal.

While Satnul was gone, a huge hyena named Jik was commander of Orluc's hordes. The hyena was much larger than most of his breed, and had fangs that were filed to be as sharp as knife points. Jik had a band of hyenas following him, and had been bribed into Orluc's army by Satnul. The hyenas were fierce and would not turn back once they had entered into battle.

However, in the face of defeat, they were cowardly. They only fought well if the battle was going in their favor. For this reason, Orluc found them invaluable, for he believed that his victory was imminent.

Orluc had a large pavilion set up for his own personal use. Inside the huge tent was his bed of hides, an ornate traveling throne, and wooden racks for his weapons. Two young hyenas attended him at all times, catering to his every whim.

The bear stretched out on the lavish cushions, devouring a platter of meat. He ate ravenously, never looking up from his feast. The hyenas stood placidly in two corners while their master ate, saying nothing and barely moving a muscle. Orluc's temper was unpredictable. So the young hyenas had every intention of remaining as invisible as possible, not wanting to do anything that could annoy Orluc.

Jik entered the pavilion, his fangs bared and glowing in the light from the torches. Orluc looked up from his meat, and a low growl emitted from his throat as he addressed the commander.

"I trust that you justify your intrusion with a *very* important report," the bear said. Jik bowed low to his master and nodded in affirmation.

"Aye, lord. That I do. Very important it is. Please forgive my intrusion," the hyena replied smoothly, his voice raspy and shrill. The bear shook his head, his coarse fur rippling with the movement.

"Continue with your report, Jik, before I lose my patience with you," Orluc snarled impatiently. Jik knew better than to stall further. He quickly continued.

"Of course, my lord. Satnul has been imprisoned by the Queen of the Jungle city called Utomia. It is as you suspected, there is a queen. It seems that you arrived just as she and King Jarlir were having a little battle over the throne of Leyowan. They have been alerted to your presence, my liege."

Orluc rolled his beady eyes. "Of course they have, you twit! We've been here for an entire month! I should hope that they know we were here. Do I command an army of half-wits?" he asked the hyena.

Jik lowered his gaze respectfully. "Nay lord." His voice was quiet and submissive, and he said nothing more. Orluc dismissed his commander with a flick of his massive front paw. Jik silently left the pavilion, leaving his slightly miffed master behind.

18

Morgo leaned against the battlements of Utomia's outer wall top, deep in thought. His scouts had just returned with a report of Orluc's movements. They worried him. The bear's army was so large and powerful that he was unsure how Utomia's strength would handle the inevitable attack.

A soft hand descended on Morgo's shoulder. Without even looking to see who it was, he knew. He reached up and placed his own hand over Kikpona's smaller one.

"The storm rises, doesn't it, Morgo?" she asked softly, her blue eyes flickering over the forest below the massive stone walls of her beloved city, and Jarlir's camp in the meadow. Her husband turned to face her, and drew her close to him.

"Yes, it does. Orluc draws closer to us with every passing day. Soon he will attack Utomia in full force. We must begin planning our strategy. We will only have one chance to defeat him. And there's something else..." Morgo's voice faded. Kikpona looked up at him expectantly.

"What else, my love?" she asked. Morgo felt uncomfortable telling her, but he knew that he needed to do it.

"Kikpona, I know that you are not going to like what I am going to tell you right now, but I just want you to listen to

259

me for a moment. I want you to let me lead the army against Orluc. And I want you to stay behind the walls. Please do not go into battle again," he whispered.

The beleaguered queen closed her eyes tightly, and Morgo could tell that she was struggling within herself. Finally, she answered him.

"I understand why you ask this of me, Morgo. But I cannot…I cannot stay behind while you and Atoru go into battle. This is my war as much as yours, perhaps even more so. I will go into battle at your side, because I must. Please understand why I must do this."

Morgo looked away, pain seeping into his heart. How could he tell her that he was not strong enough to lose her? What if he couldn't protect her, and she was injured or even worse…killed.

"I can't lose you, Kikpona. You are everything to me. I can't live without you, so please do not ask me to risk that."

Kikpona stared at him. "Morgo…I…." she paused for a moment. "I am as good with a weapon as any soldier in our army. My spear is all I need for protection. I will teach Orluc the meaning of defeat. None but my hand shall slay him. This I vow."

The mighty queen turned away from Morgo and went down the stone steps. He watched her go, and then returned to his former position, staring out over the jungle trees.

.~.~.~.~.~.~.

"We will break upon them by nightfall, my lord," said Jik. Orluc lumbered along beside the hyena as the army marched towards Utomia. The bear nodded in satisfaction.

"Excellent, commander. I will lead the main part of the army in a full front attack against the walls. You will take the left flank and attack Jarlir in the meadow. I want you to select a wise and experienced beast to lead the right flank against the walls at my side. That commander will use the catapults and timballistas to shatter the stone."

Jik smiled, his fangs showing as he eagerly anticipated the battle ahead of them. "Aye, lord, it shall be done."

The army was halted about three miles away from the Utomian walls. Jik quickly went running towards the battalion of his sister, whose name was Putra. The huge female hyena was the fiercest and meanest of the entire brood, and she demanded respect and obedience whenever she was present. She even dared to stand up to Orluc himself occasionally. Jik knew that his sister was the best choice to command the right flank of Orluc's army.

He strode through the ranks of beasts towards his sister's battalion. When he finally came in sight of her, he grinned wolfishly.

"Greetings, Putra, my dear sister. I bring good news for you from our master. He orders you to command the right flank of the army, with the catapults and heavy weaponry. Do you approve of this order?" he asked, somewhat sarcastically.

Putra's huge fangs appeared as she opened her mouth in a shrill hyena laugh. Her small black eyes gleamed evilly.

261

"I will do it. Tell Orluc to leave me to my own resources. I will not listen to that ogre's ceaseless bellowing and growling of orders during a fight."

Jik grinned again ruefully. "Perhaps it would be unwise to make your opinions known to him, sister. Patience and forgiveness are not virtues that he is well acquainted with."

The female hyena growled viciously at her brother's words. "Aye, but he would do well to learn them better. Putra the Hyena is not one to be pushed around by an oversized brute such as Orluc. I will be ready for the task when the battle begins, he may be assured."

Without another word, Putra turned and left the scene, disappearing within the crowd of her followers. Jik shook his head. Ever since they had been babies, Putra had always been independent and saucy, never quite agreeing with anyone but herself. Even Orluc's dire threats had failed in their attempt to get her to be submissive to his will. Jik was different. He was independent as well, but not so confrontational. He preferred to be assured of his place in Orluc's good will.

Interrupting his thoughts, a young hyena bowed stiffly to him. "Commander, the Master is asking for you to come to his tent."

Jik turned and followed the young messenger back towards Orluc's pavilion.

.~.~.~.~.~.~.

Horns blared from Utomia's wall tops. Kikpona sat up from her deep study of an ancient scroll, and pushed her chair back. Now what had happened? She rose and left her study room, walking briskly down the palace hallway.

Vanddai joined her, and they made their way toward the city gates. Neither spoke. When they reached their destination, Atoru and Morgo were with Makkiu, who had brought the new report of Orluc and his army. Morgo's face was grim, and Atoru was shaking his head. Kikpona quickly joined them.

"What is it, Makkiu? What news have you brought?" she asked. The cat's tail twitched nervously, as though he were hesitant to respond.

"Orluc will be within sight of Utomia by noon tomorrow."

Kikpona closed her eyes. So, the moment had finally come. The enemy was finally here. She looked at Morgo, whose face was veiled by a mask of neutrality, but she knew him too well. His fear for her was hiding just beneath the surface.

"Well, we don't have time to stand around and ponder. We must be ready for him when he arrives. Send a messenger to Jarlir. Tell him to move his army inside Utomia. We must be as powerful as possible. I want scouts following Orluc's every movement, and I will be informed of them. Atoru, prepare the army for battle. Get every soldier into their armor and sharpen all the weapons. Quetoro, help Morgo oversee the construction of the catapults and slings. Vanddai, you and I will begin planning our battle strategy."

Morgo and Quetoro bowed and left, and Atoru soon followed. Makkiu sped off in the direction of Jarlir's camp. Kikpona sighed. She regretted having to move Jarlir into her beloved city, but she had no choice. Though her stepfather was her adversary, she would not allow him to be slaughtered before the city walls. She would need every soldier he could give her.

Kikpona and Vanddai went around the palace to the Council Hall. Inside, Vanddai spread a map open on the wooden table. Kikpona paused in the doorway, and ran her hand lightly down the scrolling around the entrance. Her beautiful city in jeopardy. The very thought made her sick to her stomach. What if Orluc's invasion succeeded? Would Utomia burn?

"My Queen?"

Vanddai's voice brought Kikpona back to the present. She smiled at her sister-in-law, and joined her at the table. Vanddai studied the surrounding forests and meadows.

"I think our best chance lies in using the forest to our advantage. We know this jungle like the back of our hands. Orluc is in a new territory. We can attack more efficiently from the cover of the forest. That way, we can draw him to us, and the advantage will lie with us, not him."

Kikpona nodded in agreement. "That is my thought also. I do not want to see my city destroyed. If we can keep him in the jungle, Utomia has a better chance of surviving this battle unscathed."

Turning back to the map, Kikpona frowned. "There is another problem. What of the citizens? We cannot ask them to stay when their very lives are in danger. I would send them away, but where would they go?"

Vanddai shrugged. "Send them to Nenamene, after your family. They would be safe there, and you already know that King Amezon has offered them protection. He is our ally."

A nod from Kikpona confirmed the action. Vanddai called for a messenger, and a young wolf stepped into the hall.

"Yes, my Lady?" he asked, awaiting orders eagerly. Vanddai quickly told him his task.

"You will spread the word around the city that all the citizens of Utomia are to be moved to Nenamene for their safety. Those that stay may do so of their own free will, but at their own risk. The army will not be able to offer them absolute protection. Do you understand?"

The wolf bowed low. "It shall be as you command, Lady Vanddai. I go at once," he said, and raced out of the hall to obey his order.

Morgo entered the chamber, and behind him strode Jarlir, bedecked in a velvet cloak secured by a solid gold brooch. His crown rested on his head, proclaiming his kingship. Kikpona fought back the urge to scowl at him. Instead, she moved forward gracefully, her scarlet robes flowing behind her. She extended her hand in a sign of friendship.

"Welcome to my city, Jarlir of Ichoda," she said formally. The king took her hand hesitantly, and with an air of feigned grace, bent over it. Kikpona kept her expression neutral. Now was not the time to commence a fight over the past. The only way that she or Jarlir would survive this battle was if they fought together.

"I am honored, your ladyship," Jarlir replied cordially. He straightened up, and continued. "My army has joined yours, and my commanders await my orders. What is our plan of battle?" he asked.

Forgetting their past differences, Kikpona moved toward the map. "Vanddai and I have agreed that our greatest chance of moving the advantage to our side is to use the jungle as our fortress. We know these forests better than anyone, and your soldiers will benefit from the knowledge of mine."

Jarlir nodded, a thoughtful line creasing his forehead. "That's true. Orluc will expect us to hide behind Utomia's walls. And in doing so, he would most likely destroy the city, and gain the advantage. Though I would someday like to see your city fall, to lose it now would mean death for both my people and yours. Ichoda is already lost. No doubt he's plundered it and burned it to the ground by now," he said, a sad note in his voice.

Kikpona felt a tinge of pity at the back of her mind. Though she hated Jarlir and his cause, she too, had lived in

266

Ichoda, and had been born there. It was her home too. Shaking her head, she disagreed with herself. Utomia was her home now.

Jarlir sighed. "So tell me...what orders shall I give my commanders?"

.~.~.~.~.~.~.

Kikpona entered her bedchamber regally, closing the door behind her. She closed the heavy drapes that covered the windows, and opened the door of her wardrobe. Inside, her armor glinted in the candlelight. The great golden lion that stretched across the breastplate gleamed. Reaching out, Kikpona's fingers brushed the black plume of her helm.

Her maid stepped forward from the shadows. "My Lady? May I help you dress?" she asked cautiously. Kikpona nodded mutely. It was finally time. The greatest and most bloody battle of Leyowan's history would be fought tomorrow. And she, Kikpona, Queen of Utomia, would fight beside her soldiers.

The maid lifted the chainmail skirt out from the drawer, and fitted it carefully around her Queen's waist. She added the leg guards, and drew on the heavy black boots.

Removing the breastplate from its stand, the woman secured it over the chainmail sleeves, which covered the leather tunic. Then she tied the bracers over Kikpona's forearms. The gauntlets were drawn over the Queen's hands.

A black battle cloak was secured to the shoulders of the breastplate. Kikpona looked at her reflection in the mirror. A grim smile came to her lips. She looked every bit the warrior queen. She looked over at her maid, who was holding out the war helm to her.

Taking it, Kikpona looked at the iron helm. The gold and silver that had been melted onto the helm shone brightly. Etchings of great warriors covered the helm. Kikpona sighed and drew it over her head.

"Haya, please bring me the spear."

The maid quickly went to the huge cedar wood box that stood on a golden stand in the corner of the room. Unlatching the clasps, Haya opened it, revealing the heavy iron spear that was encased within, shrouded in pure white silk.

The servant gave the weapon gravely to her Queen, who ran her hands over the shaft lovingly. Her beautiful weapon had seen her through many battles. It had protected her from countless enemies. And now, she would have to face the greatest enemy of all.

Turning from Haya's troubled face, Kikpona moved toward the door. It opened, revealing Morgo, also dressed in his war armor, standing there. She drew a deep breath and looked away from his eyes. Morgo's gaze moved to the servant.

"Haya, please leave us."

The woman did as she was ordered, and Morgo shut the door behind her. He moved toward his wife slowly. He saw her downcast eyes through the helm, and gently pulled it from her head. Her hair fell down in a river of scarlet.

"Kikpona, my love," he whispered. His hand gently touched her cheek. His gauntlet smoothly slid over her skin. He bent down and dropped the softest of kisses on her neck. She closed her eyes, but did not speak. Morgo gently took the spear from her hand and leaned it against the wall. Taking her in his arms, he held her close. She rested her head against his breastplate.

"What will become of us, Morgo?" she whispered. He caught his breath slightly. He had known she would go into battle, but had prayed night and day that her mind would change. Hearing her words made him realize that she would be fighting beside him. He sighed.

"I don't know…but you must promise me that you will be careful. You will not put yourself in his path, Kikpona. Promise me!"

Kikpona did not have to ask of whom he spoke. He wanted her to stay away from Orluc. But she could not promise him. She knew in her heart that no hand but hers could slay the great bear. No one else was skilled enough to bring him down. Even Morgo would never cause him to fall.

"I cannot promise you that, Morgo."

Her words struck him deeply, and he felt pain flood into his heart. He stepped away from her, hurt flashing in his eyes. She knew that she had made him angry, and frightened.

"Morgo, I'm sorry, but I must fight in this battle. I will not leave my people alone in this time of darkness. I will not."

He looked down, and after a long moment, he nodded. Turning away, he left the room. Grief filled Kikpona, and she sank to her knees on the floor, tears streaming down her cheeks, making soft *plink*ing sounds as they hit her breastplate.

.~.~.~.~.~.~.

Torches burned in their sockets along the wall top, illuminating the soldiers who stood before them. Quetoro wore full horse armor, which glinted in the torchlight. Morgo stood beside him with Atoru. The three Warriors looked out over the multitude of trees in silence; waiting for the dawn's rising.

The trees were bathed in a golden light as the sun began to rise over the forest. The skies shone brilliant shades of yellow, pink and orange.

But the beauty was dimmed slightly by the sound that the soldiers heard over the jungle treetops. It was the shout of a gigantic horde, a vicious war cry from beyond the trees. It was only barely audible, but the words were clear.

"DEATH TO LEYOWAN!"

Quetoro's eyes narrowed angrily, and Atoru suppressed a shudder. The hatred and lust for blood emanating from those words was powerful and clear. Morgo gripped the handle of his battle axe tightly.

A trumpet sounded, and the soldiers turned to look down to the city's main street. Hooves thundered as Jarlir and Kikpona rode their warhorses down the dirt road, each bedecked in their war regalia. They both were the very image of splendor and royalty.

Jarlir rode a large bay stallion, while Kikpona was mounted on a Hupeg horse, one of Quetoro's kin, called Gundir. The big white stallion pranced about as Kikpona halted him. She looked up fiercely at her soldiers, and removed her helm.

"Soldiers of Utomia, my brothers and sisters! You have come with me to the very edge of battle. For this, I honor you! What lies before us is great trial, perhaps death itself. If any of you wish to go to Nenamene with your families and loved ones, I will not stop you. Let those who wish to go, go now."

Not one soldier moved from their position. Kikpona felt a hot pride rush into her at the loyalty of her people.

"Then so shall it be. Who among you will fight for me?" she shouted up to them. Thunderous roars, shouts, cheers and bellowing followed as each soldier lifted their voice in allegiance to their queen. Kikpona could not help herself. She looked over at Jarlir with a small smile playing about the corners of her lips. He looked extremely surprised at the loyalty that surrounded his former adversary.

The war cries of Orluc's army were now closer and louder. Kikpona raised her sword, and brought it down sharply. The first battalions of soldiers moved into the forest silently, taking their positions among the jungle growth. Vanddai was leading the archers into battle, to take the enemy by surprise. The last of the archers silently disappeared into the trees.

And so it began.

19

Orluc led the charge through the trees. His scimitar was clenched in his fangs as he lumbered forward, his massive bulk traveling swiftly through the dense undergrowth. He suddenly stopped and held up a heavy forepaw.

"Halt!" he roared. His battalion stopped behind him, huffing and panting from their long run. The bear rose up on his back paws, swinging his head from side to side as he smelled the air. Though the scent was faint, he could sense that the Utomians were closer than he thought.

A strange whistling sound filled Orluc's ears. He didn't have time to shout an order before a fusillade of arrows rained from the treetops in all directions. The battalion scrambled for cover as Morbians were felled by the deadly storm of Utomian arrows.

Orluc slapped at his ear as an arrow passed through it. He snarled angrily, and shouted for his archers. The longbow archers stepped forward and began firing into the trees.

Vanddai sat high above the Morbians in a huge old tree. She barely stifled her laughter as the Morbian archers wasted their arrows, firing away from where the Utomians were hiding. Fitting another arrow to her bowstring, Vanddai drew it back, aiming for the great bear that was in plain sight. Sighting in on her target, she released her weapon.

Orluc moved aside just in time. A young hyena yelped and fell dead, Vanddai's arrow lodged in his chest. The bear had seen where the arrow had come from, and motioned to his archers.

Vanddai swore under her breath as the Morbian arrows flew toward the Utomians. Two archers fell from the trees, landing among the Morbians. Vanddai knew that their advantage had been reversed now that the enemy knew where they were. Emitting a sharp whistle, Vanddai signaled her warriors to retreat.

The archers vanished through the jungle, heading back toward Utomia. Orluc laughed hideously as he watched them go. They had been defeated easily. But his triumph lasted only a moment longer, for a war horn blew through the jungle, echoing through the trees. .

Another blast followed, and then another. Orluc felt his spine tingle as an eerie war cry was shouted from the throats of hundreds of Warriors.

"Leeeeyyyyooooowwwwaaaaaannnn!!!"

And then they came, crashing through the trees and brush, weapons drawn, the light of fire and battle flashing in their eyes. The Utomians were ready for battle.

Kikpona led the charge on Gundir, her spear upraised, the black plume on her helm streaming out behind her above her cloak. Morgo followed her astride another warhorse, followed by Quetoro and Atoru.

Orluc roared, "Rally to me!" at his awestruck soldiers, who obeyed quickly, raising their weapons in anticipation.

274

Orluc raised his scimitar and shook it in the air, and the Morbians cheered.

The two armies clashed together with blinding speed. The air was suddenly filled with the sounds of metal striking metal, cries and shouts of pain, the whistle of arrows and javelins.

Kikpona was unhorsed almost instantly. Gundir fell to a javelin, crashing to the earth with a mighty thud. Kikpona was thrown clear, and she leapt to her feet. Brandishing her spear, she brought down a boar, and whirled her spear free just in time to thrust it into an archer who was aiming for Quetoro.

She battled her way toward her friend furiously, seeing that he was beset by more enemies than he could handle. The old stallion's strength was undimmed, and the light of battle shone wildly in his eyes. But blood flowed from a spear wound in his side, and the loss of blood was making him weaker.

Kikpona slammed the shaft of her spear across the head of a wolf who was preparing to leap for the stallion's throat. She whirled her weapon swiftly, bringing down all comers. Having cleared the area momentarily, she smiled up at Quetoro, who blew softly into her face.

"Many thanks, your Majesty," he said. She shook her head, and took up her battle stance once again.

.~.~.~.~.~.~.

Atoru was in trouble. His steel tipped horns were doing their deadly work, but he was surrounded by Jik's hyenas. They were dodging his big horns and nipping at his unprotected legs and belly. The black bull stamped his foot in preparation to charge away from his tormentors, when a wild yell sounded from behind him. Morgo was there, his battle axe flying among the hyenas, dealing bereavement and death wherever it was allowed to land. Atoru took advantage of the distraction, and his sharp horns found Jik.

The hyena commander yelped as he was lifted bodily into the air and hurled into a huge tree. The last thing that Jik saw was Atoru's maddened eyes as the horns were thrust downwards.

Morgo and Atoru stood together, breathing heavily from their efforts, but the hyenas all lay dead or fatally wounded. Morgo shouted to Atoru above the din of battle.

"Where is Kikpona?"

The big bull shook his head, and set off to find her. Morgo followed him, twirling his heavy weapon and barreling into a pack of wolves.

.~.~.~.~.~.

Orluc killed a mighty black horse with his scimitar, and straightened, pulling his blade free. Licking it, he glanced around for a new victim. He saw the big black bull advancing toward him through a pack of Morbian wolves, and the bear smiled wickedly. Here was an opponent of equal size and

276

strength as he. A true challenge, Orluc thought to himself, and was content to wait for the bull to reach him.

Atoru did not see Orluc until it was too late. The huge scimitar curved up and then down, cleaving one of Atoru's horns completely off, leaving only a two inch long stump in its place. The bull shook his head as blood trickled down into his eye. Bellowing with rage, he shook his remaining horn at Orluc threateningly.

"Come to me, bear!" he shouted furiously. Orluc obliged, swinging his scimitar. Atoru managed to block the sword with his horn, but was then helpless against the attack of Orluc's outstretched claws, which ripped through the thick muscles on Atoru's chest.

The bull backed away, the pain dulling his senses momentarily. Orluc grinned evilly, waiting for the next chance to bring down the bull. Atoru drew a deep, shuddering breath, and stomped his forefoot down, shaking the earth beneath him.

Summoning the last reserves of his strength, Atoru charged, his horn lowered and eyes closed. Orluc grabbed the horn and dug his back claws into the earth, attempting to halt the bull's charge. But Atoru's strength was greater than Orluc's, and the big bull knocked the evil Warlord off his feet. Orluc gripped the horn with all the strength he could muster, and tried to push Atoru off.

The muscles stood out from Atoru's neck and shoulders as he bore down, desperately trying to impale the bear on his horn. The steel tip was so close...

277

Putra came from out of nowhere. She leapt onto Atoru's back, her teeth locked on the back of his neck. Atoru bellowed with pain and reared up, giving Orluc the chance he needed. Grabbing his scimitar, he extended it upwards just as Atoru came back down, and the blade went home.

Seeing her duty done, Putra jumped off of the bull's back, and retreated into the trees, seeking battle elsewhere. Orluc stood, and a snarling laugh came from his throat.

Atoru's whole body shook. His eyes rolled white, and his mouth lolled open as blood dripped from his mouth.

Orluc pulled the blade free and backed away. Turning, he left Atoru alone. The big bull fought to keep his feet, but weakness came over him, and he went down on his knees.

Kikpona heard a bellow from Quetoro, and turned to see if her friend needed help. But the red stallion was racing away from his opponent with as much speed as he could muster, toward Kikpona.

"Get on my back!" he shouted at his queen. As he galloped past, Kikpona grabbed a handful of his mane and jumped on. Looking ahead, she saw then what Quetoro had already seen. A cry of anguish escaped from her throat as she saw Atoru on his knees, blood pooling around him.

Kikpona leapt from Quetoro's back and knelt beside Atoru. Tears of grief rolled down her cheeks as her childhood friend gazed up at her through pain-filled eyes.

"Kik…pona…" he gasped out. The Queen took his mighty head in her arms and cradled it lovingly, her tears falling down to land on his cheek. The huge bull's eyes began

278

to dim. Reaching down, Kikpona placed the palm of her hand on the white star that graced Atoru's forehead.

With a shuddering sigh, Atoru's eyes closed. Kikpona choked back a sob as she saw that her best friend was gone. She held Atoru's head closer to her, and dropped a gentle kiss on his muzzle as her tears dripped down to wash away the grime on the big bull's face.

.~.~.~.~.~.~.

Orluc and his army retreated back to their camp, leaving the battlefield behind them. Morgo ordered the army back to Utomia, but many stayed behind to administer to the wounded, and to bury the dead. Atoru was borne back to Utomia on a velvet covered stretcher. Kikpona had found his second horn lying several feet away from the place he had fallen, and now, as she walked behind the sad procession, she clasped it to her.

It was the only piece of Atoru that she had left. Quetoro walked beside her, his grime and blood crusted face streaked with tears of his own, for Atoru had been his friend also.

In the sacred Warrior graveyard, Kikpona stood by and watched as the big black bull was lowered into the earth, and was lost from view. Morgo stood beside her and held her close, kissing her hair. Vanddai was standing off to the side, her longbow gripped tightly in her hand.

Atoru's Steer Warriors bellowed, filling the night air with their salute to the general that they had respected, honored, and loved.

.~.~.~.~.~.~.

Kikpona, Morgo, Vanddai, Makkiu, Jarlir, and Quetoro gathered silently into the Council Hall. Battle plans were discussed without any disagreements. The commanders were all exhausted and filled with grief for their fallen comrades. Makkiu was called upon to report on the casualties of the battle. The cheetah stepped forward slowly, limping from a leg wound.

"Orluc's losses are estimated at twenty-five thousand. We began with eighteen thousand Ichodian Warriors, and fifteen thousand Utomian Warriors. The Ichodian losses were numbered at nine thousand. Utomian losses numbered…ten thousand. Commanders lost were: General Atoru, General Jahere of Ichoda, Lord Naruo of…"

Makkiu's voice faded in Kikpona's ears. She had only five thousand warriors left. Such a devastating loss! And Jarlir had only nine thousand left. That meant that while Orluc still had an army of twenty-five thousand at his command, she led only fourteen thousand!

Morgo touched her hand gently. "My love? Are you alright?" he asked, concern emanating from his tone. Kikpona was jerked back to the present, and she saw the worried looks on the faces of her friends. She smiled shakily.

"I'm fine. The report has simply…disturbed me," she said, looking down at her ringed hands.

Jarlir's fists were clenched. "I lost Jahere, my loyal general. He was a brilliant leader and a strategic genius. I have paid dearly for my alliance with you, Kikpona."

Quetoro's eyes darkened. "We have all lost friends and loved ones, Jarlir. Do not think that you are the only being in this room whose heart aches with grief!" the stallion's voice had nearly risen to a shout.

"Do not dare accuse me, Quetoro the Betrayer! It is a wonder that you have not run away from the danger yet, leaving your Queen in peril by herself!" Jarlir flung back at him, standing up from his chair. Quetoro stepped forward, his normally calm nature completely gone.

Vanddai rose also, eyes flashing. "How dare you speak such words to Lord Quetoro, you worthless, greedy, honorless scum! He is our Queen's most trusted advisor and closest friend!"

Seeing the fight that was about to occur, Kikpona rose from her throne, leaning heavily upon her spear for support.

"Enough!" she shouted. The room fell silent. Vanddai blushed hotly and returned to her seat. Quetoro stepped back, but his eyes still burned with hatred. Jarlir fell back into his chair, as though the argument had weakened him. Kikpona gazed sadly at the three of them.

"By fighting amongst ourselves, we hand a sure victory to Orluc. Do you not think that this is what he wants? He would be only to glad to hear that the people of Leyowan have divided themselves over petty differences."

A guilty silence covered the room as the three combatants returned to their former relaxed stance. Kikpona placed a hand over her eyes, and sank slowly back to her throne. Morgo knelt beside her.

"My love, you cannot fight in the battle tomorrow. You are exhausted and filled with grief for Atoru. Please let me lead the army into battle."

Kikpona would not hear of it. "No, Morgo. I must fight tomorrow. I will wreak vengeance upon Orluc for the death of my friend," she said. Raising her eyes to Morgo, she made a solemn vow.

"I swear by my own blood that no hand but mine will slay that foul creature and avenge Atoru's death. None but mine!" she said vehemently. Morgo was taken aback by the glitter of hatred that burned in his wife's eyes.

Gathering her battle cloak up in her hands, Kikpona silently descended from the dais and left the room, leaving her friends watching after her worriedly. Vanddai stood up once again.

"I fear for her," she said softly, echoing the thoughts of everyone in the room except for Jarlir. The Ichodian king's eyes gleamed with anger at being ordered around by his stepdaughter. As the other commanders filed out of the room, he made his own vow. To see that Kikpona never came out of the battle alive.

.~.~.~.~.~.~.

Kikpona shed her grime-covered armor and donned her heavy velvet and furred robes. Taking up her brush, she swept through her hair carefully, smoothing out the tangles. Sighing deeply, she felt tears come to her eyes as she saw Atoru's horn lying on its newly made cedar stand.

Before leaving her bedchamber, she touched the horn lightly. The ivory colored piece gleamed slightly in the firelight. The Queen wandered aimlessly down the hallways, and finally decided to go into the bath chamber.

Inside the dimly lit room, she took off her robe and laid it over the arm of a chair. She went down the marble steps into the warm pool, and breathed in deeply of the rose scented water. She lifted a floating rose bloom from the pool and held it against her nose appreciatively.

She leaned back against the bath pool's edge, letting the soothing water lap against her body and ease the aches and bruises from the battle.

A soft step caused her to whirl around in surprise. She relaxed when she saw that it was Morgo. Her husband stood against the wall, dressed in his brown breeches. She smiled faintly up at him, and rested her chin against the pool's wall.

"Hello my love," she greeted him. He smiled back at her half-heartedly. Kikpona saw that something was wrong.

"Would you like to join me? The water is very warm," she invited. He nodded slightly. After a moment, he joined her in the water. The warmth and comfort brought a smile to his lips. Kikpona swam over behind him, and gently rubbed his broad shoulders with her fingers. His tense muscles relaxed slowly, and he leaned back against her.

"Thank you, Kikpona. That was very much appreciated," he said warmly. She nodded, and looked at him meaningfully.

"What's wrong, my love? You seem so distracted. I hate seeing you like this," she said worriedly. Morgo turned around and held her at arm's length. His dark eyes flickered over her briefly.

"You shouldn't go into battle tomorrow, Kikpona. You're exhausted, and you don't have the strength to go through another fight."

Kikpona felt her cheeks flame with color, and she looked away. Her face felt as though it were on fire. Did he doubt her?

Morgo tipped her chin up with a gentle forefinger. "Kikpona," he said softly to her. She felt her heart leap at the loving tone of his voice. Her sapphire eyes lifted to meet his dark ones. She saw them filled with fear and uncertainty. She knew that Morgo was afraid for her.

She softly brushed his lips with her own, and then drew back. Turning, she attempted to move away. His fingers closed around her wrist, pulling her back to him. He pulled her close, holding her tightly. She leaned against him contentedly.

"Don't do this, my love. Don't lead the army into battle. I'm not strong enough to...to..." his voice trailed off. Kikpona looked up at him expectantly.

"To what, Morgo?" she asked, already knowing what it was that was so hard for him to say. He closed his eyes tightly, and his grip around her loosened.

"I'm not strong enough to lose you," he whispered brokenly. "I almost lost my sister once, and it nearly killed me. I could not live if something were to happen to you. You mean everything to me. You are my life, Kikpona of Utomia."

The Queen surveyed him silently. Her eyes traveled over his handsome features. Her eyes traced his rebellious dark hair, his dark, intense eyes that voiced his emotions so powerfully, the curve of his lips, and the determined set of his jaw. She loved everything about him.

She put her hand against his cheek tenderly, feeling the stubble that traced his jaw line. Gazing up into his eyes, she concentrated on portraying her deep love for him through that look. Morgo's shoulders dropped slightly as he let out his breath.

"Morgo, you have to trust me," she whispered softly. "I am Utomia's Queen, and I will not let my people fall alone. If it is my fate to die in this battle, then let it be said that I died a hero, and not a coward who hid behind her stone walls."

With a slight tremor, Morgo's eyes fell downcast. They closed, and Kikpona felt his deepest fear emanating

285

from him. She moved closer, and put her arms around his neck. She pressed her forehead to his, her eyelashes brushing his face. Morgo opened his eyes, and ran his hand through her hair. Their lips touched gently.

Drawing back, Morgo looked her in the eyes. "You are so beautiful..." he whispered. Kikpona smiled, and said the words from so long ago.

"Kikpona of Utomia loves Lord Morgo of Halesbra."

Morgo smiled and nodded. "And Lord Morgo of Halesbra loves Kikpona of Utomia."

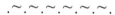

The dawn's first light streamed through the windows of Kikpona and Morgo's bedchamber, illuminating the interior. The Queen's eyes flickered open as she awoke. She rolled over and saw Morgo still asleep beside her. She drew a hand across her eyes, and got out of bed. A glance at her armor stand reminded her that a battle had yet to be waged. And today, it would be different. Orluc would not be caught by surprise in the forest again. He would come to the very walls of Utomia.

Kikpona dressed hurriedly, and had her maid help her fasten the armor. Morgo awoke, and rolled out of the bed. Shaking his head to clear it of all drowsiness, he saw Kikpona already outfitted in her armor. She smiled at him reassuringly.

286

He sighed and reached for his own tunic and breeches. Donning them, he fastened his leg bracers, armguards, and his chainmail tunic. He slid his breastplate over his head and tightened the sides and shoulders.

Kikpona brought him his dark blue battle cloak, and gently snapped it into place on his shoulders. He caught her hand as she finished, and kissed it lightly. She pulled away from him, and exited the room. Morgo followed her silently.

Reaching the palace's main doors, the Queen and her lord stepped out into the cool morning air. Together they walked toward the wall. Kikpona surveyed the trebuchets, ballistas, and mangons. The mangons were small catapults that had bowl-like wooden container supported by a thick steel arm. It was built to hurl large boulders just over the wall tops, thus providing a closer defense than the trebuchets.

The ballistas were like giant crossbows. It took three men to operate one. The arrows that it fired were nearly seven feet long, and were very thick.

Nodding in satisfaction, Kikpona joined Morgo and Quetoro at the wall top. The big red stallion was looking down at the thick stone walls apprehensively. He turned to Kikpona.

"Majesty, I do not know what sort of siege weapons Orluc may possess, and the walls may not stand."

Kikpona shook her head. "They will stand, Quetoro. They must stand, or Utomia will be destroyed. We must protect them at all costs. I want archers and javelin throwers up on the wall tops, ready to attack the men that operate Orluc's heavy weaponry."

Quetoro shouted an order, and a troop of javelin throwers, followed by two score archers marched up to the wall top. They took position, their weapons ready. Kikpona nodded.

"Good. Now there is nothing left to do but wait for him."

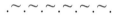

The sound of clanking armor soon filled the ears of every soldier behind the Utomian walls. The sound of thousands of marching soldiers. The sound of coming battle. The sound of death.

Suddenly, the Morbian army appeared. Orluc was at the head of his remaining twenty-five thousand soldiers. He raised his huge forepaw and roared for a halt. Instantly, the entire horde went completely silent. Then, at a motion from Putra, who stood beside her warlord, every weapon was raised, and a mighty shout went up from the Morbians.

The eerie, bloodthirsty cry rang through the city, sending an irrepressible tingle racing down the spines of every allied soldier. Kikpona felt her own confidence shaken, but stood tall until the noise subsided. Then, in the quiet that followed, she shouted down to her adversary.

"What is it that you hope to gain from a mere sound, Orluc? Do you seek to shake my courage? Well, I hope you are prepared to accept that I think of you merely as a foul creature whose evil must be wiped out from the face of this earth."

Orluc's snarling laugh drifted up to the wall tops as he replied. "Brave words for one who is about to die, Kikpona of Utomia. I will burn your city, and I will move every brick from the foundations of your fancy halls and palaces. Then, I will hang your corpse from the very gates of your city."

Morgo placed a hand on Kikpona's arm, keeping her from descending the wall steps to the ground.

"Do not take the bait, my love. He seeks merely to taunt you. Do not let him beguile you into foolish actions." The pleading tone in Morgo's voice stopped Kikpona in her tracks. She looked up at Morgo.

"I have had enough of his mockery, Morgo. It is time that someone put him in his place!" she said firmly. Morgo shook his head.

"Nay, love. The time will come soon enough."

A shout from Orluc interrupted further discussion. "I have had enough of this talk. It tires me. Trebuchets, FIRE!" he roared. Loud creaks and groans came from the three trebuchets that rested behind the Morbian army. Huge boulders were flung toward the city walls.

"Javelins, fire!" cried Kikpona as the rocks smashed into the wall. The stone shook and trembled and huge craters were formed in the wall by the missiles. The javelin throwers released their weapons. A rain of the long, deadly shafts sped down toward the Morbians, felling all who were unlucky

289

enough to be in their path. Morgo went down the steps to where Vanddai and her battalion of warhorses and riders were awaiting orders.

"Are you ready, sister?" Morgo asked her. Vanddai grinned roguishly at him, and pulled down the visor of her helm. Drawing her two swords, she flipped them in an intricate pattern around her head.

The black mare, Lumere, who was Vanddai's mount, pranced eagerly in anticipation. Morgo shook his head and mounted the horse next to Vanddai. The chestnut mare turned to look at him over her shoulder.

"My name is Reja. It is an honor to bear you, my lord," she said solemnly. Morgo smiled and placed a hand on her shoulder. Drawing his battle-axe free of his belt, he raised it up over his head.

"For love and honor!" he shouted. The gates of the city opened, and the three hundred brave horses and riders flooded out, weapons held high. Orluc sent a buffalo wolf pack lunging for them, followed by a battalion of heavily armored steers. The two groups crashed together. Horses fell to the snapping teeth and claws of the wolves, riders were scraped from the backs of their mounts by the steel-tipped horns of the steers.

Morgo and Vanddai found themselves back to back, their weapons whirling and slashing as they were attacked from all sides.

But while the Utomian warhorses were occupied, Orluc and Putra led in their secret weapon. Siege towers.

The gigantic wooden structures rolled slowly toward the wall, pushed by dozens of the strongest Morbian elephants.

Kikpona felt her blood run cold. How were they supposed to route such a terrifying advance? She turned to Quetoro and quickly snapped out orders.

"Get the trebuchets ready, I want them to attack those towers immediately. Get some torches going up here. Get the swordsmen and the wolves up here, along with Jarlir's black panthers. Hurry!"

The requested soldiers were soon positioned on the wall tops, weapons drawn, waiting for the siege towers to arrive. Archers kept up a steady stream of fire arrows going toward the huge structures.

The towers reached their destination and creaked to a halt. The drawbridges were released, and they crashed down on the battlements of the wall. Swordsmen and wolves leapt from the dimly lit interiors, followed by an assortment of other creatures.

Kikpona twirled her spear, ready for the attack. Quetoro stood beside her. The Morbians leapt onto the wall tops, weapons and fangs bared and ready. Kikpona thrust her spear into the first wolf that leapt for her, and then jerked the weapon free just in time to block a strike from a swordsman.

Quetoro reared up, striking an archer who had just come barreling out of the tower. His hooves came down as a wolf left gaping slashes along the red stallion's barrel. Quetoro bellowed and whirled on his tormentor.

Morgo and Vanddai were in the thick of the battle outside the walls of the city. Surrounded by a wolf pack, they fought from their horses. Reja and Lumere kept up a ceaseless prancing to avoid the snapping teeth of the wolves, throwing a flying hoof into the face of a Morbian every now and then.

A big black wolf came lunging up, and leapt for Vanddai. She turned just as he fell on top of her, jaws wide, teeth gleaming in the sunlight. She uttered a single gasp before the two of them toppled from Lumere, who screamed angrily as her mistress fell.

Morgo thrust his axe blade into a wolf, and then jerked away, turning Reja toward his sister.

Rolling on the ground, the two combatants fought to gain an advantage. Vanddai's arm held the wolf's snapping jaws away from her face, while she desperately tried to bring her sword down. She moved her blade down and up in a single sweeping motion, and the wolf went limp.

Vanddai stood shakily, and smiled at Morgo. "I'm alright. Send the signal to Kikpona to bring the rest of the army out here when she can."

Morgo lifted his ram's horn and blew three heavy blasts. Up on the wall top, the siege towers were retreating, having been soundly defeated by Kikpona's troops. The Queen sighed deeply as the Morbians moved away from the wall, and a great cheer went up from her soldiers.

Quetoro shook his red mane defiantly. "A good fight, my queen. We have taught them to not so easily taunt the power of Utomia!" he said proudly. But Kikpona was not encouraged, for she heard the three horn blows from Morgo.

"Come, Quetoro. We must end this," she said. The big stallion looked at her in surprise. Her tone had held dread and fear, yet also a quiet calmness. It made him nervous.

Kikpona descended the steps two at a time, and rallied the remaining army to her. Jarlir came up behind her on his bay stallion.

"It is time," he said simply, and Kikpona nodded in agreement. She looked over the thousands of loyal subjects who stood waiting for her order, and she felt a pang of sadness knowing that most of them would never see the rising of another sun. But she raised her spear to them in salute.

"My brave Utomians and Ichodians, I salute you! Now it is the time to finish the task we have started! Let the name of Utomia bring fear to the hearts of those worthless beasts!"

She mounted Gundir, who had been insistent on being with her, though his javelin wound was only slightly healed. Kikpona looked down at the dark, wise eyes of the stallion and patted his neck.

"And so it begins, my friend. The last ride of Kikpona of Utomia," she whispered. Gundir didn't have time to ask what she meant, for she tapped her heels to his sides, and the army of Utomia flooded out from the city gates. Every kind of animal and race of people followed their queen to what they knew was possible death. Yet not one turned back to safety.

.~.~.~.~.~.~.

Orluc swiped his scimitar clean on the grass, and straightened up. He saw Kikpona and her army charging toward him, and a wicked gleam brightened his eye. Here was his chance. He leapt out from the brush just as Gundir thundered past. Reaching up with a huge forepaw, Orluc swept the queen from the stallion's back.

Kikpona fell to the ground with a thud, and the wind rushed from her. She raised her spear just in time to block the scimitar's blow. Orluc backed away slowly, his huge blade twirling.

"Get up, my little queen. It is time to meet your conqueror!" he growled. Kikpona got to her feet, though somewhat hesitantly. She dragged in huge lungfuls of air, trying to replenish the breath she had lost. She shook her head to clear her mind, and straightened her shoulders proudly. Lifting her spear, she turned its point toward her enemy.

"It will be your blood, not mine that stains this ground," she said. Orluc laughed, and came at her, scimitar whirling. Kikpona readied herself for the impact, but still barely managed to keep her feet as the huge bear crashed against her. She used the shaft of her spear to keep his sword at bay, but while his right paw held the scimitar, he used his left to swipe his claws at her.

The deadly weapons snaked down Kikpona's right leg, drawing a cry of pain from her lips. Angry now, she grasped the hilt of her hidden dagger and swung it up, burying it into

294

the furry chest of her enemy. Orluc roared and staggered back. His claws reached up and jerked the blade from his hide. He dropped the dagger to the ground and looked up, his eyes glowing red. His rage boiled over, and he lunged for Kikpona once again. But his judgment had been dulled by the pain.

Orluc the great bear was halted by the spear of Kikpona of Utomia. The Queen's eyes were dark and narrowed as she pulled her weapon free of her enemy. Orluc's mouth opened, but the only sound that came out was a strangled gurgle. He raised his scimitar, but the weapon clattered to the ground as its master crashed to the jungle floor.

Queen Kikpona had defeated Leyowan's would be destroyer. At the sight of their dead leader, the army of Morbia suddenly changed tactics. They began to run, and hard on their heels were the Utomians and Ichodians.

Morgo and Vanddai led the charge against the retreating Morbians. Jarlir and his Ichodians stayed behind. Kikpona turned to face her stepfather as he rode up to her. Her face was streaked with grime and blood. She bowed her head.

"It is over. Orluc will no longer threaten us," she said quietly. Jarlir surveyed the gigantic body with scorn.

"Good. It was nigh time that he was sent back to the fiery place from whence he was birthed," Jarlir replied darkly. He looked down at Kikpona, his eyes noting her fatigue. It was the perfect time to put his plan into action. He dismounted from the bay horse and stepped toward her.

"I have decided to withdraw my forces from your city. You will rule Utomia and I will rule Ichoda, or what is left of it. We will both be the protectors of Leyowan."

Kikpona stared at him in surprise. She had never expected him to surrender to a dual throne. She smiled slightly and put a hand on his shoulder.

"I accept your offer in good faith. It will be an honor to rule with you," she said softly. She respected him for being so honorable and noble. Jarlir nodded and looked at her again. He opened his arms in a gesture of friendship, and Kikpona entered his embrace.

Suddenly, a war horn blew from the distance. Both Jarlir and Kikpona turned in surprise to see who had come. Was it yet another threat? But no, up on the hill beyond Utomia's walls was a white horse bearing an armored knight. The horse came racing down the incline, making for Kikpona and Jarlir with all speed. And it was in that moment that Kikpona knew who it was.

"FATHER!" she shouted, a smile leaping to her face, her fatigue forgotten. He was so close to her. The horse came closer with every lunging stride.

Jarlir didn't wait to see more. He jumped forward behind Kikpona and plunged his dagger into her back.

The iron spear the queen held cracked lengthways down the shaft. The mighty weapon fell to the ground in two pieces. And it seemed as though the very walls of Utomia shook.

The Queen's head was flung back, her mouth opened in a silent agony. Jarlir backed away, an evil expression etched onto his face. But his happiness was short-lived. Cyus' horse flattened its ears and doubled its strides. Jarlir didn't have time to move out of the way. The horse crashed into him, and the evil king fell beneath the big mare's hooves.

Cyus leapt from his mount's back and rushed to his daughter, catching her in his arms just as she fell. He gently lowered her to the ground, supporting her. She gasped for breath, and her eyes slowly lifted to his.

"Father..." she whispered. Tears sprang to Cyus's eyes. His daughter...he had never seen her, yet he felt an overpowering love for her. He saw so much of Elaria in her. The same soft eyes, courageous spirit, and overwhelming beauty. He held her close, kissing her hair.

Closing her eyes, Kikpona sighed shakily. Cyus reached underneath her and gripped the dagger hilt. He jerked his hand, releasing the dagger from his daughter. Kikpona shuddered violently. The big white mare stayed a respectful distance, her dark eyes watching father and daughter in sorrow.

Hoof beats sounded from the jungle as Vanddai and Morgo returned to their city. Morgo pulled up Reja and looked around for his wife. At first he couldn't find her. But then he saw an armored knight holding Kikpona under a

297

sycamore tree. Blood covered the ground. Leaping from the chestnut mare's back, Morgo raced to them.

Falling to his knees beside his wife, Morgo gripped her hand fiercely as his eyes raced over her in confusion.

"Kikpona, my love! What has happened?" he asked, his voice cracking. Cyus looked up at the young man, and instinctively realized who Morgo was. The older man laid a hand on Morgo's shoulder.

"Jarlir betrayed her, my son. He stabbed her," said Cyus. Morgo stared at him.

"No…NO!" he gasped. He bent down and laid his head in his wife's lap, tears pouring from his eyes. Kikpona's hand fluttered slightly as she struggled to raise it. Her gentle fingertips brushed through her husband's hair as her own tears mingled with the grime that covered her face.

"Morgo…it was my destiny…it must be this way…you must protect our daughter now…she needs you," Kikpona said brokenly. Morgo shook his head vehemently.

"No, I will save you!" he begged, his voice filled with pleading. "Please, don't leave me alone here," he said. Kikpona closed her eyes, tears flooding down her cheeks. She stiffened, and her hand gripped Morgo's ever tighter. Her eyes rose to her father's, and she gave him a meaningful look. He nodded understandingly.

"I promise that I will protect all of them," he whispered. Kikpona smiled faintly, contented. She relaxed, and exhaled slowly as the life passed from her body.

298

Cyus laid his daughter's hand on her stomach, and stood up, pulling Morgo to his feet. The younger man's shoulders shook unashamedly as he cried. Cyus pulled his son-in-law close to him, and Morgo stood like a small boy in his father's arms. Quetoro and Vanddai rode up, and saw the scene. Grief filled Vanddai's eyes as she saw the body of her sister in law.

"The day is dark…Utomia has lost her queen," Vanddai whispered. Lumere's head lowered, and the mare touched her muzzle to her front hoof in a salute to her ruler.

Quetoro moved over and nuzzled the body of his friend gently. "And so ends the life of a great one. Eternally may her name be spoken with reverence from the lips of her people. Long may her soul find peace in the land of light," he said respectfully.

Cyus began to lead Morgo and Vanddai back to the palace. The white mare and Lumere followed silently. But Quetoro stayed behind for one more moment. Looking down at Kikpona's peaceful face, his eyes softened.

"You built a mighty city, my Queen. A city that will never forget you as long as its wall stands. I make you this promise: that as long as I draw breath, I will protect and teach your daughter so that she may be raised to be as great of a Queen as you have been. She will make you proud. This I swear to you."

Quetoro turned to leave, and walked a ways toward the city gates. He looked over his shoulder to see her one last time, and awe passed over his face. The Queen's body lay against the sycamore tree, bathed in a stream of sunlight.

The End...

Epilogue

Kikpona was buried next to her best friend and loyal general, Atoru the Black Bull. Her headstone was made from the very statue that had held her crown. On it was inscribed:

A Mighty Queen Lies Here
May Her Memory Be Etched Into the Minds of Her People
Just As This Inscription Is Etched Into Her Gravestone
A Monument to Her Courage and Love for the City She Built

The story will continue in the sequel: "The Iron Spear"

Pronunciation Guide

Oppolo – oh-poe-loe
Ichoda – I – code – ah
Leyowan – lay-oh-wahn
Kikpona – kick-poe-nah
Quetoro – kay-tore – oh
Magiro – mah – jeer –oh
Pernog – pear – nahg
Cyus – sigh – uhss
Utomia – you-toe-mee-ah
Kalmenor – call-mehn-ore
Makkiu – mah-key-you
Halesbra – hall – ehs – brah
Uytopia – why-toe-peeh-ah
Kiunee – key-you-knee
Hanre – hahn-ray
Atrobius – ah-troe-bee-uhs
Hyutana – high – you – tah – nah
Juilorien – jew-lore-ee-ahn
Lylu – lie-loo
Weremun – wear-ah-moon
Luluk – loo-luck
Jahere – jah-here-ray
Hakasye – hah-kah-see-eh
Nenamene – nen-ah-mean
Hhuru – who-roo
Nenkin – nehn-keen
Orluc – ore-luck

About This Book

I am Victoria Kasten, author of the well known and loved "Mighty Stallion" series, and I brought IronHeart to life over the course of eight months. The country, culture and characters were carefully created to give you an epic story of love, courage, honor, and the battle for the throne of a country.

The inspiration for this story came from a dream I had almost two years ago about a Queen talking to a black bull (Atoru). From that dream, I created the land of Leyowan and the story you have just read.

This project definitely holds a special place in my heart. The deaths of Kikpona and Atoru were very hard for me to write, because I had become very close to my characters during those eight months.

I am planning on a sequel to this book, and it will concern the life of Kikpona's daughter, Kona, as she struggles to find her place in her mother's world.

I hope you enjoyed reading this book as much as I enjoyed writing it.

"May the stars shine over you, may God lead your footsteps, and may you find peace…"
  -   Utomian Blessing

Sincerely,
Victoria Kasten

SNEAK PEEK AT IRONHEART'S SEQUEL

THE IRON SPEAR!

1.

The Queen's head fell back, and her mouth opened in a silent scream of agony. The spear cracked and split, falling to the ground in two halves. The man behind her backed away, an evil smile on his face. Hoofbeats sounded, and then faded into silence. All that could be heard was the labored breathing of the queen. All that could be seen was the slow dripping of blood to the ground, staining the hard packed earth a deep crimson. A scarlet river of royal blood...

"NO!"

The fifteen year old girl bolted upright in her bed, throwing the blankets aside in her haste to rise from the dream. She heaved in a deep lungful of air, shaking her head to clear the nightmare from her mind. The door to her bedchamber opened, creaking softly.

"Princess Kona? Are you alright?" said a familiar voice. The girl turned her head slightly, looking at the big red stallion that had just entered the room. She sighed in relief at his presence.

"Quetoro! I'm so sorry that I woke you."

The old stallion regarded her kindly. "No matter, Princess. That is why I am here. What ails you?" he asked quietly, eying her with a look of concern. His graying muzzle betrayed the gleam of youthful vigor that shone in his dark eyes. Kona looked down at her hands.

"It was the nightmare again, Quetoro. I saw her...I saw her die. I saw the spear, the blood...it was so real," she whispered, her long eyelashes brushing her cheeks as she closed her eyes tightly.

Quetoro shook his head. "Ah, poor child. Many nights I have wished that it was your mother, not I who came to comfort you. But it was not meant to be. The dream is terrifying, but you must know that it is only a dream, nothing more. Your mother would not have wanted you to be so afraid."

Kona blushed and felt the heat rise in her face. She lowered her head so that the soft tendrils of her golden hair fell between Quetoro's eyes and her face, keeping her embarrassment hidden. She felt so sorrowful whenever she thought of her mother. The mother that she had never known, but had so much wanted to meet. The great Kikpona of Leyowan, whose name was spoken in reverence by everyone in Utomia.

A soft breath blew aside her hair, and she saw Quetoro standing next to her. His eyes surveyed her comfortingly.

"Try to sleep, my Princess. Dawn comes swiftly, and tomorrow does not wait for anyone. You must rest." The old stallion's logic was inarguable, so Kona lay back against her velvet cushions and closed her eyes. This time, however, her sleep was peaceful and undisturbed.

Victoria's Books

- Mighty Stallion
- Mighty Stallion 2 Fury's Journey
- Mighty Stallion 3 Glory's Legend
- Mighty Stallion 4 Dancer's Dream
- Mighty Stallion 5 A Stallion's Heart

Others are coming soon!

To get the latest information on Victoria's books, appearances, and more, log on to www.epicscrolls.com or write to:

Epic Scrolls
5465 Glencoe Ave
Webster, MN 55088